THE SEVENTH JEWEL

THE SEVENTH JEWEL

J. J. Pritchard

iUniverse, Inc.
New York Lincoln Shanghai

The Seventh Jewel

Copyright © 2005 by Jeffrey J. Pritchard

iUniverse books may be ordered through booksellers or by contacting:

iUniverse
2021 Pine Lake Road, Suite 100
Lincoln, NE 68512
www.iuniverse.com
1-800-Authors (1-800-288-4677)

Special thanks to Anne Gregory.

ISBN: 0-595-33674-4

Printed in the United States of America

In Memory of
George R. Senner

One of the Great Mountaineers

CONTENTS

▼

PART I

▼

1458 AD

CHAPTER 1

▼

MUNRAY
THE OFFERING

I was a small girl—only an infant—when the night visions began. I remember awakening, seeking the safety of my parents' blankets. My mother held me as I sobbed in her arms.

"Do not be afraid, Munray," she gently whispered. "It is but a dream. You are safe now."

But the dream continued to haunt me.

   *   *   *   *

"Why do they stare at us, Munray?"

"We are their last hope, Sisay."

"But there are so many." Thousands had silently lined the roadway leading from the temple.

"Yes, I know," I whispered, putting my arm around Sisay to comfort her. "It's as if we carry the empire on our shoulders."

It was the time of a thousand sorrows. A terrible blight had ravaged the land in the twentieth year of the reign of Pachacuti. The seasonal rains had abandoned Tavantinsuyu, our empire in the clouds. Irrigation ditches were dry. The thirsty earth was cracked and brittle. The terraced hillsides gave little nourishment without the moistening breath of life. The potatoes were black and bitter; the maize was small and misshapen. Desperate women roamed the streets, grieving the fate of their starving children. No elder could remember a time—nor could they recall tales of times before—when so many among our people had wept for water.

I am Munray. I had been chosen, along with Sisay, to climb to the highest *huaca*, or holy place, and beg for mercy from the greatest gods—Viracocha, the creator; Inti, the sun god; and, most importantly, Illapa, god of thunder and rain.

For most of my fifteen years, I had lived within the protective walls of Coricanchu, the Sun Temple, in the city of Cuzco, center of the universe. Like several hundred other pure ones, I had taken vows to remain untouched so that I might maintain my purity of spirit. It was a great honor for Sisay and me to be considered most beautiful of the Sun virgins. As such, we were chosen for this journey.

"When will we wear the feather headdresses?" Sisay, only twelve years old, was full of questions.

"When we reach the mountain's top. But that will take several weeks." I carried all our ceremonial clothing in my pack.

Sisay pouted for a moment and then brightened.

"We're dressed like sisters today." She looked up to me.

I smiled. "We could be twins."

Our black hair, thickly braided, hung outside our bright red *aqsus* and swayed at our waists. Our heavy clothes were woven from the alpaca to protect us from the mountain's bitter cold.

I had not always lived in the temple. My village was in the Conchuco nation, one of the many conquered by Pachacuti, one of the many upon which the empire was built. The dream from my childhood carried me to Cuzco.

Our local priest declared my recurring dream a sign, and so I was brought to the Temple of the Sun while I was still a child. Since that time, I had never described the nightmare again. Not to anyone.

Chaqara led our journey. As third high priest of Coricanchu, he carried the ceremonial lance adorned with black and purple plumes. The pilgrimage had been hard on the aging Chaqara, and it would become even more so. He gasped for breath with every step. The mountain demanded much from old legs.

Yuyarinu also made this journey. At the temple, Sisay and I were under her wing. We called her the "jaguar" for Yuyarinu was not afraid to speak harshly to Chaqara. She was given much freedom in the temple. Her eyes, unlike the familiar nut-brown color of mine, were strangely pale. This was a sign that she was touched by Inti. To many of us, including myself, Yuyarinu was like a mother. And, for that, she was dearly trusted and loved.

Beneath my blouse, in the rhythmic motion of my steady, labored steps, the four amulets of my necklace gently tapped against my breast. The touch was reassuring. When my family brought me to the Sun Temple in Cuzco, before they bid me farewell, my father gently circled my neck with this strand of flat stones.

"Remember us always with this, Munray." He touched the necklace. "Know that, with it, you can always find your way home."

My necklace was plain and simple compared to those made of brilliant *q'ori*, the metal of the Sun god that adorned our temples and shrines. Yet it was my most precious possession. My father made it with the sacred metal of our village.

It is said that, in the beginning of time, the stars and planets rebelled against Mamaquilla, goddess of the moon, and cast her aside. She came to rest near our village and lost all hope of ever returning to the sky. But Tuncha, a mythical warrior, said he would return Mamaquilla to the sky if she would promise to send our tiny village a gift. When she agreed, Tuncha hoisted the moon high and hurled her back into the night sky.

Mamaquilla, to honor her promise, scattered a moonbeam near the village. There, the silver-green light remained amongst the rocks as a *huaca* to the moon. The amulets of my necklace were formed from these stones.

"What are you dreaming about, Munray?" Sisay interrupted my solitary reverie.

"Home."

"Cuzco?"

"No. My village. My father and mother." I never considered Cuzco my real home. My most cherished memories lived amongst my youngest childhood.

"Happy memories?"

"They are happy and sad at the same time."

"I have no memories of my parents," Sisay said.

"Sometimes I think that would be easier." Thinking of home—of my mother and father—made my heart ache.

"I would trade with you if I could." Sisay smiled wistfully. "At least for a day."

Supporting us on our journey were three *chasqui*. They carried the heaviest loads now that the way was too steep, even for the llamas. *Chasqui* were the men who relayed messages between cities on the high, mountain roadways. It was an honor to be chosen in boyhood and trained to become a *chasqui*, but it was a great responsibility.

Awaqapak, the powerful, was the eldest and commanded the two others. No longer a *chasqui*, Awaqapak was now a warrior in the emperor's army. His scar-streaked face bore witness to many battles. Awaqapak strained beneath the greatest load as he guided our small procession. He had been on the mountain many times and had reached the high *huaca* twice before.

Phanchi was the tireless one. Tall and thin, he never grew weary. When we reached the high ground, where ice and snow never melted, it would be Phanchi's perilous task to cut our footholds with the stone end of his *piacha*.

Tequsi, in his seventeenth year, was the youngest of the three runners. He was only six when his *chasqui* training began. Much like me, Tequsi grew up without his mother and father.

The weeks that followed did not pass easily. The way was grueling, far more difficult than Sisay or I had foreseen. We struggled through dense jungles and through the cloud forest's bands of twisted, stunted trees whose roots curled and coiled like black snakes. We traversed fiery grasslands and desolate plateaus that were eerily quiet and sparse of life. We were baked by the burning midday sun, then frozen by night's icy embrace.

It wasn't until our sixteenth day that we reached the base of the twin mountains, the highest in the empire. They were called *Matararaju*, mother's milk. We were meant to reach the *huaca* atop the farther of the two peaks—an empty world of stone and ice.

That evening, Sisay and I lay silently in our shelter, listening to the *chasqui* gathered around their small fire. It was fascinating talk. They had seen much of the world.

"Last year, I met a messenger who claimed to have reached the great river in the black valley," young Tequsi told Awaqapak. Then he lowered his voice, "He spoke of unimaginable horrors."

"Nonsense," Phanchi snorted.

"The stories are true." Awaqapak spoke quietly. His voice was somber and gravelly deep. "I have seen them."

"How are such things possible?" Phanchi could not mask his disbelief.

"There are lands that are best left unconquered. Beyond these mountains is such a place. At the farthest edge of Pachacuti's empire are jungles so thick that the sky is hidden. These jungles seethe with giant serpents that swallow men whole. Beneath the brown waters of the great river live fish that devour men's flesh."

Awaqapak leaned forward; his voice was barely a hoarse whisper.

"With my own eyes, I saw six warriors unknowingly wade into the river. Soon the calm surface boiled in frenzy, and, one by one, the men fell beneath the thrashing waters. I could hear their muted screams beneath those waters. Only their bones were found."

Tequsi's eyes were wide with wonder. Suddenly, Phanchi roared with laughter and slapped Awaqapak on the shoulder.

"Awaqapak, you are a magical storyteller. I believed you for a moment. And what of you, Tequsi? Do you believe his ghost stories?"

Tequsi smiled nervously.

Awaqapak turned his thoughtful gaze back toward the fire. "I too did not think such horrors could exist until I saw them." The usually confident warrior was strangely subdued.

Yuyarinu emerged from the darkness into the fire's orange circle of light. Her eyes burned with anger.

"What is the meaning of this? Do you realize where we are? The entire mountain is a *huaca*. Yet you defile it with your laughter. Have you forgotten the sanctity of our journey? Our mission is sacred! Will we sacrifice so much in vain because of your foolishness?"

Any one of these men could have picked Yuyarinu up like a pebble, but, with the strength of her wrath, she shamed them into submission.

"You are correct, Yuyarinu." Awaqapak obediently lowered his head. "We have acted like fools. I am responsible. I ask your forgiveness."

"It is Illapa's forgiveness you must pray for. Not mine."

"Yes."

"See to it." She spun around and returned to her blankets in the darkness.

Sisay and I were reminded once more of our enormous responsibility. Sleep provided welcome relief from the weight of our burden.

It was now the morning of our seventeenth day. We had but two more cycles of the Sun to reach the mountain's height. Chaqara had grown more fearful with each passing day that we would not reach the *huaca* before sunset on the eighteenth day. I could hear the others waking around me. Phanchi was preparing tea. The day had just begun, yet

I was weary. Once again, the night vision had come to me…unchanged from countless visits of the past.

In my dream, I am seated upon a high ledge, far above a field green with young stalks of spring maize. The faint mist of dawn still clings to the ground. I must be very old because my children and their children are below me. They are all playing a game, laughing happily and running as one.

Then, upstream in the river, a huge wall of black water roars toward the field. I scream to my children, but I have no voice. I cannot warn them. The dark floodwater crashes onto the clearing, devouring all in its path. I watch in helpless terror as my family is swept away by the blackness. Nothing remains.

At this moment, amid the terror beneath me, I realize my eyes are dry. I am unable to shed tears for my own children. This is the most horrifying. And this is when I always awake.

This morning, our progress was slow. Cautiously, we stepped from rock to rock to cross a steep hillside of jagged boulders.

"Have you ever seen anything so wonderful, Munray?" Sisay gazed wide-eyed over the landscape. Craggy white sentinels surrounded us, stretching to the horizon, guarding the empire.

"Never. The higher we climb, the more beautiful it becomes."

"We have a friend. Look." Sisay pointed down the mountian. "See him?"

For a moment, I didn't see anything. Then I spotted a solitary *kuntu* riding the mountain breezes on its outstretched wings. It was graceful as it circled in search of prey far below on the valley floor. The same cold morning wind blew on our faces. It carried the faint scent of cedar groves.

Yuyarinu hiked up beside us.

"We have been blessed with a clear sky." She offered water to Sisay and me, but we weren't thirsty. "The high grounds are often haunted by terrible winds and black storms. This is a good omen."

I believed it was the gods, favoring our mission with safe passage.

Among the jagged boulders, the weary Chaqara clumsily stumbled, causing a large rock to slide. The stone tumbled onto Sisay's foot, crushing it with a dull crack. Sisay collapsed and cried out in pain.

"Sisay!"

We rushed to where she lay. The combined strength of Awaqapak and Tequsi against the stone allowed Yuyarinu to carefully remove Sisay's foot.

"Can she continue?" Chaqara asked with concern.

Yuyarinu examined Sisay's limb. "Of course not! Her foot is broken. She cannot walk."

"No!"

This was terrible for Sisay and for our people.

Awaqapak stepped forward. "I can carry her in a sling across my back."

"There isn't time, Awaqapak." Chaqara looked skyward, shielding his eyes from the bright sun. "Tonight, the Ukumari constellation passes through the southern house. At that moment, Illapa is at his strongest. We must stand atop the mountain tomorrow."

"The girl is a feather. I have carried grown men in this manner. She can still reach the *huaca*."

"Please, Chaqara," Sisay pleaded tearfully. "I am very light."

"No!" Chaqara's voice was firm as stone.

"Is it not the emperor's wish for the prayers of both Munray and Sisay?" Awaqapak openly challenged Chaqara. Disobedience to a high priest was unthinkable.

"Do not question my judgment, Awaqapak! Do you profess to know the gods' will better than myself? Munray is the chosen one. Her prayers will be heard. We will take her alone to the high place."

Sisay began sobbing. Yuyarinu had remained strangely quiet until now.

"And what of Sisay?"

Chaqara looked down thoughtfully at Sisay. Her face was ashen with pain.

"Phanchi can make her a small shelter. We will leave her food and water. Enough for two days. We will return by then. She will be fine. Phanchi can catch up to us tonight."

"Thank you, Chaqara." Yuyarinu bandaged Sisay's broken foot with cloth.

"But it's not fair," Sisay said between sobs. "I was chosen. I'm supposed to go. It isn't fair."

"Don't cry, Sisay." I leaned down and hugged her. "Your prayers will be heard by Illapa. I am sure of it."

"What do you mean?"

"The entire mountain is a *huaca*. Your prayers will be heard here, and mine will be heard higher on the mountain. Together, our voices will save the people."

I felt such sorrow for little Sisay to have journeyed so far, to have faced so many hardships, and to be turned aside now when we were so close. My heart ached for her. I gave her one last hug as Chaqara grew impatient.

"I'll make one of my songs for us to sing when you come back." Sisay wiped the tears from her cheeks.

"We'll sing it together as we return home."

We resumed our deliberate journey toward the ice and snow above. Sisay, with Phanchi nearby, waved a long good-bye as we left them farther and farther behind.

By late afternoon, our long shadows on the rocks and snow marked the coming of nightfall's bitter cold. While the others made our highest and final camp on the frigid ground, I walked around a short ridge, carefully navigating the frozen surface with each cautious step. Alone for the first time in many days, I basked in peaceful solitude—a stolen moment. Then I saw Tequsi.

On the other side of the ridge, hidden from camp, Tequsi crouched near snow-covered rocks. A lone *vicuna* stood just beyond his outstretched hand. The poor creature appeared sick and shivering; its normally beautiful wool was scraggly and thin. I wondered what had made it stray so far from home to this desolate, unforgiving place.

Tequsi made a rapid chittering sound, like a squirrel, which calmed the nervous beast. With a few halting steps forward, the animal cautiously nibbled from Tequsi's palm, then stepped back to chew its prize. At the sound of my approaching footsteps, the *vicuna* darted an anxious look at me. Tequsi turned to me and noiselessly placed a finger upon his lips as he beckoned me to his side.

"Move slowly," he whispered.

Under the suspicious eye of the *vicuna*, I crept to his side. Tequsi's palm held dried and salted kernels of maize. With his squirrel-like sound again, the *vicuna* visibly relaxed. It nosed forward, just enough to snatch more kernels.

"That's wonderful," I whispered.

Tequsi's warm smile and bright eyes had a childlike joy. At that moment, I realized we were alone together. This was not permitted.

"I should not be here." I quietly began to rise. I didn't want to bring Tequsi trouble.

"Shhh. It is all right, Munray. No one can see us. And, if you leave, you will frighten our friend."

"I suppose so." I felt both reluctant and excited.

"Here. You try it."

Tequsi gently took my hand and poured a small mound of the salted kernels into my palm.

"Hold your hand out. Like so. Hold it still. Let him come to you to take the food."

I did as he explained. The *vicuna* looked confused that I—not Tequsi—extended my hand. Once more, Tequsi made the chittering sound. The animal blinked several times, decided to trust me, and stepped forward toward my outstretched palm. First, it nuzzled my fingers. It then sniffed the maize with its warm breath, licked at the salt with its dark tongue, and, at last, gobbled all the kernels. As it contentedly chewed the hardened grain, it stared directly into my eyes.

"He likes you, Munray," Tequsi whispered.

"I think he likes the salt."

"That too." Tequsi's smile was infectious. It seemed unfair I was not permitted to speak with such young men.

"Can I try it again?" My voice betrayed my excitement.

"Yes."

I gave my hand to Tequsi, and he cradled it as before. As he held it, our eyes met. I could feel my heart race and my face become flushed. Suddenly, my hand felt awkward in Tequisi's tender grasp.

"Munray." His eyes were serious. "If only I could take your place."

"What do you mean?"

"Tequsi!" Chaqara's angry voice bellowed across the mountainside.

Frightened, I jumped away from Tequsi. The kernels spilled on the ground. The terrified *vicuna* dashed away as its hooves scattered the rocks and ice.

"This is forbidden!" Chaqara roared with rage as he approached us. "Munray, return to Yuyarinu at once."

I confronted him.

"It was nothing, Chaqara. We were feeding a hungry *vicuna*. It is my fault, not his."

"Please go, Munray. Tequsi knows our law. I must speak to him alone."

"I am sorry," I said to Tequsi.

I began picking my way back across the snow-covered rocks. At the ridgetop, I looked back just as Chaqara severely struck Tequsi's hand with his staff. Tequsi barely flinched. All the way back, I could still hear Chaqara unendingly berating Tequsi. I felt guilty that my indiscretion had created such terrible trouble for Tequsi; I also felt ashamed that I felt as I had at the touch of his hand.

It was now our eighteenth day. We only had a half-day to attain the upper *huaca* before the sun reached its highest point. The way before us was perilous, and our progress would be slow. And so, we began the day well before dawn, guided only by moonlight and starlight. There was no time to prepare our morning tea. No time for talk. There was only time to tightly wrap ourselves in layers of heavy clothing in preparation for our final ascent. May the gods watch over us.

In the frigid half-light of the moon, Yuyarinu cautiously picked her way across the frozen ground and carried two small pouches, which she solemnly hung around my neck. From the largest, she withdrew several dark green leaves.

"Do you know what these are, Munray?"

"Yes." I examined them in the moonlight.

"And have you seen the men use them?"

"Yes. The men who visit Cuzco from the mountain villages are never without it."

"Good. Then you understand," Yuyarinu said. "This will warm your heart against the bitter cold and keep you well in the high ground."

Throughout the empire, the sacred *cuca* leaves grew on the hillsides in the higher foothills. Outside of Cuzco, nearly all the men—and many women—chewed the leaves. Sometimes their cheeks bulged so full that they could not speak. They sucked in silence in their inward quest for higher spirituality. Yet I had also seen those who were unable to be without the herb. Their lost souls stared blankly from lifeless, sunken eyes as they constantly chewed—from first light and into night's darkness—great quantities of the leaves. Crumbling, black teeth betrayed constant use. One of my earliest memories was of helping the women of my village harvest the leaves. But, in my village, the leaves were only used in sacred ceremonies.

"Put them in your mouth, chew for a moment, then place them between your cheek and gums. You need only suck upon them after that. This second pouch contains the powder of baked shells. Wet your finger like so," Yuyarinu demonstrated. "Dip it into the powder, and coat the leaves inside your mouth. It will strengthen their powers. Each time you stop to rest, replace the leaves, and again apply the powder."

"What will the others think?" I was reluctant to place the leaves into my mouth. My father had often spoken harshly about those who fell into dependence.

"They understand. Please do this, Munray. It is important."

I nodded. I knew little of the gods' will. But I trusted Yuyarinu.

Setting out on the snowfield, I obediently chewed the leaves. I grimaced at their bitter taste. Then, as Yuyarinu instructed, I tongued them into a corner and covered the soggy clump with the powder of the shells. My teeth and gums grew numb, and I stirred with a curious sense of energy. As the darkness gave way to the first hints of dawn, waves of warmth slowly pulsed through my chest. Slightly light-headed, I felt a strange tingling behind my eyes.

Later, as Inti's fiery sphere emerged to paint the heavens, I caught myself staring mindlessly across the horizon. Pink-orange radiance streamed through a cold purple sky, transforming to remarkable shades and hues I had never before seen.

Still hours from our goal, we slowly climbed through a terrifying, frozen landscape—monstrous blocks of ice rising overhead and gaping caverns beneath our feet. Our pace was a crawl as we cautiously wound—first one way and then another—amid a myriad of obstacles. Awaqapak bravely led us, probing with his staff in search of cracks hidden by snowfall that could easily swallow us.

As we tenderly treaded the lip of a great abyss, our eyes were drawn down its throat. Each of us knew that, beneath the sheer blue ice walls, bottomless caverns led to the underworld at the earth's core. It was there—deep in the darkness below—where evil ones wandered bitterly cold eternally in the afterlife. Stones were their only sustenance.

Once we passed the shattered ground, we faced the steepest leg of our journey. By now, Chaqara gasped for breath with each labored step. Even Phanchi struggled for air as he cut step after step for us in the frozen snow.

"Why have we stopped? We are so close the high *huaca*."

"It is time for you to breathe the vapors of the leaves, Munray," Chaqara said.

"No, Chaqara. I feel wonderful now. My heart glows within. It is as though I am floating on the sea of clouds below."

"You must, Munray." Chaqara's voice was unyielding.

"But I am afraid, Chaqara. I am afraid."

While many chew the *cuca* leaves, breathing their smoke was reserved for shamans and dream watchers. Those who inhaled the sacred vapors separated from their bodies and crossed into the spirit world. If one did not possess strong magical powers, they could not return across the bridge of smoke to reenter their earthly form. They were lost forever.

"I have had so much of the *cuca* already," I pleaded wearily. "So very much."

Yuyarinu stepped forward. "Please, Munray. It will make the final part of your journey easier. Do it for me." Her voice and eyes were filled with sadness. I panicked.

"Yuyarinu! I cannot remember my sacred prayers. I cannot remember anything. Everything is so confused. So many depend upon me. How shall I face them if I fail?" Awaqapak had warned us that many become foolish high on the mountain. Is that what had happened to me? I only wanted to help my people.

Yuyarinu tenderly held my face in her hands.

"I will pray with you, my beautiful joy. All of us will pray with you."

Chaqara and I crouched beneath my thick *chusi* to shield us from the wind. He crushed dried leaves into the bowl of a stone pipe. He sparked the leaves, blowing the tiny embers into a flame. Obediently, I received the pipe and deeply inhaled.

The mystical energy of the blue smoke surged like a wave through my young being. The burning began in my lungs, rushed into my blood, and flowed to my heart and mind. My skin quivered like a hummingbird as the leaves' magic seemed to flow from each pore. The acrid fumes released the spirit from my body. I rose far above our small group that was huddled on the mountainside. I was becoming the blueness of the sky, the rush of the wind, the warring clouds below. I felt the *huaca's* sacred power reaching for me. I summoned all my strength to resist the spirit world's powerful allure. I must not abandon my earthly presence. I was here to serve the empire and save our people. I could not forsake our journey's mission.

My body had become clumsy. I repeatedly tripped and stumbled on the frozen slopes. In spirit, this did not matter. I no longer needed my limbs. I could soar up the great mountain with the wind. Tequsi and Awaqapak were at my sides, one on each arm, helping my body climb upward. How foolish they looked, wrapped and bundled so tightly. It was so warm. My legs took one step…then another…one step…then another.

Closer to the mountain's peak, I gazed at my fingers. They had turned a beautiful, iridescent bluish-black color, like the sunset before a storm.

"Look," I held them out to Tequsi. "Are they not beautiful?"

Tequsi turned away, refusing to look. I could feel him tighten his grip on my arm, but he seemed distant, far away. My legs continued plodding upward. One step…then another…one step…another.

Were we at the top so soon? The highest *huaca* in the empire? Surrounding us were the snow-capped crowns of many mountains. The three *chasqui* dug the frozen snow with their *piachas*. What were they searching for? Something hidden beneath the snow? Where was Sisay? Why is she not at my side?

Many hands guided me into the small pit in the snow. I was gently eased into a sitting position; my knees were placed tight against my chest. Yuyarinu removed my sandals. Chaqara took my bright *chusi* that had warmed me on the journey. Why did I not understand?

Through a fog, I saw their faces peering into the pit, down upon me. Tequsi looked so sad; tears were streaming down his handsome face. Then I saw the truth in Tequsi's tears. I would not return to the Sun Temple. I would remain atop the mountain forever.

As the ice and snow was replaced around me, I could faintly hear my voice—my own voice—softly humming, "*Wanuyulla, wanuy wanucha, amaraq aparuwaychu karraqmi puririnay.*" Death o death, do not take me away yet. I still have a long way to go.

PART II

▼

PRESENT DAY

CHAPTER 2

▼

JAKE
HIGH GROUND

The tungsten point of my climbing axe shattered the frozen surface, penetrating a half-inch into the ice. It was just enough so that I could momentarily shift my weight. I kicked two front crampon points into the mountain's sheer face and inched upward a half-step. The steel prongs strapped to my boots barely held me. My heart pounded with each step as I gasped for breath. At 6,400 meters, there was only half the oxygen of sea level. I was exhausted. My legs felt like I was carrying an anvil.

This climb was way out of my league. I wasted precious energy using brute strength instead of technical skill. The 1,000-meter drop below, nearly straight down, scared the hell out of me. It took all my effort to block the fear that makes climbers weak and tentative. I couldn't wait to get down.

The mountain made it clear I was no longer Jake Morgan, the gifted athlete. Instead, I was an over-the-hill, thirty-eight-year-old, bundled in black wind pants and blue anorak, sucking wind where I had no business being. No matter how hard I physically trained, my best years were behind me. I couldn't compete any longer with climbers half my age. And clinging to a sheer wall of ice and rock probably wasn't the best place to make that realization. Sixty feet above me, my younger, stronger, and more capable cousin, Tom Lucas, smoothly took in rope on an anchored belay. Our red nylon lifeline, anchored by a mere seventeen-centimeter ice screw, was the same thin margin that had permanently betrayed two French climbers on this same mountain only last week.

In another ten minutes, I dragged myself up over the small ledge where Tom crouched, shielding him from the biting wind.

"Good job." Tom shouted encouragingly above the gales, even though I was inches from him. "Just a bit more."

"That's a relief." I was heaving to catch my breath.

"What?" Tom shouted back. I signaled it was nothing.

"Clip into the anchor," Tom yelled into the howling wind. "I'll set another screw while you belay Jorge,"

"Right." I clipped the ice screw's locking carabiner into my harness' yellow webbing. Only then was it safe to remove myself from Tom's belay. It was a fundamental law of high mountaineering to never remove yourself from one safety anchor until you were attached to another. Most climbing deaths resulted from a moment's carelessness—a poorly placed anchor, a loose-fitting harness, a broken crampon, or a single misplaced step.

In preparation for this climb, I'd trained in the mountains of British Columbia, culminating with a climb up the Coleman headwall on Washington State's Mount Baker. But, even that regimen left me ill-prepared for the technically demanding north face. And the draining effect of altitude only made things worse.

"How's our time?" I signaled my wrist, just in case my words didn't carry.

"We're okay. You did great, Jake," Tom shouted close to my ear. "We've got two hours to summit. As soon as Jorge's up here, we'll take a quick break."

"I can use it."

I threaded the red line through the figure eight belay device. I took in several meters of rope to eliminate slack between the anchor and Jorge, our Peruvian guide, who was waiting eighty feet below.

"On belay!" I shouted down the face, signaling Jorge it was "safe" to begin climbing the steep pitch. But the wind carried my signal across the empty void of space before it reached Jorge. I waved my arm until he caught sight of me. I gradually pulled in rope through the braking mechanism as he methodically worked his way up this portion of the face.

"Keep the line taught," I kept telling myself. "Keep it taught, so, if he falls, this anchor might just hold."

Huascaran Norte reaches 6,654 meters, towering over the high Peruvian plains. Long considered higher than its sister peak, Huascaran Sur, a 1938 survey showed Norte was actually 114 meters shorter. Though the twin mountains are Peru's highest and among the tallest in the western hemisphere, the backside of these peaks contained routes of only moderate difficulty. They can be scaled by intermediate level mountaineers—amateurs in the eyes of climbing's elite.

Yet the north face of Huascaran Norte—where Tom, Jorge, and I struggled—presented some of the most dangerous climbing in the world. The face is a sheer wall; its pitches range between sixty and ninety vertical degrees, jutting 1,400 meters above the frigid glacier below. On the southern routes, the final 1,400-meter gain could be accomplished in a day. Here, it required three.

Norte's final pitches were the mountain's worst. The rock was rotten and honeycombed with hidden cracks.

Tom had picked the Spanish route—up the left side of the massive headwall—even though it hadn't been summitted this way since that one Spanish climb via the route in 1983. My cousin was obsessed on being the second to summit by this approach. But technical difficulty wasn't the only problem. The Spanish route required unusually dry conditions. Only now, two decades after the route's first ascent, had a window of opportunity appeared. Peru suffered a devastating drought last year, even worse than the severe spell in 1983. Never had Norte's ice and snow levels been so low.

Tom twisted a second ice screw into place and then threaded the handle of his ice axe through the eye of the screw for additional leverage. After he placed the second support anchor, he glanced in my direction.

As cousins, Tom and I saw little of each other growing up. My father and Tom's mother (who were brother and sister) were never close. Besides, Tom's family moved from British Columbia to Whitehorse (in the Yukon Territory) when he was six years old. With rare family gatherings, the two of us barely knew each other…until four years ago when I discovered my twenty-four-year-old cousin was one of the most respected mountain climbers in western Canada. I'd been looking for an experienced guide so I could take a business associate up Mt. Slesse. Tom showed up on my short list. I hired him on the spot, and we've stayed in frequent contact ever since.

One glance at Tom and it was obvious we'd inherited looks from opposite gene pools. Tom's straw-blonde hair and blue eyes gave him the handsome looks of a mythological Nordic hero. On the other hand, my deeply lined face was covered in a scruffy three-week-old beard. My green eyes were tired and bloodshot. Fortunately, my black, dirty, matted hair was hidden beneath a fleece hat. In short, I looked about the same way I felt.

Tom also was the most gifted climber I'd ever seen, possessing a rare blend of strength, agility, and grace. Where most climbers struggled and groped, Tom moved effortlessly with calm, inner confidence. I sensed it from the first moment we climbed together.

The last of our trio was Jorge Morales, forty-one years old, who, at first glance, appeared wholly miscast to approach any summit. Far from imposing, he stood only five feet four inches high. He had the thick, black hair and dark, innocent eyes of the locals. Two large gold teeth punctuated his wide, ready grin.

That said, I'd bet Jorge was the most dependable leg of our group. A professional guide for twenty-three years, he'd ferried climbers to every major summit in the Cordillera Blanca range. A native of Huaraz (elevation 3,055 meters), the jumping-off point for climbers entering the region, Jorge had spent a lifetime becoming acclimated to altitude stress. Tom and I marveled at his stamina.

Halfway up the sheer pitch, part of the ice-covered rock supporting Jorge cracked free. His feet shot out from under him. His face slammed against the sharp frozen rock. The red line snapped tight, rigid as a piano wire. My single ice screw strained under Jorge's full weight.

"He fell!" I shouted into the violent gusts of wind. "Tom, I can't raise him. I'm stuck!"

Carelessly, I had my hand between the line and the ground as I fed the rope through the figure eight. It was a stupid mistake. When the rope sprang tight, my right hand was instantly pinned between the lip of the ledge and the line. I'd belayed climbers dozens of times. I knew better. It was fatigue I thought. Fatigue and altitude.

The moment Tom turned to face me, the rope slipped another inch. Stress fractures spider-webbed the ice around the straining anchor.

"The screw's slipping!"

"Hold on! I'll anchor it!"

If the ice screw gave way on this sheer face, the rope would act as a deathtrap, pulling me...and then Tom...down with Jorge to our deaths.

Quickly, Tom secured and tightened a support line from the second ice screw to the first, but the menacing cracks still continued to appear. Once the first anchor was relatively safe, Tom scrambled to the front of the ledge where my hand was pinned and in pain. With the handle of his ice axe, he levered the line, taut as a bowstring. I extracted my hand, shaking the numbness from my fingers.

"I'll take the belay. See if he's okay."

Tom held a third ice screw. If Jorge was hurt or unconscious, he'd be ready to place it for an additional anchor. Cautiously, I craned over the overhang, peering down the massive precipice to where Jorge hung. Bright blood ran from his slashed cheek and forehead. Droplets blew and scattered, quickly freezing into tiny red pellets before disappearing in the void below.

This wasn't the first time Jorge had slipped and fallen on so unforgiving a route. But I knew, when he did, it terrified him. He had confided to us his hatred of the rope. Dangling, he was like a toy on a string, suspended above a horrible death. His life was now beyond his control. It was at the mercy of a few pieces of metal screwed into ice by another's hand.

Every climber in Jorge's tenuous position hears the same mental questions: Was the anchor properly set? Would the belay hold? Would the sharp edge of the ledge sever the line? How badly am I hurt? Can I move? Are my partners capable?

After a few moments, I could see Jorge regain a foothold. He swung his northwall hammer with ferocious force into the windswept ice. He was back on the mountain and moving up.

"He's climbing!" I squeezed Tom's shoulder. "He's okay!"

The rope slackened. Tom began taking in line.

We helped Jorge up and over the shelf's final lip. The blood from his facial abrasions had frozen; the bleeding had stopped. The right lens of his goggles was a mass of cracks where he struck the rock.

"Your belay saved me, Señor Morgan. It saved us all." Jorge squeezed my arm. "I am greatly indebted."

"Tom's the one you should thank."

"*Muchas gracias* to both of you." The Peruvian grinned. "Let's hope I never have to return the favor."

"Likewise," Tom shouted. "You strong enough to continue?"

"Jorge is A-okay."

"Jake?"

"Fine."

"Good. We'll take a quick break before the final push."

Precariously perched atop the narrow ledge, we rested briefly and gazed down on the world below. Low clouds in the east obscured the sprawling Amazon Basin that stretched thousands of miles into Brazil.

"How much further?" I hoped we were close. I wasn't sure how much I had left in me.

"Should be one more pitch. About 150 feet." Tom scanned the face. "Once we reach the high ridge, it should level out to the summit."

"We'll descend the southern traverse," Jorge said. "Much easier. Only twelve hours to base camp? Yes?"

I withdrew one of the three insulated water bottles from my pack, taking several long gulps. Iodine-purified water. The first I'd drunk for several hours. Jorge had repeatedly warned us that, above 5,000 meters, we needed five to six liters of fluids a day just to keep pace with the water lost through breathing.

Jorge handed us sections from a frozen chocolate bar and then gestured toward the multitude of snow-covered peaks of the northern Cordillera Blanca.

"All the mountains are out today." He slipped a piece of the rock-hard chocolate in his mouth.

"They're fantastic." Tom had a sincere appreciation for the Andes.

"Five of them are over 6,000 meters," Jorge said, wiping away the frozen blood from his face. "Chacraraju, the Huandoy massive, Artesonraju, Cariz, and Quitaraju."

Tom scrutinized the nearby peaks. I drifted off, lost in private thought.

The title on my business cards read, *Historical Salvage Engineer*. Formal verbiage. The truth? I was a treasure hunter.

Ever since my earliest childhood, I'd been fascinated by legends of lost treasures—from hidden diamond mines to lost pirate loot just waiting for someone clever enough (or committed enough) to unravel their ancient secrets and wrestle the prize from its hiding place.

I wore several hats in my line of work: researcher, fund-raiser, publicity manager, logistics expert, payroll master, and engineer. Sometimes father confessor. But I always knew my most valuable contribution was to inspire, that is, to shake up every financial backer, media representative, and, most importantly, members of my expeditions. I was to instill a sense of the unlimited possibilities that lay beyond the next bend in the river, over the next mountain, beneath the next shovel full of earth, and just over the horizon. I was to awaken in them the enthusiasm and passion to discover long-lost riches, the same two drives that fueled my every action.

Yet recently, my armor of confidence had suffered some dents. I'd begun to doubt myself—or more truthfully—doubt the merits of my craft. The fact was that my salvage failures far outnumbered my successes. I was wondering if it was finally time to grow up and stop chasing dreams and rainbows just out of reach. Was it time for me to settle down to something respectable, something less self-serving?

I had accepted Tom's invitation to attempt the north face as an escape. It had been eight months since my salvage project on Oak Island, Nova Scotia, had gained so much attention. But, within an amazingly short amount of time, the limelight lost its luster. Here, thousands of miles away from the glare of the press, I could focus all my thoughts on the pure challenge of reaching this summit.

The trip would serve as a test beyond the mountain's physical challenge. The Andes were a storehouse of legend. The forgotten emerald mines of Ecuador. The lost ransom of Atahualpa. Bolivia's mountain of silver. The legendary Incan gold mines. Perhaps, if I could resist the temptation of these local legends, I could conquer my obsessive fortune hunting—a compulsion for which I'd paid dearly. Over the years, it had cost me my marriage, my inheritance, most of my friends, and even my most recent relationship. In many ways, I was like a recovering alcoholic entering a bar just to prove I'd beaten the cravings. Only, deep down inside, I wasn't honestly sure if I really wanted to pass this particular test.

"Damn!" Tom jumped to his feet, paying for the sudden movement with a shortness of breath and a racing pulse. I awoke from my private reverie.

"We've got to get moving. We've been here nearly forty minutes!"

He was right. We had to be vigilant against the deterioration in judgment and distorted sense of time that fatigued climbers experience at altitude. Mount Everest was littered with the corpses of climbers who had lain down to rest momentarily near the summit and simply dozed off into oblivion.

The final pitch followed a steep, sixty-degree *couloir* of frozen snow.

After thirty minutes of slow, cautious climbing, we topped a knife-edge ridge. Its sides dropped off sharply, but the top of it offered a gently sloping pathway to the summit, now only several hundred meters away. That was the first moment I realized I was going to make it.

For the first time, the three of us had a clear, unrestricted panoramic view. The majestic sweep of the snow-capped Cordillera Blanca filled the horizon in every direction. To the south, beyond the dominating form of Huascaran Sur, rose Tocllaraju, Chinchey, Pucaranta, and Palcarayu. Now Tom and I knew why the Andes were considered the most spectacular range outside the Himalayas. This view made each day of the prior three weeks worthwhile.

Looking north, past several peaks jutting through the sea of clouds, Jorge pointed out two distant mountains, barely visible on the far horizon.

"That is Ecuador. Chimborazo has the great dome summit. The white volcanic cone is Cotopaxi. They are volcanoes *extinguido*…dead."

A few moments later, we reached the summit, a circular area approximately sixty feet in diameter.

"Congratulations!" I shook Tom's hand and then Jorge's. "I couldn't have made it without the two of you."

I had summitted by one of the most difficult routes on the mountain, and I was about to burst my blue and black get up with pride.

"Señor Tom, you are the best climber I've had the honor to guide." Jorge smiled broadly. "And Señor Morgan, you have accomplished something few others in world ever will!"

We were rightfully jubilant.

"You both pulled my sorry ass up this thing, and I know it," I conceded.

"It was a great team effort," said Tom. "Although I don't think Jorge broke a sweat." He then looked out to the southwest, his joy transforming to concern.

The clear weather was visibly deteriorating. Dark storm clouds had gathered.

"The storm will be here in several hours." A hard edge had invaded Jorge's easy manner.

Tom snapped into action.

"Okay. A few minutes for pictures. Then we need to head down."

Jorge and I readily agreed.

We had each carried small, lightweight cameras for this occasion. Tom and I posed several times with my small Canadian flag. Jorge attempted a number of self-timer shots to snap the three of us together. I volunteered to take a final shot of Jorge and Tom.

Peering through my Minolta's tiny viewfinder to center the two, I noticed a small scrap of red cloth, no bigger than a dollar, frozen to the ground but violently whipping in the wind.

It is common practice for successful climbers to leave small remembrances at the summit of major peaks: prayer flags, nostalgic trinkets, pictures of loved ones, or pictures of dearly departed. And, each year, the fury of ferocious winter storms sweeps the summits clean of these lonely keepsakes. Perhaps rightfully, the simple objects, so personally sacred, disappear somewhere into the mountain's vast permanence.

I lowered the camera. I was fixated on the flapping red blotch. I felt drawn to it for some unexplainable reason.

"What's wrong?" Tom shouted.

"Something left behind." I bent to the cloth.

"Just leave it, Jake. We don't have time." Tom frowned at the dark storm clouds in the distance.

I stopped, yielding to Tom's leadership. He was right. The pillar of clouds in the southwest would soon be upon us. We needed to get off the mountain as fast as possible. We put on our packs and coiled the rope between us to descend down the easier southern side. Then I caught sight of the red cloth again.

"Oh hell, Tom. It'll only take a second."

"There's no time, Jake!" Tom's composure was gone.

I knelt near the red material. "Occupational hazard." I grinned. I couldn't explain why I was drawn to it. I hoped exhaustion hadn't pilfered all my judgment.

Tom and Jorge approached with reluctance. No doubt, they wanted to dissuade me from wasting precious time.

"It's woven." Jorge examined the wool cloth in his glove. "Looks like llama or alpaca. Very old."

I carefully chipped the ice-like snow from around the cloth, revealing a larger and larger piece of red.

"It's a blanket."

Jorge reached down and tugged at the woolen cloth.

"Whoever left it up here…" Tom's words were cut short as Jorge ripped the stiffly frozen blanket free.

We knelt in stunned silence at what lay before us.

CHAPTER 3

▼

JAKE
THE MOUNTAIN'S DEAD

Gazing at us was the upturned face of a perfectly preserved young woman. A peaceful expression fixed on her delicate features, long since frozen in time.

"Holy Jesus!" This was the last thing Tom expected.

"Inca. Human sacrifice to their gods." Jorge made the sign of the cross. "*Que Dios tenga merced hacia ella.*"

"Up here?"

"A lot of their sacrifices were on mountaintops," I explained. "They believed it brought them closer to Inti, the Sun god."

Jorge nodded in agreement.

It's hard to describe how I felt. It was a mixture of horror and fascination. Horror in being face to face with the hideous practice of human sacrifice; fascination over the historical significance and perfection of what we'd stumbled upon.

"How old is it?" Tom had to shout above the wind.

"Don't know. Four to five hundred years, I'd guess. I can't tell just by looking at it."

"Yes. Very old," Jorge agreed.

Even without extensive knowledge of South American culture, Tom knew this was a phenomenal archaeological find.

In 1999, Johan Reinhard found three frozen mummies in Argentina on the summit of Cerro Llullaillaco (6,739 meters). The discovery shook the archaeological world. Prior to that time, it was inconceivable that these ancient people would have climbed such heights in deference to their gods. Yet our discovery was of even greater importance.

Even the simplest route on Huascaran Norte is vastly more difficult than a climb up Cerro, which is actually more akin to a steep hike. How had this frail young woman reached the summit of so daunting a mountain? Her people must have been incredibly tough.

But, more importantly, previously discovered mountain sacrifices had been partially exposed to the elements, which had marred their preservation. The girl huddled before us was so lifelike that she looked as though she was in the midst of a peaceful sleep and might awaken at any moment. I could almost imagine her eyes slowly opening, her hands gently wiping away the crystals of ice clinging to her fragile lashes.

The small figure was in a sitting position; her knees were pressed closely against her chest. Her arms were tightly folded as if she had tried to warm herself against the cold. The remains of a white, feathered headdress held her thick black hair in place. A cape made of intricately woven, multicolored feathers covered layers of heavy wool clothing. A crude necklace with four black amulets hung from her neck. Her skin had taken on a bright ivory hue, long since drained of its true color by the frigid temperature. I'd never seen anything like it. It was a vivid reminder that she would never wake from her slumber.

Tom gently reached to touch the ornate cape. Jorge seized his hand.

"Do not touch!" Jorge's voice had a hard authoritative tone, completely unfamiliar.

"Bad luck to disturb the dead."

I agreed with Jorge, although not for the sake of curses or bad luck. I was worried Tom might inadvertently damage precious archeological data.

A piercing blast of wind brought us back to the present. We stood atop a barren mountain, utterly exposed in the path of a storm.

"It's moving in fast! We've got to get down." Tom was rightfully worried. The wind was growing stronger. I was visibly shivering. My fingers were getting numb.

High-altitude storms kill. Savage winds plunge the chill factor deep into minus territory, and visibility deteriorates to less than a meter. In the midst of such a tempest, we could blindly stumble over a cliff, literally be blown off the mountain, or freeze to death if we couldn't dig a snow cave. It was not exactly the way I wanted to end things.

"Tom, do you have any film left?" I shouted.

"Sorry. We used it all for the summit shots."

"I've got six shots left. Jorge?"

"Just one."

"We need to shoot this and cover it back up. It's an important find, Tom. We've got to protect it." Historians searched their entire lives for this kind of discovery. I couldn't leave it exposed to the elements.

"All right, but hurry."

I photographed the forlorn little figure as rapidly as possible, double-checking the camera's settings to ensure the photos were properly exposed and focused. These pictures were far more important than our self-congratulatory summit snapshots.

Reburying the figure was more difficult and time-consuming than we anticipated. We had to scrape and cut ice chips. The top of Norte was windswept of any loose snow from the summit's frozen surface. The brunt of the storm was nearly on top of us. I hoped I hadn't caused a fatal error.

Jorge and I turned to gather more ice while Tom delicately packed the sad figure. When I turned back around, Tom was coughing hard into his orange handkerchief.

"You okay?" I shouted.

"Altitude." Tom was the last person I'd expect to have trouble. He clumsily zipped the cloth back into his parka and returned to the burial task.

We made a small mound over the young Inca and marked the spot with several short bamboo trail wands. The appropriate authorities could recover her under better conditions. Tom and I would be returning home to Canada.

"Let's see how fast we can get off this beast!" Tom quickly gathered the red line. "Jorge, how far till the icefall?"

"Nearly 1,000 meters, but easy climbing. Thirty-five- to forty-five-degree slope the whole way."

"All right, Jorge, you lead. Let's look sharp! No letdown! No mistakes!"

I needed to concentrate on the climb for the moment and ignore our incredible discovery. I was physically spent from our effort and weak from both dehydration and altitude. I'd read about climbers who, once having achieved their goal, psychologically drop their guard just enough to allow a moment's carelessness. I planned on getting down in one piece.

We crossed the south rim and immediately began our descent. Jorge had been correct. The south side of Huascaran Norte was a much more gradual decline. There were occasional frozen snow pitches of fifty vertical degrees, but, for the most part, it was straightforward climbing. There was no need for belays.

Pursued by the storm, we made excellent time and reached the icefall in less than three hours. We were still ahead of the foul weather. Looking back, the summit was entirely enveloped by a dark gray cloud cover.

Descending is always easier, and, with each step down the mountain, the air progressively thickened with energizing, rejuvenating oxygen. The farther we hiked from the summit, the stronger we felt.

It took us another two hours to pass through the icefall, the most dangerous part of the glacier where the thick ice buckles and cracks. We were surrounded by massive ice blocks, or seracs, towering fifteen, thirty, or forty-five feet high, and crevasses, the deep glacial cracks that drop off into black nothingness.

Lacking the high snows of previous years, which form snow bridges over crevasses, the ground was now a maze of gaping fissures. We repeatedly belayed one another—once we repelled down the face of an otherwise impassable fifty-foot drop—and often backtracked around crevasses too wide to leap across. Jorge repeatedly lamented the mountain's poor condition. Sadly, the great glaciers across the world were all slowly melting. As we left the icefall, the wind began to wane. The storm apparently content to punish the mountain's summit. That's when it happened.

Face down, Tom slid by me with his arms limp at his sides and his ice axe trailing behind him.

"Falling!" I shouted. Jorge and I threw ourselves into self-arrest, sinking our axes into the snow. We only had a few seconds to arrest Tom's fall. The rope on my harness pulled tight as Tom jerked to a stop. A rock-like projectile of ice bounced down the slope. We rushed to Tom and turned him over. His eyes were open, lifeless and blank. I shook him. No response. The snow beneath his head was turning red.

"Tom!" I ripped off my gloves and pressed bare fingers to his throat.

"I can't find a pulse!" I was frantic. Not Tom. It couldn't be. I shook him, as if to wake him, but his eyes never registered. "What's happened?"

"Blessed Mary." Once again, Jorge made a sign of the cross. He looked down the mountain. "It was the ice."

The ice chunk had been no bigger than a grapefruit and probably weighed less than ten pounds. But the momentum gained in its long free fall made it deadly. It could have struck any of us because we all had our backs to the upper mountain, but Tom was in the rear. It smashed the base of his skull and killed him instantly. Jorge and I hadn't even heard it.

"Jesus." The finality of the situation sank in. A split second and Tom was gone.

We wrapped Tom's body in a bivouac sack and bound him to a makeshift sled. It was unbearable, seeing him lying there so lifeless in a cocoon. I was the older cousin and felt responsible. I'd let him down. I should have been able to prevent this. We tied two lines to the back of the sled so we could control its descent. Jorge held the shorter piece. I trailed behind. I was glad Jorge couldn't see my eyes.

It was nightfall by the time we reached base camp. Our porters had already arrived from the northern route. Camp was set up. I made arrangements for Tom to be transported down to Musho by burro and then on to Lima by bus, where we would fly home to Vancouver. It was well past midnight by the time Jorge and I had a moment's solitude.

Numbly, I stared into the hissing fire of the gas cook stove, seeking inner warmth and solace from the sterile blue flame and familiar smell of propane. Jorge handed me a plastic cup of coca tea and squatted beside me. He had a cup as well.

As a climber, I could never fully separate myself from the specter of death. No climber could, no matter how practiced or skilled. Mountain climbing contains elements of the unpredictable and random—an unexpected avalanche, unforeseen rock fall, collapsing serac, or failed snow bridge dropping the unsuspecting into frigid darkness. Simply put, some climbers are just in the wrong place at the wrong time. Call it a twist of fate…or just plain bad luck.

"Señor Lucas was the best climber I have ever guided." It was the first time that Jorge had referred to Tom as Señor Lucas. "The Spanish route up the headwall. Only a few men in the world could have led it."

People react differently to tragedy. Some keep to themselves; others talk. I was surprised to find that Jorge was a talker. I think it helped both of us.

"I had another man die with me once, seven years ago, but he was not a climber. He was a good man, but he did not belong high on the mountain."

"Do you ever wonder if this is all worth it, Jorge? The mountains? The climbing?"

"The mountains are my life, Señor Morgan. This is all I know."

"Your family doesn't worry?"

"They understand I cannot change who I am." Jorge drank from his cup. "You told me you hunt treasure. That is who you are. It cannot be changed. As Señor Lucas could not change who he was."

"He had family." Just saying the words brought pain.

"Yes, I know. He showed me pictures. Beautiful children. I am very sorry."

Quietly, we sipped our tea and stared at the stove's small flame. The wind had mellowed now and was merely a breeze.

"There is an old saying, '*Sí se aman a las montañas, nunca se envejecera.*' If you love the mountains, you will never grow old. But I think this has two meanings, no?" Jorge said. "Señor Lucas loved the mountains very much."

"Yes," I answered. "He loved them very much."

I had already selfishly begun to dread the grim task of calling Susan with the news. Her husband, the father of their two children, was dead. He would be coming home in the cold belly of a cargo plane.

"At first, I blamed myself. I am responsible. It is my job to guide you down the mountain." Jorge spoke quietly. "But I thought again and again of our route, and I don't understand how it happened. We traversed away from the icefall. We weren't under it. There were no overhangs above us for the ice to break off. It's as if it appeared from nothing."

I was too self-absorbed in my grief and guilt to ponder Jorge's words.

Chapter 4

▼

Emma
Laid to Rest

I was named after my great-great grandmother, Emma Day Morgan, but everyone calls me Em. I had always hated funerals.

Only fifteen years old, I had already been to four funerals—three for my grandparents. Then Tom. I honestly didn't know Tom Lucas very well. He was a third or fourth cousin so I only saw him at a few family gatherings. I remember him from years ago as an obnoxious teenager who threw my doll up on the roof to tease me. But Tom was family, and that meant we attended his service. And that meant our grief was real. We Morgans put a lot of stock into family.

Lately, I had to lean on the family myself. My first year at high school, as a freshman, had been hard. There was a whole new group of students to gawk and stare at me. I encountered everything from naïve curiosity to really hurtful jokes. I could hear it all as I passed by. But I'd overcome it at middle school, and I knew I'd get past it now. It just seemed worse this year. There's so much more pressure in high school to be in the "popular" crowd, wear the right clothes, have the right make-up, be seen with the right people, and, of course, always look good.

My friends considered me cute and perky—although perky sounds to me like a fox terrier—with my thick, reddish-brown, shoulder-length hair and a bunch of freckles splashed across my cheeks and upturned nose. I had inherited the dark green Morgan eyes and—thanks to eighteen months of braces—my mom said I had a perfect Hollywood smile. So maybe before, I was cute.

Then, a little over a year ago, my dad and I were driving home from a movie. A drunk driver ran a red light and smashed into my side of the car. My dad was okay, but I spent five weeks in the hospital and lost my right arm. It was my prosthetic arm that attracted so much of the unwanted kind of attention. Kids stared at it; adults seemed to think it was a testimony to my bravery. While most of the time I was just thankful to be alive, there had also been lots of nights when I cried in my room. Honest. Sometimes I was repulsed by the cold metal attached there...where my arm should have been.

We waited in line to crowd into the small chapel at Vancouver's Mountain View Cemetery, a pretty peaceful oasis in the heart of such a cosmopolitan downtown. As the name implied, the green hillside of gravestones had an unobstructed view of the mountains just north of the city. Today, we drove down from our suburban home in Brackendale, a little town forty-two miles north of Vancouver, British Columbia.

My immediate family was hopelessly middle-class. I used to think we could have been the poster family for the "Average Canadian Family of the Year." My parents were high school sweethearts who married right after my dad had graduated from college. They had two kids: Joel, my eleven-year-old brother, and me. We had lived in the same three-bedroom house since before I was born.

My dad, John, was forty years old, but he looked and acted more like a fifty-year-old. He had been bald as long as I can remember, and he had started to get one of those little paunches right around the middle. He had the same job, an accountant for Griffin Markets, for fifteen years. I used to be embarrassed about my dad. He just seemed so boring and clueless.

Then, last year, when Uncle Jake was in real trouble with no one to turn to, for the first time in his life, my dad stuck out his neck to help his little brother. I was really proud of him after that.

Alice, my mom, was the same age as my dad. A lot of people underestimated my mom because she was so small—only five feet—and often so patient. But, on important stuff, she was a fiery spark plug. She would stand up to anyone if she believed she was right. That could be fun to watch.

We quietly filed up the concrete steps into the somber little church and joined the eighty or ninety people already seated. I slid into one of the dark wooden pews, polished smooth by decades of skirts and pants. The room had the fragrance of the orchids and lilies arranged atop the altar. An usher silently handed us each a small printed memorial about Tom. The photocopied pages had pictures of Tom from toddler to manhood. In the middle, it listed the four people who would give remembrances. Uncle Jake would be last. On the back of the booklet were spectacular mountain scenes that Tom had photographed all over the world. Beneath these pictures was a short Bible passage:

> "I have fought a good fight, I have finished my course. I have kept the faith." II Timothy 4:7

As I glanced around at the sad faces packed in tight in the narrow pews, it struck me how different this service was from the others. The funeral services for each of my grandparents were crowded with their contemporaries, friends, family, and acquaintances—most in their seventies or eighties. The air always seemed stagnant with an odor of mothballs. Today, this drab little chapel was filled with the much younger faces of Tom's friends.

It made me think how cruel climbing fatalities are to friends and family. They don't allow anyone to say good-bye. There wasn't any lingering illness or old age to prepare a family. There wasn't an opportunity to close old wounds between brothers, sisters, or parents. There wasn't a chance for final visits with old friends or to lay to rest petty issues that had festered over the years. Climbing deaths robbed everyone.

As I finished my surveillance of the mourners, my gaze came full circle and settled on Joel. I hated to admit it, but my little brother was growing up. He was only in fifth grade, but he was already as tall as me. His brown hair was still short, practically a buzz-cut, and his brown eyes had that same mischievous spark, like he was about to launch a great practical joke. But my brother was starting to fill out through his chest and shoulders. And, although he didn't admit it to any of us, I could tell he was starting to take notice of girls.

Joel was the natural athlete of our Morgan clan, which had naturally made him popular at school. Lately, to my father's great dismay, he'd lost interest in football and hockey and become completely enthralled with snowboarding in the winter. And in the summer? Paintball! Those two sports weren't exactly cheap, so Joel did odd jobs around the neighborhood for pay. We had to give him credit for that. I knew my mom wasn't exactly thrilled with some of Joel's new friends, but, deep down inside, my kid brother was still the same old Joel.

Recently I'd cut Joel a lot of slack, even when he was being an obnoxious cretin. I remembered how brave he'd been last summer on Oak Island, basically saving Uncle Jake's career as a salvage expert. Today, in the chapel, Joel was blankly staring into space, deep into a daydream about someone…or something.

Uncle Jake walked to the front of the chapel, took some notes from his suit, and put them on the podium.

If my dad was the Morgan family's anchor, Jake was the wind propelling the ship. He was six feet tall, and, although he was two years younger than my dad, his features were craggy, carved stone-like. His face was gaunt and prematurely wrinkled—no doubt the result of countless hours of physical work outdoors in the sun.

Jake had a can-do personality. He was part-dreamer, part-salesman, and part-visionary. Uncle Jake believed anything was possible. He lived by those mottos motivational speakers love to spout. Never give up. Champions never tire. Make no excuses.

He had so much enthusiasm and passion for everything he did; it made you want to believe right along with him—at least if you're my age. I imagined a lot of adults thought Jake was impractical and irresponsible. My dad once called him a flake chasing rainbows. But to Joel and me, Uncle Jake and his endless stories represented fantastic adventures in awesome, exotic lands. In fact, a lot of the places he hunted for treasure weren't even on the map.

Joel and I knew Jake had been with Tom on that fateful climb in Peru. I wondered if Jake felt guilty or somehow responsible for Tom's death. I know my dad blamed himself for the car accident, even though it wasn't his fault. I suspected my Uncle Jake felt the same. As he spoke, I couldn't help thinking how hard this all must have been for him.

"In the past, whenever anyone asked me, 'Why would anyone climb mountains?' I flippantly replied that, if they had to ask, they'd never understand. But I want to explain it now because I think Tom would want all of you here to understand."

"Climbing represents the ultimate challenge. It is a test of our stamina, our perseverance, our determination, and a test of our will to succeed. Climbing forces us to confront our fears and to conquer them. And, in so doing, we grow courageous. It pushes us beyond our limits. And, in so doing, we realize there are no limits. It is knowing we struggled mightily and triumphed in something that many will never even try."

"Some believe mountain climbers are merely thrillseekers, addicted to the exhilaration of treading that narrow path between safety and danger, life and death. I don't believe that's true. But, because the risk of death is ever present, those who step onto a mountain gain a greater appreciation for life. Tom used to say, 'Being on a mountain is living. Everything else is just waiting.'"

Jake's voice cracked, and he paused a moment to steady himself.

"But I think, more importantly, Tom taught many of us to climb for the solitude, the peacefulness, the self-reflection that's only possible while surrounded in an alpine wilderness. Climbing allows us to enter a pristine world, untainted by the hand of man. We leave behind our political bickering, false trappings of society, or the frantic rush of modern civilization. In the mountains, time slows to nature's pace, marked by freshly fallen snow, the passing of the seasons, timeless glaciers, and the rhythms of the earth."

I had told myself I wouldn't cry during the service because I wasn't that close to Tom, but my eyes were burning, and I could feel the back of my throat tightening up. Hearing Jake's words, I realized Tom was someone a lot of people would miss.

"Tom gave so many of us a chance to stand among snow-dusted peaks and crags afire with the crimson glow of dusk. We could awake to dawn's pink light, reflected like a million glimmering diamonds on the frozen glacier. Tom gave us the smell of heather underfoot, a pure wind on our faces, and a silent world above the clouds."

"Tom once told me that, years ago, in a high school English class, he'd read *The Innocents Abroad* by Mark Twain. He said there was a single paragraph between those tattered covers that represented all he felt, perhaps what all climbers feel. He recited it to me one night in camp. 'What is that which swells a man's breast with pride above that which any other experience can bring him? Discovery! To know that you are walking where none others have walked; that you are beholding what human eye has not yet seen before; that you are breathing virgin atmosphere...'"

Jake paused for a moment and then continued in an uneven voice.

"This was Tom's gift to us. He taught us to appreciate the mountains and to love them. He taught us what they meant; he shared their incredible beauty and the healing solitude they offered. I think those of us who were lucky enough to climb with Tom became better people because of it. I know I did. Thanks, Tom. We'll all miss you."

When the service was over, a reception was held in a room next to the chapel. Two long tables, draped in white tablecloths, held large steaming coffee and tea urns, a crystal punch bowl of red fruit punch, and a large assortment of homemade desserts. There were eight different pies, two large berry cobblers, three pans of brownies, a white cake with a great many tiny fingerprints in the frosting, and a dozen or so platters of cookies—from large chocolate chip to some sort of powdered sugar puffballs.

Then I spied it. The glistening, green-brown monolith perched atop the table like some alien life form—Aunt Winnifred's zucchini-marmalade nut loaf. God help any guest who naively bit into a slice. It was like trying to digest a flannel bathrobe.

Joel's precariously bending paper plate was threatening to collapse. It looked like he had taken some of everything. I nervously nibbled a snickerdoodle as I watched. He'd better not spill everything in front of all these people. I gave Uncle Jake a wave at the far end of the room. Joel and I would get to stay with him in Vancouver for a week while our parents headed to Calgary. We'd never visited Jake's apartment before, but staying with him would be a welcome break from our boring routine.

Joel and I were heading Jake's way, but, before we reached him, Susan Lucas, Tom's widow, took his arm. I'd only met Susan once before, but I felt really terrible for her. She looked pale, and her eyes were red and swollen. Her long blonde hair was tightly held in a bun at her neck. A small silver crucifix hung on her black simple dress. A toddler clung to her hand, one of two young children. I eavesdropped…a little.

"Thank you, Jake. Tom would have liked what you said."

She spoke quietly. Jake nodded in appreciation.

"This morning, I boxed up Tom's climbing gear from Peru and sent it to your apartment. It's just not something I can deal with right now.

Do what you want with it. Keep it. Sell it. Burn it. Throw it away. I don't care. I don't want to see any of it again."

"Why don't I just hang onto it for awhile, Sue. Johnny and Davey might want it someday."

I could understand Susan's bitterness, but I think my Uncle Jake was right. They could never replace Tom's climbing gear once it was gone. They might wish they still had it in the future.

"I've made up my mind. I've kept a few things he didn't take down with him, but that's not how I want the boys to remember him." She pulled Davey closer to her leg for support.

"You sure?"

"This whole mountain climbing thing has always been extremely hard for me, Jake. While Tom was out conquering the world, enriching all *your* lives, I was home alone with the kids nine months every year." Small tears began to well in the corner of her eyes. "What was I supposed to do? If he'd been seeing another woman, I could compete with that. But how was I supposed to compete with his climbing, Jake? How was I supposed to compete?" Tears streamed anew down her pale cheeks.

"Damn," she said softly. "I'm so tired of crying."

"It's okay." Jake put his arm around her. She stared numbly down at the ground.

"I guess Tom was our gift to all of you." She sniffed.

"I suppose so." He kept his arm there until she was ready.

Finally, Susan wiped her eyes with a handkerchief that had no more dry spots. "I've got to thank everyone else. I didn't mean to dump on you, Jake."

"I understand."

She squeezed his hands and then blended back into the crowded reception room. Jake looked sadder than I'd ever seen him before. Susan was probably right. Everyone seems to have loved the dashing, charismatic image of Tom. Everyone was in awe of his climbing skill and was thankful for everything he shared with them. But I guess, when you really thought about it, by doing all those things while he ignored his family, Tom had been incredibly selfish. I could see that it stung Uncle Jake.

CHAPTER 5

▼

EMMA
LAST MESSAGE

Uncle Jake parked his car under a dilapidated carport that badly needed new paint. He hopped out to help with our suitcases and then led us to his apartment on the top floor of a fourplex, just off Kensington Street in Burnaby, outside Vancouver. Our low energy matched the setting. We plodded up the flights of steps carpeted with an outdated orange color; it was threadbare and dirty. The stairwell was pathetically lit by two low-wattage bulbs.

"Not exactly the Ritz-Carlton," Jake said. I had figured that out from the outside. "I haven't had much time for cleaning. I've been in and out a lot the last few days."

Our dad had warned us about Uncle Jake's housekeeping. Joel wouldn't mind, so long as there was a TV and plenty of junk food, but my standards were a few notches higher. I was a tiny bit apprehensive. After all, we were going to be staying here a whole week. Jake opened the front door and led us to a spare bedroom that was just inside.

"Your room." He gestured grandly. "The bathroom's around the corner. You can get settled after dinner. I'll help you pick up after we eat."

"Whoa!" Joel entered the room before me, startled, even by his standards. "It's a mess!"

"There are beds in here aren't there...somewhere...Uncle Jake...aren't there?" Twin beds were buried under stacks of boxes, a huge mound of laundry (dirty at that, which I had no intention of touching by the way), mud-caked climbing equipment, and what must have been a folded tent that was splotched with mold and reeked of mildew. Jake opened the room's two small windows. I hoped his whole apartment wasn't like this.

Joel held up a lethal-looking ice axe. "Is all this from Peru?"

"Yep. Sorry, guys. I haven't quite finished unpacking. We can move this into storage later tonight. Let me show you the rest of the place."

Thank goodness. At least he was going to help.

Jake led us down the narrow hallway past his own bedroom to a wide-open living room. Unlike the cramped, messy bedroom, this was bright and sunny. Huge windows were framed by bookshelves that were overflowing with journals, texts, and monographs of every size and shape.

"This is great!" I was immediately drawn to the bay windows. They faced east, overlooking Burnaby Park, a serene island of green within the city. Uncle Jake concurred.

"It's a great place to contemplate the sunrise over a cup of coffee."

Joel was already studying Jake's furnishings. "Em, check out the size of this globe."

Near the computer desk stood a huge vintage world globe. I guessed it was possibly from the 1920s or 1930s. It was more than a three feet in diameter and was lit from the inside. It was as tall as me but much more fascinating. Its political boundaries were woefully outdated though.

I glanced around the rest of the room. Jake had converted half of it into an office. The other side had several easy chairs, a sofa, a television set, and a battered dining table. A faded runner covered part of the oak flooring. At the far end I could see a tiny kitchen.

Joel spun the globe, and the countries and water blended in a blue-green blur. Just because Joel was almost a teenager didn't mean he was finished being an annoying little brother. In Jake's apartment, Joel reminded me of kids I'd seen on museum tours, running from one exhibit to the next and being more interested in being first than seeing the display.

A large map mounted above the battered table was the next item to grab Joel's eye. Measuring three feet by six feet, it was lavishly hued with deep reds and rich golds.

"That's Mexico isn't it?" Joel looked toward Uncle Jake.

"Part of it. It's the Gulf of Mexico, Florida, and the West Indies. See those little drawings of sinking ships? They're the ones lost by some of the region's earliest explorers—Columbus, John Cabot, Gaspar Corte Real, Alonso de Hojeda, Luis Guerra, and Juan de la Casa. How good are your eyes? If you look real close, under each illustration, you can read the date the ship was lost and the cargo it carried to the bottom."

While those two studied the map, I examined the bookcases.

"Are there any treasures you *don't* have books on?" I pulled out an old leather journal and blew off a disgusting layer of dust. "It doesn't look like you've read them. You *have* read them, haven't you?"

"Long ago, Em. But, if it's got something I'm working on, it gets a thorough going-over. Believe me"

The shelves were overflowing: obscure journals, scholarly monographs on famous treasures, unsolved mysteries, lost mines, missing tombs, hidden cities, and major shipwrecks. *The Treasure of the Dead Sea Scrolls. The Lead Coffin of Sir Francis Drake. The Greek Statues Wreck. Sodom and Gomorrah. The Tomb of Antiochus of Commogere.*

"Jeez, Uncle Jake. I've never even heard of most of these."

The Battlefield of Alesia. The Grave of King Arthur. The Basing House Hoard. The Tomb of Herod the Great. The Lost Tombs of the Ancient Egyptians. The Missing Gold of Custer's Last Stand. The Oak Island Treasure. The Greek City of Helike. King Solomon's Mines. One whole shelf was devoted entirely to lost pirate treasure buried by the likes of William Kidd, Jean Laffite, Kanhoji Angria, Charles Vane, Samuel Bellamy, and the Knights of Malta. And all that was only one of Uncle Jake's bookcases!

A week just wouldn't be enough. I wished I could read every one. Surely each one contained long-lost secrets or mysterious hints of hidden treasures. Maybe I had some treasure hunter in me after all.

I grabbed the one about Oak Island and started reading. Joel looked too, but he was more intrigued with Uncle Jake's unusual odds and ends that were intermittently dispersed between the texts. A bleached gorilla's skull gaped beside the books on African diamond mines. At the other end of the shelf was a small brass telescope. A baseball-sized rock with a thick vein of gold served as a bookend for three manuscripts on the Lost Dutchman's Mine in Arizona. An antique silver flask with a bullet hole smack through its center leaned against a thick maroon volume explaining the Lost Rhoades Mine of Utah. A gold miner's pan and pouch were propped by a text about the Beale Treasure Ciphers of Virginia. A long, curved dagger—its handle encrusted with colored gemstones—sat atop a leatherbound book on the lost mine of Pitt Lake in British Columbia. An old-fashioned, deep-sea diving helmet sat at the far end of a shelf dedicated to shipwrecks. These included everything from early Greek traders and Spanish treasure ships to the naval casualties of World War II.

Jake's unusual souvenirs—what most adults would call clutter—was just the sort of stuff Joel and I found fascinating. I was going to enjoy our stay.

"This is the coolest stuff." Joel carefully examined the skull. "Is this thing from a monkey or chimp?"

"Bigger, buddy. That's Zaltor, the great 500-pound albino gorilla." Jake's tone had gone grave.

"Albino gorilla?" Joel looked skeptical.

"I was deep in the Congo. I'd been lost for days. No food. Running low on water. But…" Jake's voice dropped to a whisper, "I carried the golden treasure of the Lost Temple. The natives had warned me about a white demon that lived in the jungle."

When we were growing up, Jake used to entertain us like this for hours. When he really got going, it was better than any movie. Of course, we never completely swallowed our uncle's outlandish tales, but we had to admit that it was really fun to listen. We were pretty surprised when our mom finally told us that a lot of those wild stories were actually true. But certainly not this one. Jake went on.

"The sun was setting just as I reached the darkest part of the jungle. Suddenly, Zaltor sprang from the underbrush, howling and baring his long, pointed fangs."

"Fangs? Where? There aren't any fangs on this." Joel held up the skull for me to see.

I tried interrupting my uncle. "Jake." No such luck.

"We stood face to face. I realized I'd have to fight him to the death with my bare hands." Jake curled his hands like claws.

"*Jake!*"

He finally relented. "Okay."

"He's making it up, Joel."

One of my roles as big sister was to keep Joel in line.

"Duh! I just wanted to hear how it ends."

"Later," Jake smiled and then he led us into his small, spartan kitchen.

"Anytime you want a snack or anything, just help yourselves. When it comes to meals, I'm pretty informal. Habit."

Joel picked up a small framed picture of Jake and a smiling woman with short brown hair.

"Was this your girlfriend? She looks pretty young."

"Jeez! Nice going, bonehead," I thought. We weren't supposed to mention her.

Jake took the picture from Joel and set it back on the yellow Formica countertop, next to the phone. "*Was* my girlfriend. We split up. And, for your information, she's nearly thirty."

"You must still like her if you've still got her picture out."

That was too much.

"Joel! Shut up! That is totally not your business!"

How could my brother be so smart sometimes and then so stupid the next?

"That's all right. I just haven't put it away yet. No harm done, Em."

I felt sorry for him. Our mom said Jake just couldn't find anyone who could handle his globe-trotting fascination with treasure hunting. Of course, I was hardly one to pass judgement about relationships. It's something I'd tried to not think about all this past year.

Joel opened the refrigerator in search of a soda.

"Uh, Uncle Jake?"

"Oh, yeah. I forgot to go to the store. I'll do that tomorrow morning. We'll just scratch something together for dinner."

"From what? Hey, Em, check this out."

I looked. Pathetic.

"This is rich. Let's see, one hot dog. That ought to make us all a hearty meal. One empty jar of extra hot mustard…"

"That's gone already?"

"Two cans of beer. I think we'll pass on those. A half-package of Oreos. Shriveled carrot sticks."

"So they've been in there a while."

"A bowl of popcorn…"

"In the fridge?" Even Joel was dismayed.

"Think of it as cold storage, Joel."

"Oh. This is especially nice." I withdrew a small dish covered with a layer of blue fuzz. "Concocting penicillin?"

"Okay, okay. You've made your point." Jake was laughing. What else could he say? "I think in its former life it was guacamole."

"Gross!"

"Good thing you saved it, Jake. It'll really come in handy."

I'm not always this sarcastic, but Jake was one of the few adults I felt close enough with to tease. Besides, kidding around was a welcome diversion from the depressing events earlier in the afternoon. I reached to open the freezer door with my good arm.

"Stop. You win. I'll order pizza."

"Why? What's in here?" I opened the freezer, expecting boxes of popsicles, but I recoiled at what I found.

"It's full of garbage!" Joel exclaimed.

"Yeah, I had a little extra garbage, and the next pickup was while I was in Peru, so I just put it up there. It keeps it from smelling up the apartment. It's actually pretty clever." Then our uncle chuckled at his own cleverness.

He couldn't be serious. I thought the messy bachelor stereotype was an old-fashioned myth. Apparently not.

"You two have a seat, and I'll call for pizza. What do you want on it?"

We sat at the table, careful not to bump the large map of the shipwrecks. Ten packets of photographs were piled on the table. Joel started to open one.

"Are these from your trip?"

"Yes. Just got 'em back today. Em, what'll it be?"

"Mushrooms." I watched Joel from the corner of my eye. I really didn't care what we had on our pizza, but Joel detested mushrooms.

"Mushrooms!" Joel looked up from the photos. "You always get mushrooms. I hate mushrooms. Let's just get pepperoni."

"We had that last time." Actually, I had no idea what we ordered the last time we ate pizza.

"We did not! We had mushrooms!"

"Hold it, you two! You sound like a couple of six-year-olds. I'll order half-mushroom, half-pepperoni. Okay?" Obviously, Jake wasn't too hot on a week of our bickering.

Joel returned to the photographs. I took a packet as well.

"Where was this?" I held up a picture of a woman selling handmade silver jewelry atop a colorful blanket carefully laid out on the sidewalk.

"That's in Huaraz. It's the closest town to the mountain we climbed."

"Is this the mountain?" Joel held a photo of a huge, snow-covered cliff.

Jake nodded and then traced a path on the photo.

"Huascaran Norte. That's the mountain's northern face. You can see the route we took. There's no way I'd have made it without Tom."

Joel looked up.

"Are you going to give some of these to Aunt Susan? She'd probably like to have the ones with Tom in them."

"Maybe I'll suggest it in a couple of weeks, Joel. Right now, she doesn't want anything to do with climbing. I'm not sure I do either."

Joel found the pictures of the Incan mummy. "Ugh! Dude, this is really gnarly. She looks like she's asleep."

I took one of the six mummy photos. Joel continued thumbing through the stack of pictures, but I couldn't seem to take my eyes off the girl. Normally, that sort of thing really grosses me out, but there was something about it. Something compelling. Something familiar.

"Em, let me see that one." Joel impatiently reached for the picture. "Em. Earth to *Em!*"

"What? Oh, sorry. Here." I reluctantly handed it over.

"Let me clear these phone messages, and I'll order," Jake said.

The answering machine was blinking "4"—four messages while Jake was at Tom's service. Jake scrounged for a pen, selected a piece of junk mail to write on, and then pressed "Replay."

"First message, today, at 12:21 PM," droned the machine's electronic voice. Jake waited for the message, but all we heard was a heavy mechanical thumping noise, far in the background. After a few moments, the line disconnected.

Jake shrugged. "Probably a salesman." Then he pushed the button again for the next message.

"Second message, today, at 1:42 PM." Same heavy factory-like noise. I could make out faint, unintelligible talking in the background as though the caller was talking to someone else at the same time. We listened for twenty seconds before the line cut off. We couldn't make out a single word.

"That doesn't sound like someone selling magazines," Joel observed.

"Sure doesn't. Sounds like somebody has the wrong number. Let's see if we're three for three." Jake expectantly pushed the small button.

"Third message, today, at 3:14 PM. Jake, this is Judith Wrenford. You remember, from the Spencer's barbecue this summer? Listen, what you said today for Tom was really nice. It sort of helped pull things together. So that's all. I'm really sorry. Let me know if there's anything I can do. I'm in town all week. Well, good-bye."

"You know her?" I asked.

"Yes, she's one of Susan's friends, but I didn't see her at the service. There were a lot of people, and I wasn't looking around much."

He pushed the button for the final message.

"Fourth message, today, at 3:29 PM. Morgan, Jake Morgan." A deep, gravelly voice slowly enunciated each syllable. It sounded like someone who'd smoked cigarettes nonstop for twenty years. When we heard the familiar thumping sound in the background, the three of us snapped to attention. The mystery caller. "We want the last piece. We can be very generous. One hundred thousand dollars. No questions asked. Think about it, Morgan. We'll be in touch." Click. The answering machine was silent.

CHAPTER 6

▼

JAKE
THE COURIER

By the morning after Tom's funeral service, Emma, Joel, and I had settled in for the week. We'd made a list, stocked up, and now waited in the checkout line at my local Griffin Market. Since my big brother John had been an accountant with this run-down grocery chain for more years than I can remember, I felt it was my family duty to shop here, even if they didn't have the best price in town. I'd promised Joel and Emma that, once the apartment was restocked, we could spend the day visiting Stanley Park or the zoo, or see a movie. Whatever they felt like doing. Still cautious about my culinary limits, they insisted on accompanying me to the store. I smiled, remembering their examination of my fridge.

As we neared the cashier, I scanned the sensationalist tabloids and then froze. I was stunned to see a grotesque full-page photo of the mummy we'd discovered only last week. I felt like I'd been slammed in the chest. *The Courier*'s banner headline read: "Mummy's Revenge!"

I snatched a copy from the rack. How the heck did they get this picture? It must have been the Peruvian government.

The kids saw it as well.

"Isn't that the mummy you found?"

Joel's voice carried further than he intended. I gestured for him to lower his voice.

"It's the one *we* found."

The people behind us in line looked up from their shopping lists and critically scrutinized the three of us, particularly Emma.

Emma had endured a lot of stares the last few years—both the curious and the cruel. One of the less attractive traits of humans is that we gape at anyone who's different, and upper body amputees are extremely rare in Canada. Even those unintentional stares that meant no harm used to take a toll on her. Teenage girls are self-conscious enough about their appearance. I couldn't imagine how hard it had been for her. But Emma didn't cringe now or look as if she wanted to crawl inside herself. That was quite a change in the months since I'd seen her. Now, she looked the nosy shoppers right in the eye and turned to face them, challenging their rudeness. In response, each one sheepishly looked away…to their grocery lists, purses, or checkbooks. She might have gotten right in their faces if they hadn't looked away when they did. I was proud of her defiance.

"What's the story with her eyes?" Joel looked closer at the front-page picture. "They totally changed them."

Below the spurious headline, the altered photograph transformed the mummy into a ghoul. *The Courier* had distorted the young woman's peaceful expression into a contorted mask of terror. The eyes, originally closed, now stared back with blood red pupils. The mouth had been elongated into a sneer. The tabloid had twisted an important historical find into something from *Night of the Living Dead*. It was degrading, infuriating. I could feel my face redden. It was like something private and personal had been taken from me.

The caption beneath the picture read: "Five hundred year-old mummy reaches out from the grave. (See page 24)" I thumbed through, anticipating an atrociously fictionalized story. The interceding pages contained the predicted farcical parade of the absurd: Martian abductions, six-headed calves, vegetables resembling Hollywood film stars, and a woman giving birth to a goat.

"Hey, this isn't a library," the cashier barked. "You going to buy that or not?"

Irritated, I tossed the tabloid in my cart, my loyalty to Griffin Markets waning.

Emma retrieved the pulp newspaper from a grocery bag while I eased the car into traffic.

"Let's hear it," Joel said from the backseat. Emma cleared her throat and began.

"'Curse of the Mummy. What began as a recreational hike...'"

"The north face? A hike?" These writers were clueless.

"It gets worse," Emma said. "'What began as a recreational hike in the Peruvian Andes turned into a ghoulish nightmare for three outdoorsmen who unknowingly unearthed an Incan mummy and, experts believe, released an ancient death curse on those who disturbed the mummy's slumber.'"

"That's ridiculous."

It was just what I'd feared. They were exploiting Tom's death, humiliating his memory, just to sell copies of their rag. My hands on the steering wheel clenched in a white-knuckled grip.

Emma continued reading in a flat, monotone voice. "'The young woman, a likely victim of human sacrifice, was found atop Mt. Huascaran, one of the tallest mountains in the Andes. Peruvian authorities confirmed the remains are the most perfectly preserved of any mummy yet discovered from the Incan period. But did the mountain climbers foolishly awaken a long-dormant evil?'"

"That's trash!"

"'Only minutes after discovering the frozen corpse, Tom Lucas of Vancouver, British Columbia, one of Canada's premier alpinists, was mysteriously struck down and dead.' Oh no!"

"What?" At this point, nothing would have surprised me.

"There's a picture, Jake. I guess it's Tom. You can't really tell."

"Let me see." I took my eyes off the road long enough to check the blurry photo. Tom's face was hidden, but I recognized the parka and wind pants on the lifeless figure by huddled porters. Base camp. Some son of a bitch had taken a picture and sold it to this piece of literary garbage. "Christ! This could push Susan over the edge. This isn't something she needs right now."

"Look out!" Joel yelled in my ear. I swerved just in time to avoid rear-ending a diesel-stained delivery truck stopped in our lane.

"Sorry, guys. You both okay?" They nodded. "Go ahead, Emma."

"The article says that an unnamed historical scholar from the Midwest is convinced it was a curse that killed Tom."

"Unnamed because he probably doesn't exist. Or she…"

Emma looked up with disbelief. Welcome to the world of fictional journalism. I couldn't let this slide.

"Joel, hand me my cell phone. It's back there somewhere."

He handed it up to me. "Who you calling?"

"Susan. I don't want her to discover this thing the way we did."

I wondered why I was always the one who had to call Susan with terrible news. I punched the numbers into the phone. It rang five times before I heard her subdued voice.

"Hello?"

"Susan, it's Jake."

"Oh. Hi, Jake."

"How are you doing?" A lame question under the circumstances.

"Okay, I guess." She sounded drained. "I've gotten calls from a lot of Tom's friends who couldn't make the service yesterday. Everybody's been very supportive."

"Listen, I hate to be the one to tell you, but *The Courier*…you know, the sleazy tabloid…is running a story about Tom."

"What?"

I couldn't blame her for sounding apprehensive and victimized.

"It's trash, as you can imagine. It says Tom died because of a curse connected to the remains we found." I eased up the accelerator. I'd been inadvertently tailgating.

"Jesus. First the midnight phone calls. Now this. You'd think they'd just leave us alone."

"I'm sorry. I just wanted to warn you. They put a picture on the front page that's something out of a horror movie."

I wish I could have done something to change all this. Susan didn't deserve such a public violation.

"Of Tom?" She nearly shrieked. Here I'd called to warn her and I was making things worse.

"No, no. The mummy. But the whole thing is slimy and upsetting. I wanted you to know…in case you were in a store…"

"Thanks, Jake," she answered weakly. "I doubt I'll be out shopping for a while. But at least I'll know what to expect if I get strange calls."

"Okay. Well, take care. Let me know if there's anything I can do."

"Are the kids staying with you?"

"Yes, for the week it looks like. John and Alice are at some sort of convention."

"Maybe you can bring them by later this week. Johnny and Davey would love to see their older cousins."

"I'll give you a call once we know our plans, and we'll schedule it. Talk to you later."

"Bye, Jake. Thanks for calling."

I decided whoever was responsible for this shouldn't go unscathed. Somebody should have to pay for making a mockery of Susan's grief.

Back at the apartment, I went straight to my Rolodex. Steve Stinsen had been a friend since high school; he was also one of British Columbia's best litigators. I dialed his firm on my cordless while Emma and Joel put away the groceries. They joined me at the table just as my call was transferred to Steve.

"Stephen Stinsen speaking." He answered in a deep professional voice.

"Steve, Jake Morgan."

"Morning, Jake," he said, his voice relaxing. "I've been expecting you. My assistant brought in *The Courier* yesterday. I'm assuming that's why you called."

"I just saw it this morning." Joel and Emma were rereading it at the table. I never thought of myself as particularly vindictive, but this was the worst kind of cowardly journalism. "Have you read it?"

"More than once."

"Well, can we go after them? Legally? I hate this kind of crap, Steve. They've turned Tom Lucas into a freak show."

"You want to sue them?"

"Wouldn't you? Wouldn't anyone?" I was pacing back and forth, wanting to wring somebody's neck.

"Probably. But I reviewed what they wrote pretty carefully, Jake. If you're asking me as your attorney, I'd advise you not to pursue it. I'd say you don't have much of a case."

"Not pursue it?"

Steve was a courtroom pit bull, a barracuda. I couldn't believehe'd back away from something as infuriating as this.

"Look, Jake, we can file a lawsuit, but you haven't got any grounds for damages. The only person they might have libeled is the mummy. They quoted a couple of fruitcakes with nutty theories, but they covered their asses by claiming it's just opinions."

"What about the photo of Tom's body? Don't they need permission for that?"

I was trying to rein my frustration. This wasn't Steve's fault.

"Yes, if it's clearly apparent it's him. But his face isn't shown. Theoretically, it could be somebody else."

"It's him." It was probably the only thing the tabloid had correct.

The front doorbell interrupted us.

"Hold on, Steve. Joel, can you get that?"

Joel dashed down the hall.

"Jake, all I'm saying is that these kind of guys are extremely careful that anything they print is technically legal. Occasionally, they slip up…but not here."

"Uncle Jake," Joel called from down the hall.

"Hang on, Steve." I walked to the door with the phone.

Joel was dwarfed by a large shipping carton in the doorway. A deliveryman impatiently waved an electronic signature pad.

"Has to be signed for by an adult," the man said, thrusting the electronic pad and plastic stylus to sign with. "No offense, kid."

Joel looked offended.

I quickly scribbled my name. The man wasted no time rushing back to his truck.

"Jake, you still there?"

"I'm still here, Steve. Just one second more."

I looked at the shipper's address. Susan Lucas. It was Tom's climbing gear. Going through Tom's equipment was the last thing I intended to do. I'd already decided to sell it on consignment at a local climbing shop and then find some excuse to give the proceeds to Susan.

"Joel, can you wrestle this into your closet? I'll have someone pick it up tomorrow."

"Okay." Joel lifted the large box with surprising ease and disappeared into the guest room. I still tended to think of him as a little kid because he was my brother's youngest, but he was growing up and filling out. In a few years, he'd be as tall as me.

"Okay, Steve, I'm back." Steve billed clients over $300 an hour. As a friend, I didn't want to impose any longer than necessary.

"What's going on over there?"

"I've got my niece and nephew staying with me a little while."

"That'll keep you busy."

"Definitely." All those tourist attractions they wanted to see.

"Anyway, Jake, the problem is you have no actual damages that can be attributed to the tabloid. From my understanding, the underlying information is accurate. I wouldn't want a case that hinged on a photo of someone's legs. These guys are pros, Jake. If this went to trial, you could sink $60,000 in legal fees. And, even if you won, they'd appeal. But it wouldn't get that far. Any experienced judge would dismiss it for lack of merit. Regardless of how mad you are, there just aren't sufficient grounds to proceed."

Joel gave me the okay sign when he returned, indicating the box was out of the way. He sat at the table across from Emma.

"You'd be wasting your money, Jake. That's the best advice I can give you."

"Okay, Steve. I appreciate it." I hated legal loopholes like this, but I didn't have the money to pursue this thing on principle.

"Anything else?"

"No."

"Hang in there, buddy. By next week, this story will be long gone. Nobody ever remembers this kind of junk."

I knew Susan wouldn't forget.

"Thanks, Steve. Talk to you later." I clicked off.

"Jake?" Emma had laid my mummy pictures out on the table. "Did you take a close look at the picture in the paper?"

"Close enough," I answered curtly.

"I'm just curious about the way they changed it."

"It sells more papers, Em. A mummy with a hideous expression and satanic eyes is a lot more interesting than what we actually found up there—at least to the voyeuristic folks who buy this junk."

"I know that. I meant changing the necklace."

She pointed to the sets of photos and then to the paper.

"In the pictures you took, there are four medallions on the necklace. But, in the newspaper shot, there's only three."

I called *The Courier* right away to confirm Emma's observation, containing my anger just long enough to get the information I wanted. The tabloid had only doctored the mummy's face. The rest of the picture was exactly as they'd received it from the Peruvian Archaeological Society. Emma and Joel awaited my report.

"Looks like you're right, Em. Between the time we found her on the mountain and the government's expedition, one of the medallions on her necklace seems to have disappeared."

CHAPTER 7

▼

EMMA
TODAY

I awoke with a jolt. Joel's bed was empty. The small clock radio flashed 9:38. Rats! I never slept in this late, even in summer. I quickly washed up, brushed my teeth and hair, strapped on my arm, and got dressed.

It used to take me fifteen frustrating minutes to slip into the harness connected to my arm, but it was now second nature. After the accident, I'd gotten what's called a myoelectric arm, a prosthetic covered in flesh-colored plastic so the hand looks real. But it was awkward. It weighed a ton, and I was never supposed to get it wet. So I'd switched to an old-fashioned transradial. It's the kind with two metal fingers and a thumb. The harness slips over my other shoulder, and, when I move my good arm, a cable squeezes the thumb open or closed. It doesn't look so hot, but it's lightweight so I don't feel like I'm lugging something around with me.

Actually, no prosthetic arm can grip anything very hard. When I first came home, Joel thought I was going to become the bionic woman, sitting around the house cracking walnuts and bending iron bars. Lately, I'd even thought of not using any prosthesis at all, so I wouldn't feel like I was strapped into something all the time. But not yet. That step was still a little further down the road.

I walked toward the kitchen, expecting to find Joel. Instead, Jake sat at the table. His pictures were spread before him. I was embarrassed I'd slept so long.

"Morning, Em. You must have been tired."

"I don't know what my problem is." Sometimes I felt really tired when it was my period, but that wasn't the case today.

"Well, we covered a lot of ground yesterday. The park, the zoo, and then the movie. I was pretty tired myself. Joel's in the kitchen eating breakfast. You want me to make you something?"

"No thanks. I'll just have cereal."

I was still groggy. I felt like I hadn't slept a wink all night. Yesterday, I couldn't stop thinking about the mummy's necklace and the mysterious phone messages. They were obviously connected. When we returned last night to Jake's apartment, we hoped there might be another message about the $100,000…but no such luck.

Joel was slurping loudly from the bottom of his cereal bowl, simultaneously studying the back of the cereal box as if it was some best seller. I found some orange juice in the restocked refrigerator and sat down next to him.

"Hey, Em, what was with you last night?" Joel asked, his mouth full of milk.

I was immediately on my guard. My brother had a nasty way with practical jokes. "What do you mean?"

"You were talking in your sleep. I had to throw a pillow to make you stop."

I downed my juice in one gulp. "You're kidding." I remembered when I was in camp one summer. A girl in our cabin always talked in her sleep, and she was really loud. By morning, everybody's shoes were scattered all around her bunk. We'd thrown them at her all night long to try to make her stop. It never worked. The worst thing was that she said some really embarrassing things.

"So what did I say?"

"I woke up, and you were sitting up in bed, looking at the closet and asking if it was today." Joel poured himself a second bowl of cereal and even more milk.

"If *what* was today?" I figured Joel was only giving me half the story.

"How should I know? You were the one doing the talking. You just kept asking, 'Today? Today? Today?' over and over until I nailed you with the pillow. Then you finally laid down and went to sleep."

"That's weird. I don't remember anything. I don't even remember dreaming." At least I hadn't said anything Joel could tease me about.

"So, you two solve the mystery?" Jake walked into the little kitchen.

"No," we said in unison.

"I'm betting the answer will be pretty straightforward," Jake said. "Most likely, the amulet just dropped off when the Peruvian government was bringing the figure down the mountain. It could be anywhere up there now. Impossible to find. We covered the figure up pretty thoroughly with ice after we took the photos, so it's not likely another climbing party would have found it. And I don't think it could have gotten lost while we were up there."

"You don't think…"

"I was kind of loopy on the summit. High altitude makes you a pretty stupid. Only half the oxygen and all. I suppose I was a bit sketchy."

"Gosh, that sounds safe," I said sarcastically.

"Why would one little piece of a necklace be worth so much money?" Joel asked.

"Well, as far as antiques go, this one's really ancient, probably 500 years old. I'm not an expert on the Inca, but I remember most of their jewelry was melted down into ingots by the Spanish conquistadors. So Inca jewelry is extremely rare. But I'd agree that $100,000 seems like a lot for one piece.

After breakfast, Uncle Jake used a jeweler's magnifying loupe to study the photos of the Incan mummy. The necklace pieces were flat, black-colored stones and were about the size of a quarter.

"Whatever these are made of, it's not gold."

Jake held the photo within inches of his left eye, squinting with the other. "Gold wouldn't oxidize and turn black like this. There seems to be a rough hole bored into the top of each medallion, and a cord or string was then threaded through it. They just look like ordinary stones to me. Hardly worth what our mystery caller offered."

In the *Courier* photo, one of the center amulets was missing. Jake compared his photo and scrutinized the missing piece.

"It looks like the top of the amulet was broken or shattered. That would explain it falling off and getting lost. Mystery solved!" he announced with aplomb. He put down the loupe and tossed the photo back into the pile. "The amulet simply broke off."

"You think someone might find it someday? Maybe it's just lying on top of the snow."

"On top of Huascaran? It's technically possible but highly unlikely. I certainly wouldn't go back up there and look for it. It's just another small piece of antiquity that was lost to the ages."

Uncle Jake began looking through the rest of the photos. He picked up a picture of himself and Tom and gulped at the broad smile on Tom's tanned face. Tom wore dark glasses, a bright red parka, and an orange bandana tucked behind a baseball cap to keep the sun off the back of his neck. The bandana made him look like a French Foreign Legionnaire.

"That bandana..." Jake thoughtfully rubbed his chin.

"What?" Joel looked over at the picture.

"I don't know. There's something about that orange handkerchief." Jake quickly scanned the summit pictures. "He wasn't wearing it on top of the mountain. So why did it seem like it was up there?"

Jake smiled at us.

"This is the problem with altitude. A lot of climbers forget the details."

"Well, what did you guys do up there?" Maybe if Jake talked about it, he'd remember.

Jake leaned back and closed his eyes, mentally reliving the climb.

"We climbed the last pitch to the ridge leading to the summit. Man, it was an incredible view! We took some pictures. I remember I had trouble getting the flag out of my pack. We saw the storm coming, and we then found the blanket covering the mummy. I took more photos while Tom and Jorge stood by. The storm was almost on top of us by then. Jorge and I chipped out ice while Tom packed it around the…*His pocket!*" Jake banged the table with his fist. Joel and I jumped to attention.

"Tom stuffed that stupid orange bandana back into his pocket. Joel, get Tom's climbing gear. Hurry!"

"What are you thinking?" I wasn't following.

"Em, I'm wondering if Tom may have helped himself to an historical souvenir…despite Jorge's warning."

Joel plopped the large box onto the floor in the center of the room. "Here it is."

Once opened, we were greeted with the pungent odor of ripe clothing that had been worn for three weeks but never washed.

"Pew!" I had to plug my nose.

"The glamorous side of mountain climbing," Jake grinned.

At the bottom of the box, Jake found Tom's parka and fished it from the heavy container. The coat reeked of mildew. The back collar was gruesomely stained with Tom's dried blood. Jake tried the left pocket. Empty.

"I'm not sure I want to find it. I'd hate to think Tom's last action was ripping-off a museum-quality artifact."

Jake unzipped the right pocket, reached inside, and withdrew the tightly wadded kerchief. Tom's orange bandana was hard and crusty, but there was definitely something inside. Joel and I didn't blink as

Jake carefully unfurled the cloth. Wrapped inside was a crude rectangular black stone, half the size of a domino. A chill trickled down my back. The hole at the top was broken. We'd found the final piece of the mummy's necklace.

CHAPTER 8

▼

EMMA VANISHED

Uncle Jake banged on the apartment door. It flew open, and there grinned Rudi Speidel, one of Jake's many longtime oddball friends.

"JM! Good to see you!" The two exchanged a hearty handshake. "How long's it been? A couple of months?"

"Almost eight," Jake corrected.

"Time flies." Rudi saw Joel and me. "And these are your long-lost kids?"

"My niece and nephew. Emma. Joel."

"Great to meet you. Well, come inside."

As we were driving across Vancouver this morning, Jake told us that Rudi Speidel was a part-time professor at Simon Fraser University. He was an expert in something to do with historical metallurgical studies. Jake had worked with him on past salvage projects. He said Rudi was a whiz at analyzing badly corroded or decayed metal—both for its exact composition and its historical significance. But Rudi Speidel wasn't what I'd expected. He had long, raggedy hair and a two-day growth of beard. His black pants and shirt were so wrinkled that it looked like he'd slept in them. He had a slight potbelly and wore old-fashioned, red high-top Converse. His bushy eyebrows met at the bridge of his nose. Jake said he was brilliant. For me, it was going to take a little convincing.

"Still seeing Linda?" Speidel asked as we followed him into the small interior.

"Umm, that didn't work out. We split up a month ago."

"Sorry. I thought she was a keeper." It wasn't what Uncle Jake wanted to hear right now.

Rudi's apartment barely held the four of us. A big table supporting six computer screens hogged most of the space. Multicolored wires and cables snaked and tangled among the screens and beneath the table adjoining five computer minitowers. The carpet smelled like fried fish, and the air was stuffy. At least it was warm. I couldn't convince Jake to turn on his car's heater on the way over.

"You kids know your uncle was quite popular with the girls back in school?"

"Hardly." Jake apparently wanted to change the subject.

"Well, pal, I'm thinking of that first Tolo. Was that our freshman year? Or sophomore?"

"Don't go there, Rudi."

Now I knew he wanted to change the subject.

"Yes, go there." I always liked teasing Uncle Jake, and, judging by the mischief in Speidel's voice, this might give me ammunition.

"Well, no one ever went out with this one particular girl, but, of course, your Uncle Jake here, he felt real sorry for her. However, the reason no one went out with her…"

"You know, Rudi, I think these two would be much more interested in your exploits a few years back. Em, Joel, remember the Y2K scare at the end of 1999?"

"Sort of." Joel was too young to remember it well. But I did.

"When everyone was worried about all the computers crashing?"

"Right, Em. Rudi, you still have all that stockpiled freeze-dried food, bottled water, and toilet paper? How many years worth?"

"I think I can find a picture of you two at that dance, JM. They're much more interested in that."

"Definitely!" Joel enjoyed their verbal fencing as much as I did.

"Or maybe I could post it on the Internet," Speidel grinned devilishly.

"Truce!" Jake held up his hands. "I can't compete if you're going to fight dirty."

Jake and Speidel were amusing, but it made me wonder if that was how boys viewed me. If I asked someone to a dance, would I become someone's private joke for years to come? 'Remember that girl with one arm? What a freak!' I had to push those kind of thoughts out of my mind. I couldn't dwell on stuff like that. I had to keep moving forward.

"You're not going to show us?" Joel asked.

"Nah. It's just our long-running gag. I couldn't do that to JM. I owe him, and he knows it."

"Owe him?" Maybe Jake had loaned him money.

"The son of a bitch saved my life." Speidel answered matter-of-factly.

"Really?"

"No." Jake tried to interrupt.

"We were scuba diving years ago, just out of high school. I had a problem at 100 feet and tried to shoot to the surface. If your uncle hadn't grabbed me and slowed my ascent, my lungs would have burst like a balloon."

"At the most, I kept him from getting the bends—if even that. Anyway, Rudi, I told you on the phone why I need your help." Jake finally steered the conversation back to business.

"Let's have a look." Speidel held out his hand. Into which, Jake unceremoniously plopped the amulet, cord and all.

"So, this is what the little lady was wearing?" Speidel slipped on a pair of brown reading glasses and began to meticulously examine the surface of the amulet.

"That and three others just like it. When did you start wearing those?" Jake shifted his attention to Rudi's glasses.

"Just wait a few years. Your turn will come. Heavy little sucker, isn't it? If it wasn't for all this exterior oxidation, I'd say gold…or even lead." Speidel used his thumbnail to scrape at the black surface.

"Jake thinks it's about 500 years old." I was trying to be helpful, but Speidel gave me a look over the top of his glasses as if to say, "Who's the expert here, young lady?"

"Thanks," he said, slipping a hint of a smile. He pulled the cord back from the broken area and studied it several moments. "Far too dense for silver. Could be a high-grade gold-silver alloy. Hell, it could even be in the *ossie* family."

"What about gold wrapped in silver?" I didn't think Joel's idea was so bad, but Speidel gave him another one of those looks before glancing at Jake.

"What do you need, JM?"

"As complete a rundown as possible. Composition of the alloy…if that's what it is…and any unusual historical significance. I put it at mid-1400s Inca, Central Peru."

Rudi was skeptical.

"This looks like something you or I would have made with Playdough, not standard Incan craftsmanship. You sure on your facts?"

"That's what we've got so far."

Rudi shrugged.

"Okay. I'll run the standard stuff at the lab this afternoon. Magnetic particle analysis. Liquid penetration. Energy dispersion x-ray. Fluorescence analysis…"

Jake interrupted the impressive list.

"Just tell me what time it is, not how to build the watch."

"Ha ha." Speidel returned his attention to the amulet. "Composition's the easy part. The computer will spit that out in a few hours. Historical? I've got some colleagues who specialize in this South American stuff—Incas, Mayans, and Aztecs. There are also half-dozen academic chat rooms for Incan buffs. I'll post some queries and see what we get back. The whole thing shouldn't take long. Call me back early tomorrow morning. I may surprise you."

"That quick?" I thought it might take days.

"You're playing with the varsity now." Speidel gave me a wink.

"Oh. And Rudi, try not to lose it," Jake added. "This little guy's very valuable to someone…as in six figures valuable."

"I'll try to hang onto it." Speidel was visibly impressed.

"Thanks. Call you in the morning." Jake signaled us toward the door.

I didn't know why, but it made me feel good there was such a bond between these two that Jake could entrust Rudi with something worth so much without the slightest hesitation or doubt.

The next morning, I walked out of the bathroom just as Uncle Jake impatiently slammed down the phone.

"Damn."

It was about quarter to nine. Joel was still rousing himself. (It was my turn for the bathroom first.) Surprisingly, I'd slept more soundly than I had for days, which is weird because I was really wound up about what Rudi Speidel might uncover. But my uncle obviously wasn't feeling as calm.

"What's the matter?"

"Oh. Morning, Em. I don't know. Maybe nothing. I tried to connect with Rudi last night. But his phone just rang and rang, so I left him a message on his pager. This morning, I tried the same thing. There was no answer to my page, and the operator says his phone is out of order."

Joel appeared in the hallway, squinting and still half-asleep. "Em, you done in the bathroom?"

"Yes." I turned back to Jake. "It's still pretty early."

Joel shuffled over to Jake's desk. "What's the matter?"

"I can't get through to Rudi, and it's bugging me. He's an early riser, and he always returns his messages. I don't like the feel of it."

Joel and I watched Uncle Jake stare at his desk for more than a minute, thoughtfully rubbing his chin. Then he slapped his leg.

"Get dressed! We're going over there. Now!"

"I just got up," Joel protested.

"Hurry or you'll be going in your pajamas."

Jake snatched his keys from the desk. Joel dashed to the bedroom. I was still sliding my good arm into my coat when Jake yelled from the door.

"Let's go!"

The situation looked bad. Rudi's outside door was ajar. Jake's face fell.

"You two stay here a minute. Let me check this out first."

Like in a B-grade horror film, the door slowly creaked open. What we saw I recall as a series of random images flashing in my mind. The apartment, Rudi's jam-packed technology nerd quarters, was stripped bare. Only one lone terminal sat atop the table. The computers beneath were all gone. Black, red, and yellow cables sprawled where the monitors had been yanked. A television cable dangled uselessly from its outlet. Half of Speidel's books were gone, and those remaining had been carelessly dumped. A lamp lay shattered on the floor in one corner near a pile of old dirty socks. The kitchen's yellow linoleum floor was splattered with chili. Half a pot remained—cold and crusty—on the stove. The refrigerator was full. Dirty dishes filled the sink. The automatic coffeemaker had dutifully made a full morning pot—still warm. The pictures on the walls were gone. The closet was empty except for three wire hangers on the floor. Empty dresser drawers were open. We were stunned. Rudi Speidel was gone.

"Panicked and ran," Jake somberly observed.

"Or left town with the loot?" Joel suggested what we all were thinking.

"Or that," Jake acknowledged. "I just can't believe he took the necklace. It's not like him. I've known Rudi for thirty years."

"It was a lot of money, Jake."

My dad always said that money changed people. I'd hoped he was wrong in this case, but this was pretty powerful evidence. "A lot of temptation."

"I suppose so, Em. It's discouraging when you think you know someone so well."

I couldn't tell which bothered Jake more: losing a hundred thousand dollars or being betrayed by a long-trusted friend. I hoped it was the latter.

We were nearly home when Jake's cell phone rang. He activated the speaker so he could still drive with both hands.

"Hello."

"Mr. Jake Morgan?" It was an older woman's voice.

"Yes."

"This is Claire Kaltreider. I'm a friend of Rudi Speidel."

Jake swerved the car to the side of the road and switched off the engine.

"Is he all right? Do you know where he is?"

"Meet me near your tree house in an hour. That's all I can tell you, Mr. Morgan. Good-bye." The caller hung up, and we gawked at the dial tone. Jake switched off the phone.

"The tree fort?" Joel asked. "What's she talking about?"

"Must be the tree house Rudi and I built in grade school. Jeez. Let's see. It's about forty-five minutes from here—if I can find it. The tree house. Jeez. Why there?"

"Maybe because only you and Rudi know where it is?" I suggested.

Jake did a U-turn and accelerated toward Highway 1. We arrived at the edge of a thickly wooded spot thirty-nine minutes later before heading down a muddy road and climbing out. After another 100 yards on foot, fighting holly and vines on an overgrown trail, we reached a clearing. In its center stood a large maple tree; its trunk was smothered in ivy as thick as my legs.

"Still here," Jake said as we saw it.

Dwarfed by the tree was a gray-haired woman wearing a red sweater.

"Mr. Morgan?" The woman extended her hand to Jake.

"Yes. You must be Claire." They shook. "What's with all this cloak-and-dagger stuff? Where's Rudi?"

"I wish I knew," she said. "He acted very strange last night."

"Rudi always has been the nervous type."

"Paranoid, you mean." She started shuffling through her handbag. "He came by my house in the middle of the night. He must have been on foot...I didn't hear a car...and he came to the back door. He just said you'd be anxious to have this back."

She handed Jake a small paper bundle, tightly bound with a blue rubber band.

"He said to tell you, 'The score is settled,' if you know what that means."

"I'm afraid I may."

The woman closed her purse and immediately headed toward a different path.

"Thanks," Jake called after her. He unwrapped the small package. Inside was the black amulet. Near the broken top portion a tiny hole had been drilled—no doubt for a sample to test the metal. But something must have gone wrong. The paper wrapping was a handwritten note:

WATCH YOURSELF, JM. YOU'RE IN WAY OVER YOUR HEAD!

CHAPTER 9

▼

JAKE
SHIMMERING SNAKE

Emma and Joel feasted on self-concocted gourmet peanut butter and jam sandwiches. It was nearly 1:30 PM, and they were famished. In our rush to Rudi's apartment and our rendezvous in the woods, I'd completely forgotten about breakfast.

Joel flipped through the TV channels with the remote while Emma intently examined the dark amulet at the kitchen table. I was trying to unravel the events of the last few days.

Obviously, the crude medallion Tom had taken from Huascaran held enormous archaeological value to somebody. But who? And why? I was increasingly frustrated by the amulet's elusive secret. My prime source for such information had just disappeared. And his abrupt departure was tied to the necklace. How? I felt responsible for getting him involved. As seductive as this little mystery was becoming, the artifact belonged to neither Tom's family nor me. It was the property of Peru, and, sooner or later, I'd have to return it to the authorities. The mystery caller's $100,000 offer a few days ago was tempting, but I'd never stolen before, and I didn't plan to start now. So the big question remained: What was it about this crudely formed necklace that warranted such fascination on the one hand and such panicky fear from Rudi on the other?

I jumped as the phone interrupted my thoughts and retrieved it on the second ring.

"Hello?" I was hoping for Rudi's voice.

"Morgan?" Instead, I heard the deep gravel of our mystery caller—minus the background industrial noise.

"This is Jake Morgan." I pushed the speakerphone button and snapped fingers at Joel and Emma. "Are you calling about the necklace?"

Joel muted the TV and rushed over. Surprisingly, Emma hadn't heard. Either that or she was ignoring us.

"Turn the speakerphone off, or I'll hang up. My business is with you and no one else."

I didn't know who he was, but, because I possessed what he so desperately wanted, he was certainly in no position to dictate terms.

"If anybody hangs up, it'll be me. I can easily sell this to someone else and easily for more than your paltry $100,000." Joel's eyes grew round. The first rule of negotiation is that the first price is never the final price. I wanted to see how far I could push this character. I'd fill in Joel on this later.

At the other end of the phone was a pronounced silence. I waited. The second rule was that he who speaks first loses. Finally, a deep, rolling laughter broke the silence.

"I see I'm dealing with a professional, Mr. Morgan. Excellent. Let me lay my cards on the table. It will be to both our advantage."

"Fine."

"I represent the interests of an international art collector who prefers to remain anonymous. As you have concluded, my client has taken a keen interest in the Incan necklace, which you and your associates discovered. He is anxious to obtain the fourth piece."

"Does he have the rest of the necklace?" What good would the single piece be to a collector?

"That is irrelevant for the time being. He is only concerned with your piece. I judge from your demeanor that you do indeed have the fourth piece?"

I envisioned a heavyset man salivating, awaiting my reply.

"I don't have it with me." I glanced across the room to the amulet Emma held and winked at Joel. "But I know where I can get it."

"Excellent." The speaker cleared his throat, but the voice remained gravelly. "Mr. Morgan, my client is prepared to make you a most generous offer—much more generous than I had advised. He appreciates your reputation and integrity."

How ironic, mentioning integrity considering the nature of our conversation.

"How much?" I looked over at Emma, purposely dangling the black medallion over her glass of Coke.

"My client is prepared to offer $250,000, subject, of course, to authentication." The voice carried finality.

"Two hundred fifty thousand dollars," Joel blurted. I signaled him to be quiet.

"Why does your client want it so badly?" I was stalling to obtain more information. Glancing at Emma again, I wondered if she might be ill. Normally, she'd be on the edge of her chair over something like this.

"Who can say, Mr. Morgan? Who can say? Some collect stamps; some collect butterflies. My client collects Incan relics."

I covered the phone.

"Em, are you all right?" I called to her, but she didn't look up.

"Well, Mr. Morgan, do we have a deal? You could chase a great many hidden treasures with that much money."

Then, Emma plopped the amulet into her glass of Coke. It furiously fizzed and foamed in reaction.

"Damn!"

Joel reached Emma first. He grabbed for the glass, but she moved aside with surprising agility.

The bidder was disturbed.

"Morgan! My client needs an answer." The thick voice had lost its accommodating tone. "We won't wait forever for your cooperation."

"Em, what's your problem?" Joel shouted.

"You'll have to call me back." I hurriedly hung up, regretting I hadn't gotten more information, seized the glass from Emma, and removed the medallion. My niece seemed disoriented.

"Em, you all right?" I felt her forehead for fever, but her skin was actually cool to the touch. This was supposed to be her holiday. I didn't want her to come down with something.

"What? Oh, yes. I'm sorry. I don't know why I did that. It's okay, isn't it?"

The black patina on the rectangular piece had turned to a gray sludge and was now oozing off in thick, opaque drops. I wiped off the muck, revealing the amulet's original color—a glistening silver-green. I'd never seen anything like it. It was stunning. The carbonation from the Coke had done the trick. I'd seen carbonated beverages used to clean battery terminals in cars with similar results. Joel was all admiration.

"That's awesome! Em, how'd you know to do that?" Joel gently took the piece from me and examined it.

"I'm not sure why I did it." Knowing Emma well, I'm sure she felt guilty about the entire matter.

"Don't worry, Em. You may have done us a favor."

"Uncle Jake?" Joel's voice cracked. "She found something. Look at this."

All three of our heads converged above the medallion.

Crudely engraved on the reverse of the shimmering little rectangle was the image of a snake. The amulet was generating more questions than answers. Was this snake a mere decoration, or did it have cultural significance to the Inca? Was it a religious symbol, good luck piece, talisman, or even a primitive warning of some sort? A lot of detective work lay ahead of me.

In the middle of the night, I awoke to the sound of voices from inside the apartment. My clock radio flashed a red 1:42 AM. Groggy, I remembered Joel and Emma were with me, and my brief confusion quickly turned to irritation. This was way too late for a teenage slumber party. True, it had been a long, exciting day, but we still needed to wake up early tomorrow.

I rolled out of bed and shuffled across my room. The floor, unusually cold on my bare feet, jolted me awake, and I was surprised to notice the voice coming from the living room, not the kid's bedroom. Cautious, I crept down the narrow hallway, realizing I might have a burglar. My stomach tightened in anticipation. But it wasn't an intruder. It was Em.

She stood alone, a motionless statue in the darkened room. The right sleeve of her nightgown hung loose and empty at her side. In the silver-white moonlight, her skin shone pale and ghostlike. Her eyes were distant and empty. I was unnerved. Emma's attention was riveted to the atrocious painting of the Toronto skyline I'd received from a friend of a friend. She stood within a few feet of the lousy cityscape. Speaking softly, her pronunciation was slurred.

"Today? Today? Today?" she softly repeated to herself.

"Em, what's wrong?"

I'd never seen her do this. I was concerned. The funeral—combined with the events of the past few days—was taking a toll on her.

Vacantly, she stared at the painting, chanting softly in the darkness without acknowledging my presence. "Today? Today? Today?"

Even when I positioned myself directly in front of her, she looked right through me. Her eyes were a black void. I gently shook her by the shoulders.

"Emma, wake up! You're sleepwalking. Em!" At last, her eyes gradually began to register.

"What? Where am I? I...What am I doing out here? What's going on?"

She seemed confused and a bit frightened. I tried to assure her she was all right.

"You were sleepwalking, Em. Do you do this at home?"

"No...never! At least I don't think so."

"Well, you sure were doing it a minute ago. I found you out here talking to yourself."

"That's weird. I'm sorry if I woke you up."

We walked back down the hall to her room.

"You were talking about some boyfriend from school."

"What!" She panicked. "Who? What did I say?"

"Just kidding. You didn't say much of anything." She crawled into her bed and pulled the thick comforter to her chin. Joel slept soundly in the matching twin-sized bed a yard away.

"You get some sleep," I said paternally.

"Sorry I woke you up, Uncle Jake," she said heavily, already beginning to drift back to sleep. "Good night."

I closed their door and silently waited outside their room for five minutes. I then cracked the door and peered in. Emma was sleeping peacefully, breathing at the same slow measured rate as Joel. I closed the door and slipped back into the living room. I sprung the hidden latch beneath the Toronto painting, which glided open on the graphite-lined hinges, revealing the dial of a small, gray wall safe.

I glanced over my shoulder. The kids didn't know about the safe, and I wanted to keep it that way. I spun the combination—left, right, left, right—until the barely audible click. Then I opened the small concrete-filled steel door.

The lower shelf held official papers: birth certificate, marriage license, insurance policies, last will and testament, divorce papers, and a few old love letters I should have burned long ago. This pathetic little stack was the sum total of Jake Morgan's *illustrious* life.

I pulled a small manila envelope from the upper shelf and withdrew the leather cord, from which dangled the shimmering medallion.

Emma's sleepwalking was just a coincidence, but something troubling gnawed at the back of my mind. I made a mental note to keep an eye on her. I closed the safe, spun the tumblers, and swung the hideous painting back into place, noting the click of the latch. Tomorrow I'd contact the Peruvian Embassy about returning the amulet. It had become too much trouble for something that wasn't even mine. I dragged myself back to my bedroom and fell into bed. If I could get back to sleep, I'd still get four hours of shut-eye before the alarm.

CHAPTER 10

▼

JAKE
OSMIUM-187

A trio of uniformed officials led me into an executive conference room where a long, mahogany table held court, flanked by a dozen leather ergonomic chairs. At the center of the massive table, a silver tray held bottled waters, cans of ginger ale, and a carafe of hot coffee. Potted ferns stood sentry in the corners of the birch-paneled room. Two men had already seated themselves. But it was a woman who approached me.

It was an unexpected surprise when the three policemen showed up at my apartment unannounced. I'd been summoned to a formal government meeting involving the Peruvian amulet. They'd even mentioned Rudi by name. That was what came from his posting inquiries on Internet chat rooms. I was about to find out what all this was about while Emma and Joel waited in an adjoining room.

"Mr. Morgan? Francine Gireau. I'll be coordinating this special task force at the request of the prime minister. Thank you for joining us this afternoon."

"Did we have a choice?" The three police officers who escorted us to the meeting stood outside the door.

"I assure you that you'll be pleased by the outcome," Gireau said.

Francine Gireau was primly elegant in a white linen blouse beneath a suit of brown cashmere. A delicate strand of pearls hung at her neck. I'd guess she was close to fifty, but she had the tawny, healthy look derived from spare time perhaps spent at tennis. Sporting a short, neat haircut that was thinly streaked silver-gray, she moved among male presence with polished ease. Though Gireau never revealed her exact government title, she had the smooth, confident tone of someone used to getting her way.

"Let me make the introductions." Gireau made it clear this was her meeting.

"Angus McPhee, special assistant to the Department of the Currency. Mr. McPhee is our government's liaison to the International Monetary Fund."

"Pleased to meet you," I said.

McPhee was immense. His girth strained the seams of his gray pinstripe suit, negating the elegance of his crimson silk tie and immaculately pressed shirt. McPhee made no effort to raise his bulk from the chair, but he simply extended a swollen paw for me to shake.

"Thank you," he said.

"An unusual greeting," I thought.

Gireau continued, introducing the man dressed casually in khaki pants and a navy blue shirt.

"Our visiting neighbor from the south is Dr. Richard Stansbury, director of Emission Control Research with Ford Motor Company in Detroit, Michigan."

Stansbury stood and leaned across the table to shake hands. His gray hair was meticulously oiled and combed off an oddly high forehead. Wire-rimmed glasses balanced atop his long, thin nose. I guessed Stansbury to be in his early sixties.

"Dr. Stansbury received doctoral degrees in chemistry and molecular biology from the University of Michigan. And you've been at Ford for how long?"

"Thirty-four years." His voice exuded pride.

Gireau took her seat, indicating the meeting could formally begin.

"I must remind each of you gentlemen that what we're about to discuss is still restricted, highly confidential information. Is that understood?"

Though she spoke to our entire little group, all eyes were firmly fixed on me. I was the outsider.

"Understood."

This was a bad start. They'd dragged me here for a meeting, clearly orchestrated on my behalf, and automatically questioned my integrity.

"Excellent," Gireau crooned. "Dr. Stansbury, why don't you begin?"

"Thank you. Bear with me while I provide some background, Mr. Morgan."

"Call me Jake." At least I'd make an effort.

"Fine. How familiar are you, Jake, with catalytic converters?"

"Somewhat, but go ahead. A review will probably do me good."

"As you're no doubt aware, the purpose of catalytic converters is to reduce harmful atmospheric pollutants in automobile exhaust: hydrocarbons, which cause smog; and carbon monoxide, which is poisonous. A converter breaks down the nitrogen and oxygen from exhaust that would normally bond with hydrocarbons." Stansbury's speech accelerated, exhibiting his boyish enthusiasm for his work. But he was losing me.

"Whoa, you're beginning to lose me."

Gireau interjected. "Think of a mixture of iron filings and sugar going down a conveyer belt. If the mixture passes under a magnet, it will attract all the iron filings, and only the sugar comes out the other end."

"Yes, that's correct," Stansbury said. "Excellent illustrative analogy."

Gireau leaned toward me, having played the part of the accommodating host.

"I get lost on the chemistry, too."

"The physical design of a converter is quite straightforward," Stansbury continued. "It consists of a ceramic structure coated with a metal catalyst. The purpose of the catalyst is to assist in a chemical reaction without actually being destroyed by that reaction. Catalyst metals are normally platinum, rhodium, or palladium, all platinum group elements known as PGEs. For cost savings, a catalytic converter is designed to expose the maximum surface area of catalyst to the exhaust stream while minimizing the amount of metal catalyst required because these platinum group elements are quite expensive—normally more so than gold."

"I'm still with you." I suspected where all this was heading, but I decided to let the meeting proceed as they'd planned.

"Now, even though catalytic converters have remarkable smog reduction properties, two serious shortcomings have emerged." The moment Stansbury mentioned the word shortcomings, his enthusiasm evaporated.

"First, the catalytic converter is ineffective when cold or when the automobile is first started and its engine and exhaust system are warming up. Until the converter heats up, it does virtually nothing to reduce pollutants. This period accounts for seventy-four percent of the hydrocarbon pollutants released from cars equipped with catalytic converters."

"Which I assume would be an even bigger problem in the colder provinces," Gireau added.

"Yes, very much so," Stansbury agreed.

"You mentioned there was a second problem?"

"Yes. Regrettably, we've now discovered that catalytic converters rearrange the nitrogen-oxygen compounds to form nitrous oxide, which is a potent greenhouse gas 300 times more potent than carbon dioxide, today's most infamous greenhouse gas."

"Which means?"

"Although the catalytic converter has made dramatic reductions in air pollution, it is a seriously threatening agent of global warming." Gireau spoke matter-of-factly.

"So, by solving one problem, you've created another, potentially much worse problem." I did a poor job of concealing my accusatory tone. Stansbury flinched.

"Let me remind you all that there is no confirmed scientific evidence that global warming is anything more than a natural phenomenon."

"What! Open your eyes!"

How could anyone with Stansbury's level of scientific knowledge possibly deny the problem's existence? The insidious effect of our warming atmosphere had already struck in the mountains, and none of the ranges had been spared. Glaciers were retreating in the Himalayas, the Alps, the Andes, the Cascades, the Urals, and the Pyrennes. Even on the white towers of the Alaskan Range, so close to the Arctic Circle. And what so many failed to recognize is that most alpine glaciers hovered right at freezing and were extremely sensitive to temperature changes. If the air increased just a degree or two, it was like putting ice cream from the freezer into the refrigerator. Slowly but surely, it would begin to melt.

"Gentlemen!" Gireau interrupted. "We don't have time for this meeting to degenerate into a playground shoving match. Regardless of respective political beliefs, we are here for the same purpose. Confine your remarks to the task at hand."

Maybe now I would learn something.

"What is the task at hand?"

"We're getting to that. Please continue, doctor."

"Thank you." Stansbury lowered his voice and quickly scanned around the room—as if checking for hidden microphones. "During our original research in the1970s, when we were searching for the ideal catalyst, we tested all the elements in the platinum family. In one particular test, an incredible discovery was made, but these results were never released to the public. Even though palladium, which is used in most cars today, is a very effective catalyst, miraculous results were achieved from a little known derivative, or isotope, of osmium and iridium. It is called OS-187.

"During testing, OS-187 neutralized carbon monoxide and hydrocarbons, but, unlike the other metals tested, OS-187 created no nitrous oxide. Furthermore, its catalyst properties worked at any temperature, even subzero. In fact, the only discharge from the OS-187 equipped converter was hydrogen and oxygen. H_2O. Plainly speaking, water."

"The perfect catalyst." Stansbury had finally impressed me. "So you're saying OS-187 could eliminate the single biggest contributor to global warming—automobile exhaust."

"I'll let that last remark slide, Mr. Morgan."

"My high school chemistry was a bit rusty, but I seemed to remember something about osmium becoming poisonous when heated."

In truth, I'd studied several volatile and potentially poisonous chemical compounds several years ago for a salvage project.

"That's correct." Stansbury failed to disguise his astonishment at my sudden command of chemistry.

Angus McPhee broke his silence and snapped to attention. "What! This stuff is poisonous?" Until now, he'd assumed a passive role, sitting like a great, silent Buddha with one hand comfortably placed on his ponderous waist while the other aimlessly spun a black Mont Blanc pen on his blank legal pad.

"No!" Stansbury burst out. Then more quietly, "No, no." He shook his head. "Osmium gives off textroxide, which is poisonous. But OS-187 does not."

"Are we going to get to the real reason I'm here?" I asked.

"Please bear with us, Mr. Morgan," Gireau said. "We feel it's important for you to fully understand the situation."

"All right." I popped the top of a ginger ale. "Doc?"

"OS-187 doesn't occur in nature. It's man-made, created in trace amounts as a by-product of platinum processing. It's exceedingly rare. And astronomically expensive."

"How rare?"

Gireau interceded as the topic swung political.

"The world's only significant source of OS-187 is Kazakhstan, which, as you know, borders Russia. Annual production is measured in ounces, as opposed to metric tons. Every few years, a few grams of OS-187 appear on the black market. When it does, it sells for more than $150,000 per gram."

"Per gram!"

"That's $4.5 million per ounce," McPhee volunteered.

"That would explain a lot." I thought about the phone calls I'd received.

"Correct," Dr. Stansbury said.

"And the Kazakhstani carefully guard their monopoly," Gireau said. "Smugglers are dealt with harshly and efficiently. For the most part, they're never heard from again."

I thought of Rudi Speidel's sudden desire to disappear. The poor guy completely panicked...and rightly so.

"As you can imagine, despite its sensational test results, the incredible price of OS-187 renders it unusable for commercial application," Stansbury said.

"Yeah. I can see where a new Ford Taurus at a half-million dollars might put a crimp in your market share." I smiled.

"Quite."

Stansbury was oblivious to my attempted humor.

"Unusable, that is," Gireau paused dramatically, "until now."

Stansbury leaned forward in his chair, his tone now hushed and conspiratorial. "You see, Mr. Morgan...I mean, Jake, the crude 500-year-old medallion that initiated your associate's Internet-based inquiries is comprised of pure OS-187."

"How is that possible?"

I'd already assumed that was the case, and they sought the return of the amulet, but I still had some questions.

"That's the point," Stansbury said. He removed his glasses and wearily rubbed his eyes. "It simply isn't possible."

"What Dr. Stansbury means is that currently we don't know quite what to think," Gireau said. "Essentially, there are only two possible scenarios."

"And they are?"

"The most obvious is that the necklace is a hoax, perpetrated by either yourself or someone else in your climbing party. This is a possibility we already eliminated based on the cost of acquiring even a small sample of the element."

I'd never been accused of fraud in such a hospitable manner.

"And the second?"

"Somewhere, hidden within the boundaries of the ancient Inca Empire, lies a vast, undiscovered deposit of OS-187. Remember, Mr. Morgan, this entire region is incredibly rich in precious metals. Combined with the fact that there are large areas in the Andes, particularly in Peru, that are still unmapped and unexplored, except by the local Indians. This is why we believe the existence of an osmium mine is a very real possibility."

"And, if such a supply existed, the price would plummet and…" I began.

"It would then be financially feasible to utilize the element in catalytic converters." Stansbury completed my observation. "When rhodium was first discovered in 1908, it cost $12,000 per troy ounce. Now it's a fraction of that."

"Are you giving the Inca enough credit?" I stood and started walking around the table. "I mean, the Inca were incredibly industrious with astounding accomplishments to their credit. A 6,000-mile road system. Advanced astronomical observations. Temples constructed with box-car-sized stone blocks fit together so precisely that today, centuries later, you still can't slip a piece of paper between them."

"Your point?" McPhee stopped his spinning Mont Blanc.

"The third possibility," I said, taking my seat again and leaning on the table with a long dramatic pause, "is that an enterprising metalsmith discovered a way of creating OS-187 500 years before our modern scientists."

"That is utterly ridiculous!" Stansbury exploded in an uncharacteristic show of emotion. "The creation of OS-187 requires temperatures exceeding 700 degrees Celsius and pressure equal to 20,000 atmospheres. Your notion is absolutely absurd!"

Gireau half-stood to referee.

"Whatever the source," she interjected, "the isotope offers hope of an environmental breakthrough that the world desperately needs."

"And you want the medallion back."

She calmly sat and then smiled.

"Actually, Mr. Morgan, we'd like you to locate the mineral deposit."

This was the last thing I'd expected. I felt off-balance and was verbally at a loss.

"I'm flattered. But the location and recovery of a large ore body calls for a geological engineer. My expertise lies in archaeological salvage work."

"Treasure hunting would be more accurate? Would it not?" McPhee's words dripped with disdain.

Normally, I ignored this kind of sarcastic sharpshooting, but it didn't sit well, especially coming from him. McPhee's corpulent face bore the self-satisfied expression of having enjoyed too many lunches at the expense of the taxpayers. He shared an arrogant trait I had noticed in others who deal with other people's money, a sense that his proximity to the rich made him their financial equal. I wondered why men like McPhee couldn't grasp the gulf between actually creating wealth and merely representing it.

"Whatever you want to call it, Mr. McPhee. What's your interest in all this?"

"Money."

He answered as if there were no other valid reason for involvement.

"Our government has loaned the nation of Peru hundreds of millions—both through our involvement in the International Monetary Fund and directly. In the last year alone, they've threatened to default four times. That's money we'd prefer not to lose."

"If there is a mountain of this miracle metal somewhere in the country, it would do the same thing for Peru that petroleum did for the Middle East. It would generate a tremendous economic boom and an instant ability to repay the billions of dollars owed to other countries around the world. The sooner we can help them locate the ore, the sooner Canada will be repaid."

"You're correct about the geological engineers," Gireau said, steering the conversation back on course. "As we speak, three geological teams are in different areas of the Andes, searching for the element: one in Bolivia, one in southern Peru, and another in northern Argentina. At the same time, just for insurance, the Peruvian government, with whom we'd like to cooperate, wishes to launch an archeological-based approach. After all, the OS-187 was part of an Incan artifact. Who knows? The quickest road to the isotope's discovery may lie in an indirect route."

"There are other salvage experts in Canada," I began. "I can think of three or four..."

"The majority of this work will be at altitudes above 3,000 meters, possibly as high as 6,000 meters," Gireau explained. "While there are archeologists with...how shall I say...stronger academic credentials, none of them have any high altitude experience. Certainly none have actual mountaineering training. In addition, you're already somewhat familiar with the country."

"I see."

She had a valid point. Working at altitude compared to salvage at sea level was different as...well...night and day.

"I don't want to misrepresent the situation to you, Mr. Morgan. The consensus in Ottawa is that the historical approach has very little chance of success. It's more an accommodation of the Peruvian ambassador. So, while it's an important patriotic endeavor, your value will be more diplomatic than anything else."

I knew she was probably right. But I couldn't see myself flying halfway across the globe to be somebody's political lapdog. The opportunity to help make even the slightest dent in global warming was worth the effort, and the potential dent that OS-187 could make was huge. Maybe it was something I could do in Tom's memory. When he was alive, the great mountains' dying glaciers was one of the few things that could dampen his spirit. It would be a fitting tribute.

And, of course, there was the mystery.

How could the necklace have been made with the osmium derivative? Did an ore deposit exist in South America, or, as I had flippantly suggested, could the Inca have actually developed an advanced refining process? The magnitude and scope of this were greater than any mystery I'd tackled in the past. It was an opportunity—a challenge—I might never have again. To be truthful, this last was the more personally compelling.

"Well, Mr. Morgan, can we count on your participation?" I sat silent for a moment.

"If I commit to the expedition, I'll go in to find the metal, not for political window dressing. I've got better things to do with my time than to be some sort of lame duck. Is that understood?"

"Absolutely," Gireau smiled. She realized she had me.

"In that case, I'm in."

"Excellent." She handed me a bulging file folder. "This contains all the preliminary information you'll need. You'll fly to Lima in a few days to confer with a Dr. Maroto, a respected authority on the Inca. The two of you will be working together on this."

"Incidentally," McPhee feigned nonchalance, "the Peruvian government is anxious for the return of their necklace."

I'd had my fill of McPhee. I swiveled my chair to face Gireau, effectively turning my back on him. "Ms. Gireau, is there any doubt on the part of our government that I'll return the amulet?"

I could tell Gireau knew where I was heading with this, but I think she realized she was being out-maneuvered.

"No," she slowly said, "you wouldn't be here if we didn't think we could trust you."

"Then I have to delay the return of the amulet."

"It's worth over two million dollars!" McPhee bellowed.

"From an archeological standpoint, it may have relevance in tracking down the mineral deposit. You do want me to try to find this metal?"

"All right," sighed Gireau. "If you think it will help, then, by all means, hold onto it for the time being. Please understand that, if it's lost, you will be held accountable. As Mr. McPhee says, it's worth a great deal, and Peru's Minister of the Interior is anxious for its return."

"I understand. Anything else I should know?" I began thumbing through the file.

"I'm afraid there is just one small catch," Gireau slid in adroitly.

"A catch?" I looked up from the file. I really didn't like McPhee's smirk.

"The catch involves the two children who accompanied you on your celebrated Oak Island expedition…" Gireau continued.

"My niece and nephew?"

"Yes," she smiled. "They will be required to accompany you to Peru."

"What!" I was flabbergasted. "Why?"

"Apparently, the Peruvian ambassador in Ottawa has become a big fan of yours. He read about your Oak Island exploits with great interest and believes the children are good luck," Gireau explained. "I believe he called them '*que trae suerte.*' She picked up a piece of stationery with the National Seal of Peru ostentatiously displayed as its letterhead and read: "If the same two children do not accompany Mr. Morgan, immigration officials will not permit him to enter Peru."

She laid the letter on the table.

"I'm afraid he was very specific and underscored it. And it isn't subject to negotiation."

"My brother's going to love this," I thought.

CHAPTER 11

▼

EMMA
OUR ADVENTURE
BEGINS

Joel and I didn't mind the VIP treatment one bit. When Jake took us to the passport bureau, the staff made a huge fuss, beginning with the uniformed official who whisked us right past the snaking queue of grumbling travelers, who were likely lined up there for hours. Their envious looks were priceless. Their sour faces were scowling, "Who are those kids?" It had been a long, long time since I'd actually enjoyed people staring at me. But this felt like celebrity. It was outstanding!

The downside of this trip though was shots! Lots and lots of them.

A special clinic had agreed to rush us through. The three of us, ushered together to a private exam room, were greeted with a grin from a young Asian intern.

"Good afternoon. I'm Katie Sung. I'm the immunization specialist."

I guessed she was in her mid-twenties. She wore her stethoscope slung casually around her neck. Then it disappeared into the pocket of her white lab coat. A pink "fight breast cancer" ribbon curled gracefully at her lapel. The photo on her I.D. tag displayed a warm, enthusiastic smile.

"I see here you two are off to Peru." She looked up from our forms to smile again at Joel and me. "Sounds like an exciting vacation."

"Yup." Joel regressed to monosyllables whenever he was nervous.

"Whereabouts will you and the children be traveling, Mr. Morgan?"

"Lima, initially. But, most of the time, we'll be pretty remote. We're not completely sure yet. Definitely the Andes. Possibly the Amazon Basin."

Katie Sung obviously disapproved of Uncle Jake's lack of itinerary detail. "I see," she answered curtly. She examined our files again, nodded to herself, and sighed. "The government currently requires immunizations for typhoid, cholera, yellow fever, and malaria."

Joel squirmed. She continued.

"There haven't been any recent reports of dengue fever, so we can dispense with that. However, if you'll be in inaccessible regions, I'd recommend rabies and hepatitis-A."

"Okay," Jake said, trying to brighten Katie Sung with his masculine charm. "Load 'em up."

Joel shot him a nasty look.

"And you, Mr. Morgan, have had all your immunizations a few months ago?"

"Correct."

Jake winked at Joel, who just glared back.

My brother abhorred needles and shuddered again. "Can't we just take pills for these?" It was one of the few things he was really chicken about. I didn't like shots either—who did—but I learned to tolerate them after those intense weeks in the hospital.

"The malaria is administered orally, Joel. But all the others require shots. Certainly a strong young man like you isn't bothered by a little poke in the arm?" She bestowed upon my little brother a very engaging smile.

He brightened and shrugged cooly. "Not much."

"Hey, Joel, if you don't cry, maybe she'll give you a balloon," I teased.

"Very funny, jerk."

"Mr. Morgan, it's not on the requisition report, but I recommend you take along some Diamox in case Emma or Joel experience altitude difficulties."

Our uncle was all charm again. "I should have thought of that. Good idea." Then Jake caught Joel's disapproving look. "They're just pills, Joel. Oh...and I'd also like to bring some antibiotics."

"Why don't I take you down the hall to the pharmacy? The lab can prepare the immunizations while we're getting those two prescriptions."

"Sounds good. You two wait here," Jake said. "We'll be right back."

The adults left, closing the door behind them. The stark room didn't even have any old magazines to read, so I was forced to amuse myself more creatively.

"I guess they're going to wait before they spring the luba-luba shots on you," I said with a totally straight face.

"Luba-luba?"

"Didn't Uncle Jake tell you? Jeez, Joel, it's the worst of all."

"Never heard of it."

"One of those creepy jungle diseases. You get it from these little bugs that fly up your nose and crawl on in. After a couple of days, your brain starts turning to pus, and it oozes out your nostrils."

"What!"

"Honest! Look it up on the Internet. Your intestines, too. They just sort of slither out."

"Slither out where?"

I rolled my eyes at him.

"Think, Joel."

He thought.

"Gross! Are you serious?" Joel wasn't as gullible as he used to be.

"The shots aren't much of an improvement. You have to get four of them, and the needle has to go right in your stomach. They're long and curved—the needles—so they really, really hurt when they go in."

Now Joel looked skeptical. Darn. I should have kept the needles straight. I talked fast.

"Of course, luba-luba only affects people with very small brains, so females are immune."

At that, Joel punched me in the shoulder just as Jake and Katie Sung walked back in.

"Ow!" It hadn't hurt, but I was in rare form. Jake took the bait.

"Hey, Joel! Knock it off! No roughhousing in here. And you know you don't hit girls."

Was that good timing or what?

After my luba-luba buildup, the real shots barely bothered Joel. Or maybe he was just showing off for Katie Sung.

Three oversized duffel bags slouched at the front door. Our taxi would be here in ten minutes. Joel snagged some last-minute television, Jake was finishing up in the bathroom, but I was antsy. Anxious to leave, I paced and ended up at Jake's desk. His passport was on top of his wallet. I picked it up, wondering if his picture was any better than mine.

Judging from my uncle's hair, the photo was probably five or six years old. He wore it much longer back then. I flipped through the pages, captivated by the multicolored, multishaped stamps from all over the world. I wasn't really snooping. I was just curious about all the places he'd been…and he'd been to a lot!

Many of the stamps were in English. India. Singapore. Tuvalu. (Tuvalu? Where the heck was that?) Bailiwick of Guernsey. I could translate the Spanish ones easily enough, like *Correos De Costa Rica* or *Estados Unidos Mexicanas*. There were three or four that looked like Arabic. Turkey? Egypt? I had no clue. I think another was from China, although telling Chinese characters from Japanese gave me trouble.

There was even a triangular stamp from Andorra, the tiny principality between Spain and France. Why in world would Jake go there? *Brasilia* was obviously Brazil. *Belgique* was Belgium. *Polynesie Francaise*! That must have been fun…and it was recent. Business or pleasure? I wondered.

I had to guess at some. I think I read somewhere that *Helvetia* was Switzerland, but I couldn't remember *Magyar*. Something in Europe. Whoa! *Republique du Congo*! Uncle Jake really had been in the Congo. That skull on the bookshelf popped back into my brain.

Jake's toilet flushed just as some papers fell out of his passport. I panicked. Jake would be out any second…and I was snooping. What were they? One paper was our electronic tickets; another was our hotel confirmation. But the third was a Spanish e-mail (that was torn in half) probably from some government office in Peru. Jake was walking toward his bedroom door! No time to read all of it. He had highlighted three words and rewritten them below with their English translations:

insecto = insect
pescar = fish
jaguar = (same?)

Surrounding the three were several big, dramatic question marks.

Jake's bedroom door was opening. Quickly, I refolded the papers and stuffed them back in his passport. He hadn't seen me.

"Well, you two, ready for our adventure?" Jake glowed with enthusiasm.

"Absolutely," Joel said.

"We're both ready." Was I ever.

"Great. Grab your gear. Let's wait downstairs. The cab should be here any minute."

I puzzled over the e-mail. Why hadn't Jake asked me to help translate? He knew I had three years of Spanish. His *espanol*, on the other hand, was limited to *enchilada* and *taco*. Obviously, Uncle Jake wasn't telling us everything about our mission to Peru.

Our parents met us at the Air Canada ticket counter. Originally, my dad had made a gigantic stink about us "running off to a third-world country that didn't have decent plumbing and was run by drug lords and blah, blah, blah." And those were his less colorful comments! However, a call from Ottawa, arranged by Francine Gireau, calmed him down. Finally, he relented and reluctantly let us go. Our mom, on the other hand, wished she could join us.

They both gave us the expected parental advice. Mind your Uncle Jake. Make good choices. Be careful. Wash your hands. Don't take packages from strangers.

Duh! Joel and I rolled our eyes for most of ten minutes, but we knew they meant well. And we'd miss them. Peru was a long way from Brackendale.

After thirteen hours, including a two-hour layover in Florida where we boarded an AeroPeru flight, we finally touched down, bleary-eyed, in Lima, Peru.

Jake told us Francisco Pizzaro founded Lima, "City of Kings," in 1535, only three years after the conquistadors had invaded. A quick takeover. Among other things, Lima was famous for a devastating earthquake in 1746 that destroyed all but twelve houses and killed ten percent of the population. Now, modern Lima and the surrounding area had mushroomed to over eight million inhabitants.

Even though only ticketed passengers were allowed inside the airport, the terminal was a boiling cauldron of frenzied travelers. The police here carried machine guns, which made me nervous. Joel thought it was cool.

I have to admit that my first impressions of Lima were mixed. The city seemed to be shrouded in gray film. Part air pollution, part haze from the nearby Pacific Ocean. A lot like Los Angeles. And then, leaving the airport, we drove past miles of poverty. Shacky little shanty towns—thousands of huts of wood and tin—clung to the hillsides all along the highway. I'd never seen so many people living in such poor conditions. Joel and I continually exchanged pathetic looks.

A long boulevard, *Avenida Colonial*, led to the old part of the city where we were to stay. Our hotel was on *Jiron de la Union*, the main shopping street. It was just a half-block from the *Plaza de Armas*, a huge plaza with statues and fountains that was ringed with colonial buildings—real old-world elegance.

We didn't have jet lag because there was only an hour difference from Vancouver, but Joel and I were still exhausted. Jake insisted we all get a good night's sleep. Tomorrow, we'd start our search for the OS-187.

PART III

▼

PERU

CHAPTER 12

▼

JAKE
SEVENTH JEWEL

Emma, Joel, and I drove across town in our rented drab green Land Rover to meet with Professor Estrella Maroto and begin our search for the OS-187.

"What do you know about this Dr. Estrella Maroto?" Emma glanced through the dossier. "There's only a paragraph about her in here. It says she studied in Lima and spent some time at Oxford. She is fluent in several languages, but there's not much more than that."

"I've read some of her articles. She's actually quite brilliant in her field. Early South American cultures and languages. Although her writing has a pretty bitter undercurrent. Cheap shots at Europeans. Stuff like that."

"Swell. I'm sure we'll really get along."

Emma was in a feisty, sarcastic mood. But, because Dr. Maroto and I would be working together, I'd made an effort to try to keep an open mind.

"She's been chasing after one particular Incan myth for the last six years…at the exclusion of everything else. Apparently, she turned her back on a promising academic career to search full-time for a mythical emerald. That's about it. But she's a respected authority on the Inca."

I was still unclear what role Maroto would play in the search for the OS-187. My instructions were to assist her in the search, whatever that might entail. The background information I'd been given was fuzzy on the theory she was pursuing.

I parked in front of a dilapidated two-story building with rusted, corrugated metal siding. We climbed out and stood in front of a badly weathered wooden door.

"Uncle Jake, do you think she might be a little intimidated by you? I mean…you were in all the newspapers last year with Oak Island."

Emma was quite perceptive for a high schooler.

"That already crossed my mind, Em. We'll just go nice and easy. After all, it's her project."

I knocked hard on the thick, rustic door.

As it creaked open, I stood face to face with Dr. Estrella Maroto.

"Dr. Maroto, I presume." I extended my hand with my most disarming smile. "Hi, I'm Jake Morgan."

Estrella Maroto was surprisingly tall for a woman of such evident Peruvian descent. She looked to be in her early thirties, though it was a little hard to tell. Her bronzed skin was deeply weathered from long days in the sun. Dr. Maroto's thick, black hair was gathered in two long braids that were tied together behind her head. Dark circles under deep brown eyes indicated too much work, too little sleep, or too much worry—maybe all three—and detracted from an otherwise wholesome attractiveness. She was clad in a dirty, loose-fitting green T-shirt; black sandals; and nylon expedition shorts revealing a pair of strong, nicely shaped legs.

But, whenever I first met someone, what I really paid attention to was their hands. You can tell a lot about someone by their hands. Estrella Maroto's hands were strong with short-cropped, unpainted fingernails. Thick, cord-like veins ran up her forearms. They were honest hands, well-acquainted with hard work. She also didn't wear a wedding band. I found myself attracted. The thought of spending several weeks working together might not be so bad after all.

Unfortunately, Professor Maroto made it immediately clear that the feeling was not mutual. Instead of shaking my hand, she placed her hands defiantly on her hips and leaned against the doorway to block our entrance.

"Let's get something straight right from the start, Señor Morgan. I'm not impressed by your pathetic treasure hunting exploits." So much for Emma's concern. "I've studied all your expeditions, and it's not an enviable record. In my mind, you are nothing but a cheap opportunist. You have no advanced degrees, not in history, archaeology, or even anthropology. In fact, you have no degree at all. I've known men like you before. You're all alike. Serious scholars do all the tedious, grueling work, sorting through petrified shit to track a civilization's diet or picking apart rotting corpses for clues on medical practice. We do hard, thankless, 'roll up your sleeves' archaeological work while men like you grab the headlines, pose for photographers, and line your pockets with antiquities that don't belong to you. And, worst of all, in the process, you totally screw up any archaeological or historical significance of a site during your clumsy pilfering of artifacts. You're an amateur, Morgan. Completely unqualified. And I'm a professional. That's all I need to know."

I could hardly believe the vindictive crap this bitter woman clung to. Here she was, itching to pick a fight with someone she had never met. She looked at me with contempt.

"When I saw it was you they'd selected to assist on this project, I couldn't believe it. Some politician must owe you plenty. And I have no idea what they were thinking when they allowed you to bring your family."

She then scoffed at Joel and Emma.

"But you're in luck, Señor Morgan. I have no interest in the headlines you crave. My only interest is in helping my people, and, from what the government has told me, this project has the potential to do just that. I'll leave the media to you. Don't worry. I'll never stand between you and the cameras. You'll have plenty of opportunities to get your picture in the papers. Just leave the real archaeological work to me. If that's agreeable to you, then we have the basis for a working arrangement. Understood?"

"That's not fair!" Emma stepped forward.

"Emma, Joel, would you excuse us for a minute?" The kids got the message and beat it back to the Land Rover. I turned my attention back to the professor. I could feel my face reddening as I readied to speak. Maroto's attitude was going to stop now.

"You're right, Professor Maroto. I don't have any advanced degrees. I didn't even graduate from college. I only went for a year. I've never denied it. I have nothing but sincere respect for people who have a dedicated commitment to legitimate scholarly research. But I have no time for pompous academics who believe people aren't capable of rational thought without a string of degrees after their name."

"Now. For the sake of accuracy, let's get a few things straight. First, I don't know who you've worked with in the past, but it wasn't me. So don't give me any crap based on what happened with someone else. You don't know anything about me."

She looked at the ground, refusing to meet my gaze. Perhaps she'd expected me to cower at her tirade.

"Secondly, every salvage expedition I've coordinated had the appropriate governmental approval, which includes giving up eighty to ninety percent of whatever I find. I take big risks for a meager piece of the pie. I've never—and none of my crews—have ever stolen artifacts. I don't appreciate being called a thief. Don't do it again."

Every muscle in my body was tensed as I waited for her response. If it wasn't the right reply, I'd be headed back to Vancouver at once. Finally, she looked up.

"You are correct. I had no basis for personally attacking you. I have worked with Europeans in the past. It has not gone well. I am sorry."

"Apology accepted."

I wondered if she always ran hot and cold like this.

"Lastly, the two children are my brother's. Bringing them wasn't my idea. That was one of the demands made by your Peruvian ambassador to Canada. And, in truth, these kids were instrumental on a recent expedition."

"Yes, I read about it."

She relaxed and casually slipped her hands in her pockets.

"They seem to be good luck."

I was proud of how they'd helped me in the past. Dr. Maroto shifted her stance.

"I believe people make their own luck, Señor Morgan."

"I agree, but Joel and Emma have a knack for being in the right place at the right time. And there may be another reason to have Emma along. It's just a hunch at this point."

"She's crippled." Maroto accused.

"Em lost her arm a year ago in a car accident."

"That's terrible. I'm sorry." It was the first time Maroto sounded genuinely human.

Emma and Joel were leaning against the car, laughing about something.

"Listen, professor, whether we like it or not, we have to work together on this project. Considering the importance of what we're looking for, I suggest we put differences aside—at least during the search."

I extended my hand a second time. She looked at it a few moments and then reluctantly shook it. Her hand was warm to the touch.

"Maybe we can get by on first names too?"

"Agreed. Why don't all of you come in? You may as well know what we're looking for and why."

I signaled Emma and Joel that it was all right to return.

"Incidentally, Estrella, if we should come across any petrified shit, I'll make sure you get first crack at it."

"I'll keep that in mind," she said with the slightest hint of a smile.

We climbed to the second floor on clanking, metal, industrial stairs that were suspended above a cluttered garage and storage area. Estrella unlocked a heavy metal door at the top of the staircase, which opened into her living and working area. The room, measuring about fifty feet by forty feet, took up the entire top floor of the building. Although there were no windows, two small skylights permitted narrow beams of morning light to illuminate a swirling sea of floating dust in the dark interior.

Estrella flipped the light switch, and dozens of fluorescent lights flickered to life, flooding the room in harsh, high-intensity clinical lighting that was reminiscent of a surgical suite. It was somewhat out of sync for the disheveled surroundings.

The room was a combination Incan museum and research library. Dr. Maroto's living facilities seemed a momentary afterthought, as if eating, sleeping, and living itself were irritating interruptions to her obsession with the jewel. I wondered how many precious years of her life had been spent in rooms like this to pursue a myth.

Estrella led us past a tiny kitchenette with a laughably miniature stove and refrigerator. A small aluminum sink was filled with a jumble of dirty dishes.

"She must use the same maid service as you," Joel said under his breath.

The room's most dominant feature was a large composite of color aerial photographs that created a six-foot by four-foot photo of Peru in intricate detail. Emma and Joel were drawn to it. The wide variety of colors and terrain provided a dramatic representation of Peru's diverse ecosystems. The deep blue of the Pacific Ocean contrasted with the brown coastal desert, which dissolved into the white tundra of the Andes and then back down to the emerald-green tropical rain forest that bordered the chocolate-brown Amazon River. Between each of those extremes were gradations of individual ecosystems. In all, Peru boasted dozens of separate climatic habitats.

Dr. Maroto's aerial map was peppered with multicolored pushpins, each with a tiny handwritten label attached. I tried reading them, but they were neither in English nor Spanish.

"What are the pins for?" Joel inadvertently removed a pushpin he was examining.

"Do not touch, please!" Estrella Maroto's voice was sharp. Carefully, she replaced the pin precisely from whence it had come.

"The pins represent different aspects of research surrounding the jewel."

"I assume that's the reason we're here."

"*Sí*," Estrella concurred. "In any event, the red pushpins signify where specific clues have been discovered. The yellow are archaeological digs that may have relevance, and the line of blue pins is the assumed route of a four-man expedition from Francisco Pizzaro's main force. I will explain this momentarily."

On the same wall as the composite were six additional Peruvian maps, or map reproductions, representing various historical periods in the nation's past. There was a copy of a crude coastline rendering (dated 1527) that included Panama, Ecuador, and Northern Peru with the interior of the map intentionally labeled "Unknown Territory." Another map reproduction, drawn in 1784, depicted the Cordillera Blanca mountain range.

At the far end of the wall was a yellow map of Peru, devoid of modern political boundaries, outlining the territories inhabited by the forty or fifty ancient tribal nations the Inca conquered and assimilated. They ranged from the Olmo Tribe in the northern desert, to the Conchuco nation in the center of the great Andean spine, and to the Uru and Lupaca Nations near Lake Titicaca in southern Peru.

Opposite the wall with the cartography mural was a small, battered steel desk, the type that was popular in the 1950s. Its surface was littered with notes, journals, typed papers, two open books, several official government reports, and three empty graham cracker boxes. Above the desk was an open-faced wooden cupboard, firmly bracketed to the wall, with dozens of built-in cubbyholes. Each compartment was filled to capacity with carefully rolled or folded slips of paper, newspaper clippings, notes, and black and white photographs. I assumed every meticulously pigeonholed scrap dealt in some manner with the missing jewel.

In the middle of the room was a makeshift table, an old door with each corner supported by three stacked cinderblocks. On the center of the table, I noticed a bright blue file folder labeled "OS-187." The folder seemed to contain a lot more information than the file I'd received from the Canadian authorities.

As Estrella explained one of the historical maps to Emma and Joel, I casually opened the OS-187 file. On top was a report entitled:

BIOGRAPHICAL DATA
SUBJECT: Jacob L. Morgan, Canadian Citizen
COMPILED: Peruvian Ministry of the Interior

Estrella Maroto had diligently highlighted portions of the biographical report. Based on our debut conversation, I guessed she was underwhelmed with its findings.

Sparsely scattered throughout the large one-room studio was an eclectic collection of mismatched secondhand chairs, end tables, and a grotesque, moth-eaten purple sofa.

Taking up half of the longest wall stood five tall bookshelves that were tightly packed with everything from dust-covered, leatherbound journals to garish paperbacks and college textbooks. One of the five bookshelves had double-reinforced doors with wire mesh embedded in thick glass. Three high-tech steel locks secured it.

Each and every volume on the shelves was dedicated to one subject—the Inca. These shelves cradled a wealth of knowledge, invaluable historical reference materials. Every scholarly work written on the Inca, or pre-Incan civilizations, in the last 200 years must have been represented. It was an exceptional private collection, especially for someone of such seemingly modest means. Yet something bothered me as I scanned the many shelves. I couldn't pinpoint it. Here was the most comprehensive private library I'd seen on the Inca, but I felt something wasn't there that should have been. Something was missing.

"This is a remarkable collection. It must rival any of the universities."

"It is the finest collection in Peru." Dr. Maroto spoke with an enormous amount of pride. "Of course, some of the rarer works are reproductions of the originals."

"Emma, Joel, you should look at this collection. Some of these books are hundreds of years old."

I peered through the bulletproof glass in the security shelf and recognized an obscure title from the extensive cramming I'd had done in preparation for the trip.

"Is that Palencia's *Historia del Peru?*"

"You know this work?" Estrella's eyes suddenly sparked with animation.

"Let's just say I know of it. Prescott referenced it frequently in his 1847 *History of the Conquest of Peru,* but it was rare even then. Isn't there only one copy, residing in Spain?"

"*Si.* Technically, that is true," she said enthusiastically. "This is a reprint of the 1571 text, published several decades later. It's the sole reason for the locks. It's in very poor condition and extremely fragile, but it provides a fascinating perspective of the Incan rebellion in the mid-1530s."

Chalk one up for my side. The mere mention of this text and her face looked years younger. There was real joy in those dark eyes. I'd scored points. No, I didn't have the academic credentials Estrella Maroto so cherished, but she at least knew I'd done my homework and then some. I also realized that, beneath Estrella's austere exterior, was a passion for her work I found appealing.

The only personal items in the business portion of the room, without any apparent historical significance, were individually framed pictures of eight small children sitting on a small end table. Perhaps they were students in a class she taught or maybe nieces and nephews. There were too many, and she was far too young for all these children to be hers.

"Perhaps we should get to work?" I wanted clarification of our expedition.

"*Sí.* Of course. If you wish to sit, I will provide a full explanation."

Emma, Joel, and I found seats. Estrella remained standing, as if to make presentation to a board of directors.

"As you may know, the government reviewed with me the circumstances surrounding the OS-187 necklace you discovered with the mummy on Huascaran Norte," she began.

"I had a similar briefing in Vancouver."

"I believe there is a strong possibility of a connection between the jewel and this osmium material that both our governments wish to locate. The jewel is the only Incan legend referring to something so unique, highly prized, and which subsequently disappeared. In my opinion, if we find the jewel, we find the OS-187."

"What is with the jewel you guys keep talking about?" Joel asked.

"I think it would help Emma and Joel if you brought us up to speed. I'm unclear myself on the connection between the two." I tried to mask strong doubt. I had assumed we'd been assigned to work with Estrella because of her extensive knowledge of the Inca. But it was beginning to sound like she was merely using the OS-187 expedition as an excuse, at the government's expense, to continue her search for this all-consuming emerald or jewel. I wasn't sure if she was trying to deceive us or if she had sought the prize for so long that she had come to deceive herself. I'd at least listen.

"The first reference to the jewel's existence surfaced in the chronicles of Garcilasso de la Vega's *Commentarios Reales*, published in 1609," Maroto said. "While Garcilasso's father was European, his mother carried the blood of Incan rulers. She was the niece of Huayna Capac, who ruled the empire from 1493 to 1527. She was ten years old when Atahualpa seized the throne.

"Garcilasso's mother learned the Incan history at the feet of the Children of the Sun themselves. She, in turn, taught Garcilasso when he was but a boy. You see, the Inca had no written language. Their history was handed down through stories and legends." With great reverence, Estrella untied a battered leather journal in which she had accumulated five centuries of clues and notes concerning the legend.

"There is a brief reference in Garcilasso's *Reales* that, 'During the reign of Topac Yupanqui, a great sadness befell the royal Inca at the loss of one of his most prized possessions—*K'anchis Llajpa*—the Seventh Jewel.' *K'anchis Llajpa*. That is, *Quechua*, or language of the Inca."

"When was that?" Emma always wanted the facts and figures. Joel preferred the big picture, the intuitive side of things.

"That would have been some time between 1471 and 1493," Estrella answered. "The Incan ruler believed the loss to be the will of Inti, the Sun god, who 'devoured the jewel in a jealous rage. This being so, none in the kingdom were to evermore speak of the jewel for fear of inciting Inti's wrath.' That is the only mention of it by Garcilasso de la Vega," she said.

"But hasn't anyone ever looked for it?" Joel asked.

"Countless treasure hunters, historians, and fools have sought the jewel. At the time *Commentarios Reales* was published, stories circulated that the jewel was a fantastic emerald, the size of a man's head. But no one could discover anything more about the mysterious stone."

"Okay, if it's the Seventh Jewel, where are the others?" Em asked. "Does someone have the first six?"

"In a manner of speaking, the other jewels did exist," Maroto answered. "Please let me continue. You must hear the entire legend to appreciate all that has gone before. By the middle of the 1700s, it was generally believed the jewel did not exist—that it was a myth, an illusion, a falsehood created by an errant historian, or by the Inca. Then, in 1831, a fantastic discovery proved its existence and fueled a century of treasure seekers."

Dr. Maroto's eyes assumed an animated brilliance.

"During the renovation of a chapel in Arucas, in the Canary Islands, the journals of Hernando de Ulloa, a sixteenth-century Spanish missionary, were uncovered," Maroto said. "For the most part, the volumes are tedious accounts of everyday life in the mission over the course of several decades, except for three incredible pages that refer to an occurrence in 1568."

As Estrella wove the legend's fabric, a vocal tapestry representing six years of solitary research, she became visibly drawn into the mystery. Her voice hushed, as if she mistrusted the very walls surrounding us. I was concerned with her ability to remain objective about the OS-187 project. She continued.

"Ulloa, the missionary, had been summoned to give last rites to an old man dying of fever. The victim refused to reveal his Christian name for fear that his sins would bring shame—or worse—to his family back in Spain. Ulloa described the man as 'delirious with the fever, possessing a soul most tormented, with a haunted look as if hunted by some unspeakable evil.'"

"The dying man claimed to have been part of the original 165 adventurers under the command of Francisco Pizzaro during the conquest of the Inca thirty-six years earlier."

"This was in the Canary Islands?" Emma asked.

"Yes."

"Isn't that all the way across the Atlantic Ocean from Peru?" Emma asked.

"But it's close to Spain," I explained. "It would make sense."

"Yes, I believe this man was hiding," Estrella said. "Hiding from his past, from his transgressions, and from something that haunted him. He had chosen a remote island for his asylum, yet he was still close to his mother country."

"Continue," I urged.

"According to Ulloa's recording of the confession, in 1533, after the Spanish defeated the Inca at Caxamalca and during the sacking of

Cuzco, Pizzaro heard rumors of a great jewel that was lost to the empire many years earlier. Yet, try as he might, Pizzaro could not discover its whereabouts. Despite inflicting the cruelest of tortures upon the Incan nobles and chieftains, none could remember—or chose to remember—any details about the jewel. Only that it had existed in the time of their fathers."

I had to admit Estrella Maroto could spin one hell of a story. The kids were completely absorbed, and I even felt myself drawn in.

"Pizzaro called upon four trusted lieutenants—this feverish, dying man claimed to be one—and instructed them to travel south with an Indian interpreter, deeper into the Incan empire. By whatever means they deemed necessary, they were to obtain from the natives the location of this remarkable treasure."

"Amazingly, this account was corroborated by Pizzaro's own journals that were scribed by his secretary. The 'great' conquistador...you see...could neither read nor write," Estrella smugly interjected. "On behalf of his General, the secretary wrote, 'On this, the 29th day of November, 1533, I have commissioned four men—Sotelo, Candio, Mexia, and Oreilana—and one Indian to travel further south in search of the treasure that continues to elude me.' Prior to the discovery of Ulloa's diaries, historians assumed Pizzaro was referring to a quest for more gold. But don't you see," Estrella said earnestly, looking at each of us as if we were particularly dense, "it was a search for the jewel. It was the jewel that had eluded him."

Emma and Joel nodded in understanding. It was evident Estrella was completely fixated upon this legend.

"Pizzaro's only other reference to the jewel—or those who sought it—was made five months later." She looked down and read once more from the leather journal. "'We continue our prayers to the Almighty for the best, but I fear the four soldiers I sent have been slain by savages. I will commit no more men to the pursuit of a phantom treasure.'"

"According to the feverish man dying before Ulloa, for reasons he could not recall, the small group turned and headed north in search of the jewel, rather than south as Pizzaro had commanded."

"So you're thinking the jewel is made of OS-187?" Emma asked. "I'm not sure I see the connection."

Estrella didn't immediately answer. I think her patience was wearing thin. I doubt she had spent much time with two overly inquisitive kids, particularly teenagers. Their incessant questioning could be annoying. Even I admit that. But their innate curiosity had already proven them invaluable.

"It may well be," Estrella replied. The odd tone of her voice suggested there was more to this legend than she was telling.

"According to Ulloa's writings, the group discovered the jewel's hiding place, but only after inflicting 'the most vile and heinous injuries to countless natives to loosen their tongues.' He said the jewel 'was hidden by the hand of Almighty God, and it was miraculous that they had found it.'"

"The dying man claimed he was the only one who knew of the treasure's hiding place. When Ulloa questioned him about his companions, the man confessed to slitting his comrades' throats, so he might seize the treasure for himself. He had intended to return and retrieve the treasure, but he believed he was pursued by the dead—not his fellow soldiers—but by what he called 'the other dead.'"

"Ulloa pressed the man to disclose the treasure's location for the benefit of the Church and to achieve absolution for his sins against mankind and the Lord, but the man died without revealing its hiding place."

Emma and Joel were speechless. Estrella's narration had achieved the intended effect.

"I've read a little bit about the jewel." I leaned back in my chair and casually crossed my arms behind my head. "As I recall, treasure hunters abandoned the search for it back in the 1930s. There were just too many other Incan legends with larger treasures to chase. The lost ransom of Atahualpa, for example."

"That is correct. I am the only serious historian who still seeks the jewel."

She answered with a thin smile. I couldn't tell if she was proud of the fact or embarrassed by it.

"It's a compelling story. I'll give you that. And you certainly tell it well."

I stood and walked over to one of the maps on the wall. "But, unless you've found something that leads us directly to it, it's a huge area in which to hide something so small. The Incan empire encompassed Peru, Ecuador, Bolivia, Argentina, and Chile. By comparison, the proverbial needle in the haystack would be easy."

"There are no clues to pinpoint the location. There is no treasure map with pirate skulls, as you'd see at the cinema. But it is you, Señor Morgan, who has considerably narrowed the search area."

And with sudden energy, Estrella rushed to one of the current maps of Peru. Emma and Joel followed.

"Prior to your discovery of the mummified remains atop Huascaran Norte, it was believed the Inca had not conquered central Peru, which includes the mountain, until the mid-1490s. Yet we know from the girl's ceremonial costume that the sacrifice took place during the second half of Pachacuti's reign, meaning sometime before 1471. Now the logical question is: Why would the Inca perform an important ceremony outside the border of their own empire? The answer is: They wouldn't. This means the Inca conquest of central Peru occurred decades earlier than previously thought."

"Which means what?" Joel asked.

"For the last three centuries, treasure hunters seeking the jewel never ventured further north than here." She pointed to a small spot on the map. "Huanuco Pampa, more than 100 kilometers south of Huascaran. Your discovery effectively opened up an entire new region where the jewel may lie. I believe we will find it between Huascaran and Hua-nuco Pampa."

"That's all fine, Estrella, but you've yet to explain how this jewel might lead us to a mineral deposit of OS-187. That's why we're here. Sure, the jewel is a fascinating mystery, but there's more at stake than a lost emerald. Even if we found your jewel, which doesn't seem feasible, how will it lead us to a mine?"

Estrella was silent several moments. She finally met my eyes with an unarmed look. "You will have to trust me."

"What!" I'd traveled halfway around the world, dragging Emma and Joel along, and she wanted me to proceed on her word.

She pleaded. "I cannot accomplish this alone. I need someone to help. I have studied this for many years. I am convinced the Seventh Jewel will lead us to the mineral. But I ask that you trust me a little longer." She placed her hand on my arm, and my insides jumped. "Please."

Damn. Jake Morgan, the sap. I was going to give in to those deep brown eyes. I only hoped she hadn't pursued the legend so long that she'd become completely self-delusional. I sighed.

"All right, we're in."

"*Muchas gracias.*" She withdrew her hand. "You will not be disappointed. I am sure we can find it!"

"What's your plan?"

"We have a meeting with the Department of Antiquities tomorrow at the National Library. It is close to your hotel. I will take a bus."

"I've got a car. Why don't we pick you up? What time?"

"Thank you. Twelve o'clock."

I stood in her doorway at the top of the metal stairs. Emma and Joel lagged behind, drawn to the research library on their way out.

"By the way," I tried to sound casual, "do snakes play any kind of role in Incan culture?"

"No, I do not believe so. Is that important?"

"Just an advertisement I saw."

That seemed to satisfy her, and I'd gotten an answer. I didn't want to mention the amulet's engraving until I completely understood the professor's intentions.

"Señor Morgan…" Estrella began.

"Please, just call me Jake. Every time you say Morgan, I look around for my father."

"All right, Jake," she awkwardly said, "I am sorry about your cousin. I didn't know him, of course, but…well…I'm sorry for his family. For the children."

"Thank you. I appreciate that." Estrella was becoming downright human. "Hey, come on, you two. We need to get back to the hotel."

"Professor Maroto," Joel said, "where are the other books?"

"The other books?" she blinked. "What do you mean?"

"You've got tons of books on the Incas, but where are all your books on jewels?"

That's what was missing! Good for Joel! Estrella fumbled with a weak response.

"Umm…I keep them at the university. But now it is time for you to go."

This extremely intelligent woman had spent a good portion of her professional life meticulously tracking down a purported giant emerald. Yet there were no reference materials—not a single book—on precious gemstones. It didn't add up.

CHAPTER 13

▼

EMMA
ESTRELLA'S SECRET

Finally. Joel and I had been waiting in the car forever. Estrella rushed down the stairs from her office. She wore sandals with faded blue jeans, a wide brown belt, and a tight white T-shirt. Her hair was still tightly braided, just like yesterday. Uncle Jake walked slowly behind her, studying her as she bounded down the stairs.

I climbed into the backseat next to Joel, leaving room up front for Estrella. Jake slid into the driver's seat, reached over, and opened the passenger side for our guest. She wasn't there. She leaned in Jake's window.

"No, it will be much quicker if I drive." She was planted by the driver's side of the Land Rover. Jake sat firm.

"That's all right. I can find it. Jump in."

"No. The traffic is very difficult in the afternoon. I will drive." Estrella looked defiant.

"I'm already here."

The two stared at each other several moments like a couple of middle-school kids, sizing each other up at a dance.

"Are you two going to argue all day?" I finally asked. "At this rate, the library will be closed by the time you guys are done. Can't we just get going?"

Reluctantly and awkwardly, Jake moved over to the passenger side and sighed. Estrella hopped into the driver's seat, turned the ignition, and revved the engine. She gunned the accelerator, and the car jumped to life. The pigtailed professor drove erratically through the narrow, crowded streets, grinding the gears with each shift.

"Put the clutch in all the way," Jake shouted above the engine. "You're going to ruin the transmission!" Estrella knit indignant eyebrows, but she did as Jake instructed.

"So what's the deal with this professor's notebooks?" Joel asked, looking ahead to the library.

"We're hoping they might help us find the osmium deposit, if it really exists," Jake answered. "It involves an isolated native tribe."

"I shall explain."

Estrella quickly commandeered the conversation, making us even more nervous when she turned back to speak.

"In the 1940s, there were unconfirmed reports of unshod human footprints found at high altitudes. And there were occasional stories by government survey teams about their campsites being vandalized or food supplies stolen, but there was never any sign of the thieves. A legend grew of a lost tribe of Incan warriors, but, of course, there was never any proof."

Estrella swerved abruptly to a faster lane and nearly sideswiped a tour bus. She drove unfazed.

"Then, in 1949, a remarkable event occurred at the Feast of the *Pleiades*. You know of this? It is an annual Peruvian festival that draws more than 70,000 pilgrims from throughout South America. That year, in the middle of the ceremonies, the vast crowd silently parted for three elderly travelers. All three wore the ancient Incan emblem of the sun, and they spoke only *Quechua*, language of the Inca. Fortunately, the festival was also attended by two noted anthropologists: Oscar Nunez del Prodo and, an Englishman, Dr. Montgomery Richardson."

Estrella made a sharp, unannounced left turn. Joel and I smashed against each other on the right side of the car.

"Jeez!" I gave Joel a nervous look. But he was loving it.

"Can you get this up on two wheels?"

Thankfully, Joel wouldn't drive for several more years.

"Go easy," Jake said. "Let's get there in one piece."

Estrella looked annoyed.

"The three pilgrims were of the Q'ero tribe, the last pure remnants of the Inca. Ancestors of the Q'ero tribe had fled to the high mountains to escape Pizzaro and the conquering Spanish invaders. For 500 years, they lived in seclusion within their hidden villages, isolated from the rest of the world. It's a remarkable story!"

Estrella punctuated this last sentence with a prolonged honking of the horn to urge four elderly pedestrians faster across of the street. She floored it and then continued.

"Professor Richardson spoke briefly with the Q'ero travelers, but, at nightfall, they disappeared into the countryside. No one knew where they had come from and where they were going. The three were never seen again. It took Richardson four years, mostly solo expeditions into the interior, but he eventually discovered the tribe. I believe he may have revealed their location somewhere within his journals."

"So you think they know about the jewel?" Joel practically shouted from the backseat.

"No, the Seventh Jewel disappeared many years before the Spanish came to Peru. I don't expect the Q'ero to actually know of the jewel's location. But I believe they may unknowingly have a small clue, perhaps a tiny thread in an ancient story or folk song that might lead us to it."

Uncle Jake, Joel, and I did a little mutual rolling of the eyes.

Estrella finally turned into the National Library's vast parking lot, squeezed into one of the narrow parking slots, and turned off the engine. She swiveled fast to the backseat.

"Think of it! The Q'ero are direct descendants of the Inca! Their ancestors knelt before Pachacuti, heard the gunshots, and smelled the powder of Pizzaro's rifles."

Joel got right to the point.

"Why didn't you or somebody else think of this sooner if the professor's notes have been here since the 1950s?"

"Montgomery Richardson refused to release his notes or reveal the location of the tribe. But he passed away six years ago. And, until your uncle's discovery at the top of Huascaran, our government has been unwilling to share the information with the public."

Eduardo Viedma lounged lizard-like against the edge of a wooden table that was loaded with thick, burgundy-bound volumes. Nearly fluent in English, Viedma was the assistant undersecretary for the Department of Antiquities in Peru's Ministry of the Interior. Perhaps thirty years old, Viedma suffered from an unwholesome, emaciated appearance. His tendons and ligaments stretched tightly over his bones; his cheekbones protruded beneath narrowed, menacing eyes. He wore a white starched shirt that was open at the collar. As he slouched, his cuffed green pants had risen to his shins, revealing black and red striped socks and hairless upper ankles. The fingernails of his little fingers were long, like a woman's. Eduardo Viedma instantly gave me the creeps.

Dr. Maroto had convinced Viedma to meet us in the basement of the National Library. The sprawling, dimly lit subterranean expanse housed row after row after row of old volumes, no longer of interest to the general public. The basement also contained books on permanent reserve, valuable collections, and research materials archived long ago that no one had the inclination—or time—to catalogue. Richardson's journals fell into this last category. The only patrons to wander through the underground maze of gray metal bookshelves were graduate students from the nearby university.

The whole area had the musty smell of yellowing pages in long-forgotten volumes. I could tell Uncle Jake relished being surrounded by so many books. He'd spent countless hours in other dungeons of knowledge throughout Canada and the United States—researching, studying, and digging for snippets that might help him unlock great historical secrets. Estrella had said the library is where the real treasure hunting occurs. I knew Uncle Jake agreed, and he enjoyed research as much as the more adventurous stuff.

The four of us pulled up seats on crates beside a small, locked enclosure that was four walls of a chain-link fence. It rose the full height of the nine-foot ceiling, measuring maybe ten feet by fifteen feet. It was reminiscent of a small jail cell. Inside, Richardson's journals, manuscripts, and specimen samples were being held prisoner. The floor of the small enclosure was littered with dust balls, paper scraps, and cigarette butts accumulated after years of janitorial neglect. Against one side of the fencing, a wall of filthy cardboard boxes, in various stages of collapse, teetered in stacks. Another chain-link wall supported a row of cobweb-covered wooden crates. A dirty lightbulb dangling from a rafter illuminated four rows of formaldehyde-filled specimen bottles that were discolored from the slowly decaying bats, leeches, snakes, and rats within. The gate, or door, of the metal room was secured by several coils of rusted chain and fastened by an imposing steel padlock. An aged security guard sat watching us, perhaps thirty feet away.

"Señor Viedma, thank you for agreeing to meet with Dr. Maroto and me. We appreciate your time. This is my niece, Emma, and my nephew, Joel."

"Of course," Viedma answered, showing absolutely no interest in Joel or me. "You forgive me if I eat. Normally, this is my time for lunch."

Viedma held a grapefruit in his bony fingers. His dark eyes examined Estrella very appreciatively. Jake postured.

"Go ahead and eat."

My Uncle Jake once told me he had dealt with pompous, self-inflated bureaucrats all over the world. I remember him saying that, with a sincerely empathetic ear and a little flattery, you could eventually get whatever you were after. Now I got to watch him work.

"We won't take much of your time."

Viedma's eyes narrowed further. "Perhaps you will explain to me why it is suddenly so urgent for you to examine Señor Richardson's journals. They have been sealed here in the archives since his death many years ago."

"Six years ago," Estrella corrected.

"Yes, six years."

I noticed that Viedma's eyes never met Estrella's. When he did glance in her direction, his gaze never left her chest. What a slimeball! Viedma methodically peeled the grapefruit and then placed a segment of the fruit in his mouth.

"The wastebasket, *por favor.*"

He motioned to Estrella to hand him the green metal basket, even though he was actually closer. Chauvinist. She reluctantly handed it to him. We all needed to cooperate. After sucking the juice from the grapefruit slice, Viedma dangled the spent pulp from his mouth and grinned grotesquely before spitting it into the trash can.

"*Gracias.*"

Joel and I exchanged looks of disbelief. Man, this guy was crude!

"As I said," Viedma looked at his long nails as he talked, "if I knew of your urgency, I might be in a better position to help."

He placed another piece of fruit into his mouth, sucked it dry, and again dribbled the remains into the pail between his feet.

"I explained as much as I could yesterday. On the phone," Estrella said. I could tell she was losing her patience.

"Yes," he said, eating more of the grapefruit, "but I also think a great deal was not explained."

"We were assured by the library's director that we would be granted access," Estrella firmly stated.

"And I hope that will eventually be the case." Viedma spit again. "But this is no longer their responsibility. It is now the jurisdiction of the Ministry of the Interior. How are these journals connected to the mining expeditions of which you briefly spoke?"

"Señor Viedma, may I call you Eduardo?" Jake interjected.

Viedma shrugged and placed another grapefruit section into his mouth. His fingers and hands glistened with the sticky juice.

"Eduardo, Dr. Maroto believes the Q'ero tribe, which Professor Richardson first encountered in 1949, might help in locating a possible deposit of a rare metal. But, in order to find the tribe, we need his notes."

Viedma picked a bit of pulp from between his teeth with the long fingernail on his little finger, briefly examined it, and flicked it onto the floor. "There is no lost tribe, Señor Morgan. The Q'ero died off hundreds of years ago, along with many other ancient people. I would not put faith in the words of this Richardson. You will find Peru is rapidly becoming a modern country. All of it." The last grapefruit segment was inserted, sucked, and spit. Viedma withdrew a soiled handkerchief from his pocket and slowly wiped his mouth, fingers, and hands.

"Dr. Richardson was a brilliant anthropologist..." Estella began.

Jake quickly cut her off.

"We understand it's a ridiculous long shot, but we're pursuing this at the specific request of the prime minister's office." The words "prime minister" had the intended effect. Jake finally had Viedma's full attention.

"This metal you speak of...Is it valuable?"

"Very," Jake said.

"Valuable like silver? Or valuable like gold?"

Joel stood up and walked over to the small metal enclosure, looking up where the metal fence met the ceiling. I'm not surprised he was bored with all of Viedma's stalling. The assistant undersecretary glanced at Joel with indifference.

"It is much more valuable than gold," Jake answered.

Viedma's eyes widened just the tiniest bit, like a poker player trying to hide a winning hand.

"Señor Viedma," Estrella was passionate, "if we can locate the metal and if the deposits are large enough, it could raise the living standard of the entire nation. We could help millions in Peru. Might we review the documents this afternoon?"

"I wish you could, but you must understand this is not such a simple thing. To gain official access will require written approval from many departments—the Department of Mining, the Bureau of Indigenous Peoples, and the Ministry of the Interior. Not to mention compliance with several irritating environmental regulations. Something of such importance cannot be rushed. Normally such an undertaking takes several months."

"Several months!" Estrella jumped to her feet, her dark eyes flashing. "This is of national importance to the people of Peru!"

I suspected this guy was slippery, and this just proved it. I hated these passive-aggressive types hiding behind phony smiles.

Joel wiggled the chain-link door, loudly rattling the coils of rusted chain.

"Leave that alone!" Viedma barked. Joel abandoned the door and nonchalantly wandered toward the maze of shelves, not the least bit rattled by Viedma.

"Eduardo," Jake said calmly, "all we're asking for is a few hours. You and I know we'll eventually get approval. Give us entry to the records, and we'll all save your government a great deal of time. I imagine your assistance in discovering the ore deposit would be quite feather in your cap, career-wise."

Viedma's eyes slit.

"I'm sorry, but my position will not change on this matter. Reviewing the material in the next few days is impossible. However, I will initiate the paperwork on your behalf," Viedma oozed false graciousness and then stood to indicate the meeting was over. "I suggest you contact me in one week."

"A week!" Estrella's fists clenched at her sides.

"A week." Viedma said with finality. "Hopefully, I will have more information for you at that time. I will certainly do my best, Señor Morgan. But, as I said, this is a complicated matter. One cannot be sure how long it may take. Now I must return to my office."

Viedma crossed the large floor, walked the steps to the main floor, and slammed the heavy door behind him.

Estrella's face was a dark crimson. "This is unacceptable!"

Jake was somehow calm.

"Relax. An arrogant, pencil neck paper-shuffler isn't going to derail an expedition his own government is backing! I'll call the ambassador as soon as we get back to the hotel. We'll be in here tomorrow." Jake's confidence calmed Estrella for the time being.

As soon as we were out of the basement, Joel dropped a bombshell.

"Uncle Jake, Em and I want to go to the movie down the street. It's a double-feature. Is it okay if we get back after dinner?"

What! Where did Joel come up with that? I had no intention of sitting through two movies I couldn't understand. I looked to Joel for an explanation, but he had that look he got when he was scheming. I decided I'd play along, at least for now.

"We'd really like to go," I added. "And it's only a few blocks from the hotel."

Joel grinned. We made a pretty good team when we weren't bickering.

"Well, I suppose." Jake sounded reluctant.

"It is very close to your hotel," Estrella pointed out.

"All right, but I want you two back no later than eight."

"No problem," Joel said.

"Okay. Have a good time. And be careful."

Jake and Estrella walked out past the book return desk. As they left the library, I could hear Uncle Jake.

"Estrella, are you doing anything for dinner?"

Joel grinned.

"Okay, Joel. What's the story? I'm not going to sit through two movies I'll barely understand."

"Duh. We're not going." Joel lowered his voice to a whisper. "We're going to sneak into that little cage and copy the professor's notes."

"Are you nuts!?" I practically shouted.

"Shhhh…Uncle Jake thinks he's smooth, but he's never going to get that creep to help us."

"We don't know that for sure."

"If Jake or Estrella got caught trying to sneak into that cage, what do you think would happen?"

"Here? They'd probably go to jail."

"Right. But what if two kids got caught?"

"I don't know…probably not jail."

"Exactly. We'd get a big lecture. Or I don't know, maybe grounded. Don't you see, Em? We're the only ones who can do it."

"I don't know, Joel. I'll have to think about it."

What bothered me was that, deep down inside, I suspected Joel was probably right. But the idea made me nervous.

"While we're here, I suppose we may as well do a little research."

Even with three years of middle-school Spanish, my *espanol* was rudimentary at best, but I wanted to read whatever I could about the Seventh Jewel. I was much better at reading and writing Spanish than speaking it. If there had been a decades-long search for the stone, as Estrella and Jake said, there must be some books about the mystery. If we were about to embark on a real search for treasure, it only made sense to learn everything I could. I also suspected that the esteemed Professor Estrella Maroto had intentionally withheld something about the emerald.

Joel and I walked down a crooked hallway on the third floor where the green linoleum flooring reeked of disinfectant. Downstairs at the information desk, we'd been told in halting English that the only person on the library staff who spoke both English and *Quechua* was a researcher with a tiny office in the old part of the building on the top floor. Señora Hoya.

It was obvious when we passed from the new building to the old. The new library's smooth yellow walls and bright fluorescent lighting suddenly degraded to rough tan plaster and dim, metal-shaded lightbulbs. Both parts were floored with the same ugly green linoleum, but the old library's floor was an inch lower than the new.

At the end of the hallway, we reached a flight of exceedingly narrow wooden stairs, which wound up around to the left. Each step was visibly worn by decades of footsteps climbing before us. Even Joel and I had to crouch down to squeeze up the narrow flight. It was no place for a claustrophobic.

We reached two tiny offices—more like rabbit warrens, if you asked me—at the top of the well-polished steps. The first space was empty, except for a discarded metal electric fan. Cautiously, I peered into the second and was met with the odor of burnt onions.

A middle-aged woman hunched intently over a massive, leather-bound volume, studying the text with a silver-framed magnifying glass and tracking it with her index finger. The office was a disheveled mess. Stacks of magazines, books, and yellowed newspapers slouched in every corner. The desktop was obscured beneath six oversized books, each one peppered with dozens of yellow sticky-notes. Two miniature windows looked out between the library's uppermost eaves. I could hear the faint cooing of nesting pigeons outside. No wonder the library directory only listed three floors. This place was more like a secret attic.

Señora Hoya's long, slate-gray hair was neatly pulled back in a bun. She wore a multicolored sweater and peered through Coke-bottle glasses, which magnified her eyes to twice their normal size. These were the eyes that greeted us when she finally looked up.

"Excuse me, Señora Hoya? They said you speak English?"

"*Sí.* Yes. How may I help you? It is nice to have visitors. No one visits my little office."

She barely took notice of my arm, as if a one-armed teenager was the most natural thing in the world. I liked her right from the start.

"And *Quechua*?" Joel asked.

"*Arí.* That is correct, although there is little use for the language today. What is your interest in this?"

"We're looking for books on...*K'anchis Llajpa*," I read from my note. Estrella had written the *Quechua* words down at my request.

"*K'anchis Llajta*? I don't understand. May I see your paper?"

I dropped the small note into her hand. Señora Hoya glanced at the slip of paper, and her puzzled expression immediately relaxed. Our cheerful helper reemerged.

"Oh, yes. I'm sorry. I misunderstood. I thought you said *Llajta*, not *Llajpa*. It is easy...is it not...to make such errors in translations back and forth?"

"Well, I probably didn't pronounce it..." I stopped in mid-sentence. That's when it hit me. Homonyms! Words that sound identical but have different meanings! Estrella had carefully explained that early Incan history had been chronicled by Spanish historians who transcribed the Incan stories told to them. But wouldn't the conquistadors have struggled with subtleties of the Incan language, just as I struggled with similar-sounding Spanish words? What if some Spanish historian centuries ago had innocently mistaken one word for another? Had Joel and I stumbled onto a missing piece of the puzzle? A clue known only to Estrella, which she had painstakingly concealed?

"What kind of jewel would *Llajta* be?" I tried to act casual.

"Oh, it doesn't mean anything like that."

"What does it mean?" I leaned expectant over Señora Hoya's cluttered desk.

"Well, my child," she said, "in the language of the Inca, *K'anchis Llajta* doesn't mean the Seventh Jewel. It means the Seventh City."

CHAPTER 14

▼

EMMA
LAST OF THE INCA

"It makes perfect sense, Joel. Estrella had no reference books on jewels. You saw that."

"Yeah. And she totally freaked out when I asked her about it."

We were alone in a quiet reading room on the library's third floor. We didn't want anyone listening.

"She also seems too smart to give up her career to search for something as small as a jewel. But an entire city lost for 500 years. That's different. She must have figured this out years ago."

I began to understand Estrella's secretive obsession with the mystery. Discovering a lost city would make her famous and give her international prominence...in the academic world, at least, and maybe the whole world.

"But Em, seriously, how could a whole city disappear? How would that even be possible?"

"Did you read that article on the plane about Machu Picchu, the city the Inca built in the 1400s?"

"Some of it," Joel said tentatively.

"Machu Picchu has more than 200 buildings, and it's only forty miles from Cuzco, the Incan capital. Yet no outsider ever saw it until some professor from Yale stumbled on it in 1911. Even though it was built on top of an 8,000-foot-high mountain, it was totally overgrown with jungle."

"Em, 1911 was almost a hundred years ago. You couldn't hide a whole city today, not with planes, satellites photos, ultraviolet cameras, and stuff."

"I thought you said you read the article."

"Well, I just sort of skimmed it," Joel admitted.

I'll bet he'd just looked at the pictures.

"At the end of the story it said that, in 2003, the remains of a small city called 'high village' or something was discovered on a ridge, directly facing Machu Picchu and only a mile away. Joel, Machu Picchu has a half-million tourists a year, and not one single person ever saw this other city. They didn't see it because it was completely hidden under vines, trees, and plants. Not only that, the article said that the Andes are covered in clouds and mist half of the time. So the idea of a whole city disappearing isn't all that crazy."

"Except for one thing, Em. Estrella said the city, or jewel, disappeared before the Spanish ever got here, not gradually over hundreds of years? How do you explain that?"

"Well, I can't right now."

I hated it when Joel asked me something I couldn't answer. He'd probably wind up being a lawyer. "But the Spanish didn't have airplanes."

"So," he said in whisper, "should we do it?"

I looked around us.

"Absolutely. We'll go down to the basement and find some place to hide until the library closes and everybody goes home. But how will we get back out?"

"That's the easy part, Em. They make buildings to keep people from sneaking in, not to keep 'em from sneaking out. Come on."

Behind the countless bookshelves, in a deserted corner of the basement, a large pile of empty cardboard boxes was near the freight elevator. Joel and I wriggled behind the pile, laid flat on the hard cement floor, and then pulled boxes around us. We were completely covered and (hopefully) completely hidden from anyone looking at the pile. It was 4:15 PM. The library closed in forty-five minutes. We figured it might take another hour or so after that for everybody to go home. There were no windows to worry about down here, so, even if they kept the lights on, we couldn't be seen from outside the building. We only worried about the security guard we'd seen earlier in the day. We laid there in silence as the time slowly passed. I dozed off at one point, only to be awakened by Joel's growling stomach.

"Quiet," I whispered.

"I can't help it. I didn't have any lunch," he whispered back.

"What time is it?"

Joel pressed his watch, and his face glowed from the green luminescent light.

"Five forty-two. Someone walked by while you were asleep, but they didn't stop."

The building had grown quiet. There was the constant hum of a boiler or generator and the muffled sound of traffic outside, but we hadn't heard the elevator or footsteps or anything inside for quite some time.

"Em, you think Uncle Jake's ever killed anybody?"

"What?"

"Well, he's been all over the world on all sorts of treasure hunts. I'm just thinking he probably has run into stuff like you see in the movies. He wouldn't tell us about that kind of thing."

"Like killing people? Joel, he doesn't even own a gun. That doesn't make any sense." I had no clue where Joel had come up with this. In our stillness, his imagination was working overtime.

"I'll bet he has."

"Whatever, Joel…whatever. How much longer? It's freezing down here."

"It's only five 'til six. How can you be cold? We're practically in the tropics."

"I don't know. I just am."

At home, I was rarely cold. But, ever since we'd landed in Peru, I'd felt a constant chill.

Fifteen minutes after six, the lights shut down. Joel and I were enveloped in darkness. We waited another few minutes for our eyes to adjust and then quietly crawled from our hiding place.

"So far, so good," Joel said.

Silently, we crept back to the chain-link enclosure, guided by Joel's tiny keychain penlight and the red dots of light overhead from smoke detectors. With Joel's light, we could see a whopping three feet in front of us. We finally reached the fence.

"Here's the door."

"What's the plan? I can't climb up over it," I said, looking up into the darkness.

"No problem. The door isn't chained very tight. I checked, remember?" He moved it back and forth. "I thought we'd squeeze in, but it looks narrower than it did today."

"Perfect," I said sarcastically. "Pull it open, and I'll see if I can squeeze through. I'm thinner than you."

I slipped through the door with a half-inch to spare. Joel had to totally squash himself to get inside.

The tiny spot of light from Joel's keychain barely illuminated the neat blue, longhand on the yellow-edged pages of Richardson's diary. Many of the words were smudged, like when I'd received letters from my grandfather that he'd written with a fountain pen. This journal was thick. I wasn't sure where to begin. I flipped through the pages. Ten minutes later, one-third of the way through, I struck pay dirt.

"Joel! Here it is! Listen! 'October 15, 1953. Redemption! The great day! At last I have found them. The Q'ero Tribe, keepers of the dying

Incan flame. It has been four years, three months, and eleven days since I first began my quest. No longer must I wonder if I had become Cervantes' fool. The Q'ero exist—untouched and unspoiled by the corrupting hand of modern man. The Inca live!'"

"Wow, Em, you did it! Now we need to find out where they are. How to find them."

"Okay, okay. I'm skimming through this as fast as I can." I spoke in a loud whisper. "If you think you can do it faster, you're welcome to try."

"Just hurry up, okay?" Joel didn't like the dark, deserted basement anymore than I did.

"There's lots of stuff here about what they used for medicine. Plants, berries, roots, and stuff like that. There's even some drawings. Weird!"

"What?"

"It says here the tribe used some sort of frog's skin as a painkiller."

It would have been interesting to read all of it if we had more time.

"Wait a minute. Here's something. 'They make their home under the watchful eye of Suchana Peak and forage within a five-kilometer radius of the landmark, never losing sight of their sacred ground.' Hold it, Joel. I'm going to write this part down." I scribbled the location reference down on my gum wrapper.

"That's it?"

"I'll keep looking." I continued scanning the thick journal for keywords. Joel suddenly interrupted.

"Shhh!" he whispered. We could hear several sets of footsteps overhead in the library's lobby.

"Who's that?" I asked.

"How should I know? Let's finish this and get out of here."

"Joel!" I startled him.

"Jeez, Em. Don't do that."

"But there's a long passage here beneath the word 'treasure.' 'I have made the most heartbreaking of discoveries.'"

At the mention of treasure, Joel ignored the basement stairway and peered over my shoulder at the text.

"'In previous entries, I have alluded to Manco's cryptic references to the wealth of the Inca, presumably an immense quantity of golden objects that was rescued from Cuzco centuries ago at the time of the invasion and subsequently hidden amongst the surrounding stone cliffs and rock spires. On several instances, Manco unknowingly confirmed my hypothesis that it was this treasure that compelled the Q'ero to live in these inhospitable surroundings. Yet I had learned the gold rests upon sacred ground, and, as such, no tribesman had seen the Incan treasure for half a millenium.'"

"How much is that? 500 years?" Joel asked quietly.

"Yes." I could barely believe what we'd stumbled upon. I wondered if Jake, Estrella, or anyone knew about this.

"Keep reading!" The small beam of light wouldn't allow Joel to read ahead.

"All right. 'Foolishly, I became seduced by talk of Incan treasure. I am ashamed that I betrayed Manco's trusting, childlike nature in order to elicit the treasure's location.'

'Last night, I scaled the pinnacle, at great personal risk, to enter the eye itself. But the forbidden sanctuary is an empty shell, save for thousands of *desmodus rotundus*, dirty and repugnant creatures. There was no hidden treasure chamber, no ancestral artifacts, and no golden figurines.'

'One might question if a treasure ever existed. I believe so. The chronicles of Molina spoke of sacred Incan relics escaping Pizzaro's grasp. It is evident that, in the interceding 423 years, the cave was looted, perhaps by Spanish invaders, modern day adventurers, or even by the Inca themselves—disgruntled renegades of the Q'ero's noble cause. For countless generations, these sad people have placed their faith in a hollow shrine, sacrificing themselves to guard an empty cavern.'

'It is now my belief that the facts I have outlined above account for the declining population of young men and women within the Q'ero population. One must assume that younger tribal members, rebelling from the Incan culture of obedience or in an attempt to reaffirm their faith, climbed the precipice—as I had—and discovered the painful truth. How could such a revelation not create a sense of betrayal?'

'I will not reveal this to the Q'ero. Henceforth, I will confine my actions to the research for which I came. The Inca have been robbed of so much that I will not strip away the Q'ero's final vestige of hope and honor.'"

I didn't have time to tell Joel how sorry I felt for the tribe. The door at the top of the basement stairs began to open. I could hear voices. Someone was coming!

"Em!"

"I heard it. Let's get out of here!" I put the journal back into one of the boxes as Joel squeezed back out the narrow opening.

"Hurry up!"

At the top of the stairs, the heavy metal door swung open with a loud bang just as I turned off the penlight.

"*Se apararon las luces.*"

"*Espere un momente busco el circuito.*"

Several figures were faintly silhouetted against the dim lobby lights. Their voices made my stomach turn. I felt my way to the door and began scrunching through the small space while Joel pulled it open. I was almost through when I dropped Joel's penlight onto the floor.

"Joel, I dropped the light!" My voice was a panicked whisper. I knelt down outside the cell, blindly groping with my good hand for the light.

"We don't have time!" Joel sounded frantic. He pulled me to my feet and away from the enclosure. Through the darkness, we heard heavy footsteps clattering down the stairs. We felt our way behind some bookshelves. Without warning, Joel and I were blinded by a bright flash. The basement lights had come on!

We immediately hit the ground, lying as flat as possible on the hard cement floor. The men hurried down the remaining steps. I thought we'd gotten further away in the darkness, but I was horrified to realize only a single bookshelf separated us from the metal enclosure. We were only fifteen feet away from it. A narrow gap in the bottom row of books allowed us to see six or seven tan-colored pants carefully tucked into knee-high black boots.

"Soldiers," Joel barely whispered. I put a finger to my lips. A trickle of icy sweat ran down my side.

We could hear the chain rattling and the click of the opening lock. The soldiers entered the enclosure, piled up all the boxes, and began removing them.

They made numerous trips up the stairs, but several men were always in our immediate area. It was impossible for us to sneak any further away. Within a short time, the military men had cleared out the entire space, leaving only the formaldehyde-filled specimen jars on the shelves. Once more, we heard the rattling of the chain and the locking of the large padlock. The black boots remained while someone wearing a pair of street shoes approached. Words were exchanged, and the soldiers then left. Their boots rang out upon the metal steps. But the civilian shoes stayed near the enclosure. Could he possibly see us?

Then I saw it! Joel's little penlight was right there, next to the man's feet. He was practically standing on it! My heart began pounding in my ears. The man turned, inadvertently kicking the light back into the enclosure, where it rolled around noisily and settled under the shelves.

With his back to us, the man knelt down on the floor and reached under the chain-link fence in an attempt to fetch the penlight. My pulse was racing so fast that I honestly thought I was having a heart attack. If he reached the light, Joel and I were toast. Not only would he realize it was actually a flashlight, but he'd feel that the bulb was still warm. He'd call the men back to search until they found us. This was turning out to be a terrible plan.

He grunted as he stretched his arm, still unable to reach it. He made a final, violent effort to jam his arm further into the enclosure. The fencing strained against his shoulder. His fingers were just inches from Joel's light.

"*Maldito!*" Angrily, he withdrew his arm. He was giving up. We were safe! As he stood back up I recognized something. Black and red striped socks. Viedma! And he wasn't leaving. Now I could see only his feet again. He stood motionless for what seemed like an eternity. Then I heard him take something out of his jacket, followed by a "click" sound. Jeez! Did he have a gun? I felt like he could look right through the books and see the sweat on my forehead. How could we have been so stupid?

Slowly and deliberately, Viedma walked into the stacks. He was looking for us! He methodically paced down one long row of books. His soft footsteps were getting quieter and quieter. Then, moments later, they grew louder and louder as he came closer and closer. It sounded like he was right on top of us! I looked through the shelves behind us, horrified to see his feet. He'd find us any second!

Boom!

The heavy door at the top of the stairs crashed open.

"Viedma! *Está usted allí todavía?*"

I held my breath. Wasn't he going to answer? Come on, answer the guy!

"*Sí,*" he finally shouted. "*Ya voy.*"

Joel and I heard his faint footsteps climbing the stairs. Then they stopped. What was he waiting for? He couldn't see us. Why didn't he just go home? Then he cursed one last time, and the heavy door crashed shut. He was gone. Thirty seconds later, the lights went out.

Joel and I lay silently on the floor another fifteen minutes, just to be sure everyone had left the library. When we both felt it was safe, we cautiously crawled from our hiding place.

"Jeez!" I said in a whisper. "I'm exhausted."

"You see his socks?"

"Yes. Let's get out of here. I'm totally freaked-out."

Prior to hiding, we had located several first-floor windows we could unlatch and slip through. Joel pressed his watch, and the green dial flashed 7:24. I was exhausted. It felt like midnight. But we had to get back to the hotel. It was time for a showdown with the *esteemed* Professor Estrella Maroto.

CHAPTER 15
▼

JAKE
CHARTING OUR COURSE

Emma and Joel were still at the movie. And, although I hoped they wouldn't get back too late, it had been nice to have some adult time with Estrella. I was surprised how personable and engaging she was when she tossed aside that chip on her shoulder. Downstairs, over dinner, we'd plotted how to circumvent Viedma's bureaucratic petulance. Estrella shared my anger over paper shufflers who couldn't look past their nose to see the bigger picture.

We knelt on the floor—each with an ice-cold beer in hand—studying the map I'd spread out on the plush hotel carpet. One thing I had to say for Ottawa, they were certainly putting the kids and me up in style for this portion of the expedition. Aside from a toilet that continually gurgled, the hotel's two-bedroom suite was a level of luxury to which I was ill-accustomed.

Estrella had garrulously explained her personal theories on where the tribe might be located. I leaned back against the glass coffee table.

"Estrella, don't the Spanish Chronicles of the Inca describe small, one-man furnaces used to refine their gold and silver?"

"*Sí*. Set upon hillsides so the wind could act as a bellows." Her face lit up whenever we spoke of the Inca.

"Is it at all possible they might have fashioned a much larger furnace that was capable of refining the OS-187?"

"I am not an expert on metals. The report we were given does not seem to think so." She had alluringly pretty, deep brown eyes that turned down at the corners. Her black lashes were long and straight.

"No, it doesn't. It definitely doesn't."

"As I was saying," she returned her attention to the map, "whether the tribe is stationary or nomadic, they must inhabit an area that is still unmapped and uncivilized. It must also be an area where the vegetation obscures them from airplanes."

I realized it was her obsession with the jewel and the Inca that I found most appealing. A passionate energy surged in her whenever she spoke of the mystery. That surge I recognized. In a very real sense, we were kindred spirits, obsessed with unearthing secrets long since buried and forgotten. This was more than having one too many drinks. With Estrella, I felt a genuine connection.

"Do you ever unbraid your hair, Estrella, and wear it down?"

Her finger stopped cold on the map.

"No, not for a very long time." There was a definite sadness in her voice.

She looked back down to the map. Back to business. Great move, Jake! I was trying to get things onto a more personal level, and I'd apparently reopened an old wound. And here she was, sharing her dearest pursuits. I wasn't exactly endearing myself to her at this point.

"Estrella, I have to confess I'm a bit unsure of this search. We're looking for something so small. Even if it's a huge emerald, there are a thousand ways it could be lost: dropped in a lake or river, buried, crushed, burnt, or simply smuggled out of the country years ago. Honestly, I'm kind of struggling with this. You really believe it's still in the same place?"

"*Sí*. I am very sure the jewel still lies where it did centuries ago." She may have been sure, but she avoided my eyes, purposely looking away. It was that same evasiveness that surfaced yesterday afternoon. She was hiding something.

In fairness, I should have expected it. She barely knew me. By nature, treasure hunters—all of us—are a paranoid and mistrustful lot, convinced everyone is out to steal the secret clues our research or field work had uncovered. To be honest, I wasn't much better. I hadn't told her about the animal figures on the medallions. Eventually I would, but, for now, I'd take things one step at a time.

We were interrupted by Joel's signature knock at the door. I could hear the kids chattering until I opened the door to let them in.

"What happened to you two?" Their clothes were a mess, covered with sooty dirt, and they smelled of perspiration. "Everything okay?"

"Jake, you're not gonna believe it!" Joel ecstatically rushed into the room.

"Joel!" Emma sharply cut him off. "Let's do it like we planned."

Then Emma strolled, a little too casually, to one of the large over-stuffed chairs, plopped into the seat, and theatrically dangled a leg over the armrest. She looked extremely confident. Her voice was studied calm.

"This is cozy. Did you two have a nice dinner?"

"*Sí*. It is too bad you missed it. How was the cinema?"

"Did you talk about the jewel?" Emma put an unusual amount of emphasis on the word "jewel."

"Yes, among other things."

"Interesting. An emerald the size of a watermelon. That's what you said. Isn't it, professor?" Emma sounded very cagey. Joel looked to her expectantly. Something was up.

"Well, that is the legend," Estrella answered.

"Really." Emma swung her dangling leg back and forth. "So tell us, professor, when were you going to tell us it's not really a jewel we're searching for...but a lost city?"

Emma stopped swinging her leg and looked directly at Estrella while her question hung in the air.

Estrella looked nervously…first to me…then to Emma…and then back to me. Classic deer in the headlights. I was stunned.

"*Maldecir.*" Estrella looked completely crestfallen. "I was going to tell you. I just wanted the right time."

"We're looking for a city?" I was clearly the dumb guy in the room.

"*Sí.* We seek a lost city," Estrella admitted dejectedly. "The Seventh Jewel is a city."

"Okay, let's hear it. And stick to the facts this time. We're supposed to be on the same team, remember?" This explained her earlier evasiveness, but how had Joel and Emma figured it out?

"Understand that everything I told you yesterday is true. Pizzaro's greed and the diary of the priest, these are well-known to other archaeologists. I discovered the key six years ago while researching for my doctoral thesis on language variations among the Incan tribes." She quietly laughed, shaking her head. "It was so obvious! I couldn't believe it hadn't been thought of before…but no one had."

"What?"

Joel chimed in, "In *Quechua*, the words 'jewel' and 'city' sound exactly the same."

"Homonyms," Emma added.

"I see!" The light bulb finally came on. "The Spanish chroniclers. They misunderstood."

"*Sí*, they misunderstood. I felt the city was just waiting for me to find it." Estrella raised her voice. The fire she felt for the Inca was returning. "I vowed I would discover the city."

"So why didn't you tell us?" Emma sounded like her old self again.

"I have told no one until this moment." Estrella turned our attention to the large map on the floor.

"During the reign of Pachacuti, six known provincial capitals were established north of Cuzco as the empire expanded. These six capitals were the most prized cities by the emperors: Andahuaylas; Vilcas; Vitcos; and Vilcabamba, which, at one time, was also lost to civilization. It was actually Vilcabamba that Hiram Bingham originally sought when he discovered Machu Picchu. The fifth capital was Sausa, and the sixth was Hua'nuco Pampa.

"Notice the capitals are somewhat evenly spaced apart." The four of us crowded around the map as Estrella marked their locations.

"She's right," Emma observed. "Aside from the cluster around Cuzco, they're spaced about every…"

"One hundred twenty-five miles," Joel jumped in.

"Correct, Joel. But look at the gap between the sixth capital, Hua'nuco Pampa, and the next provincial capital to the north, Caxamalca, established under the next Incan emperor, Topac Yupanqui."

"It's bigger! It must be…"

"Almost 260 miles, to be exact." Estrella said. "Almost exactly twice the normal distance."

"Which means it's extremely likely there's a missing capital somewhere between the two," I said.

"*Sí.* Missing or lost."

"I think you're on to something here, Ace. I really do."

I was glad she laughed at the nickname.

"We must reach the journals tomorrow," Estrella urged. "We are so close to the answer."

"The journals won't be there tomorrow," Joel said. "They're gone."

"Gone? But today…"

"Viedma and some military police took everything from the archives, including all of Richardson's notebooks."

Emma's tone left no room for doubt.

"This is terrible." Estrella's face fell, her internal lamp extinguished.

"So that's were you kids were."

That explained their filthy appearance. Nothing from these two surprised me anymore.

"He almost saw us. You have no idea how close we came to getting caught, Jake." Joel looked upon all this as one great adventure.

"Estrella, any idea why Viedma would step in and confiscate everything?"

"When you told him of the osmium's value, I could smell greed dripping from his pores," she said vindictively. "The man is a pig. I do not trust him. The way to the Q'ero may be lost."

"This won't make our job any easier." I wasn't about to throw in the towel. This whole expedition was turning into an absurd long shot. Luckily, I had a weakness for those odds.

"The secret is not lost." At Joel's remark, Estrella and I snapped to attention. "We sneaked inside."

"We only had time to skim one of the journals, but I copied down some directions."

"You have notes?" Estrella sounded as though she'd just been given reprieve from execution.

"Just a few that seemed important." Emma withdrew the crumpled gum wrapper from her jeans' pocket. I roared with laughter.

"You guys are amazing! How'd you get in?"

"We just sort of squeezed in. The chain was loose," Joel explained.

"It was Joel's idea."

Both kids wore gigantic, mischievous grins. Estrella gave Joel and Emma an admiring look, as impressed with the two as I was.

Emma referred to the small slip of paper. "It said the tribe stays within a five-kilometer radius of Suchana Peak so they can always see the eye."

"Its eye?" Estrella sucked on the tip of her long braid as she pondered Emma's words. I looked back at the large map.

"Estrella, are you familiar with a Suchana Peak?"

"Suchana is *Quechua*, Jake. I do not know it. This map is in Spanish." She knelt next to me, studying the map and pressing close against my side. I liked the feel of her next to me—if only for a moment—although she seemed oblivious to everything except the two-dimensional terrain on the floor.

"Uncle Jake, Richardson wrote about a treasure the tribe believed was inside the eye. Treasure they originally took from Cuzco."

"Inside the eye? That sounds like a cave. What kind of treasure?"

Legends were rampant in this part of the world about lost treasures.

"That's the big problem," Emma said. "Richardson climbed up and searched inside. The eye was empty. He figured the treasure was probably stolen a long time ago."

"I guess that isn't too surprising." I looked at Estrella, braid in her mouth. "Fortune hunters have combed Peru for centuries in search of Incan wealth. I doubt much could have escaped discovery after so many years."

I hated to discourage the kids, but I was trying to stay focused on the reason we were here, particularly if we were now in a race against Viedma. Jewel aside, we needed the OS-187.

"At least we can find the tribe," Joel added encouragingly.

"Jake, this is not good."

Estrella surprised me. We had discovered an invaluable clue, and the glass was still half-empty.

"It could take us weeks to discover the *Quechua* names for the hundreds and hundreds of mountains and peaks in the Peruvian Andes. The Cordillera Blanca alone has dozens that are nameless. Viedma has the journals. Within Richardson's writings, there are undoubtedly enough references for knowledgeable persons to locate the Q'ero tribe long before we are able to do so."

"Not if he doesn't have the map." And with that, Emma produced a ripped journal page with the dramatic flourish of a circus magician. She was beaming, justifiably proud of herself.

"Map!"

Estrella sprang to her feet like an Olympic athlete.

"From Richardson's journal." Emma casually fanned herself with the stolen page.

"When the heck did you do that?"

Joel was equally surprised, which I think gave Emma the most satisfaction.

"Just before I put the book back into the box. You were still trying to get out."

"When Viedma's men were coming down the stairs?"

"Yup."

"Jeez, Em." Emma laughed happily at her brazen recklessness and at Joel's obvious admiration.

"It's really crude, Jake. Just penciled outlines for landmarks." She handed the paper to me.

"But Viedma doesn't have it," Estrella grinned. "That is the important thing. No one has it but us."

The map was so simplistic that I wondered if it could help us after all. The center contained a small pyramid labeled Suchana. It was the only lettering on the drawing. The upper right corner depicted a much larger, taller pyramid. On the lower right corner was a continuous squiggly line that branched into two wiggly lines at the bottom of the page. The left side had a long row of pyramids angling downward, left to right. I set the ripped page down next to our map.

"The pyramids are obviously mountains," Estrella said.

"And the wavy line is most likely a river."

"Would that line of pyramids be the Andes?" Joel asked.

"They're all the Andes, but this suggests Suchana lies east of the major mountains. Okay, guys, concentrate on the areas that Estrella has marked as being relatively unexplored."

"Emma, was there any reference to the scale of Richardson's map?"

Estrella was right in asking. For all we knew, the scale of the drawing was so small that it might not even appear on our government-issue map.

"No. I mean, I didn't have time to see."

"Focus on the double twisting portion of the river. That's got to be unique." We were all crowded around the map. Unfortunately, Peru had an enormous number of rivers and mountains.

"Here!" Emma shrieked. We all jumped.

All eyes instantly focused on the tiny spot under her finger. It was a small area in south-central Peru, about 500 kilometers east of Lima, just within the boundary of the Manu Wilderness.

"Em, I think you're right," Joel said. The river is a perfect match. And there are the two mountains."

I carefully studied Richardson's drawing…then the map…and then to the sketch again. We had it. It was a solid clue, a foothold with which to locate the tribe isolated from the outside world for half a mil-lenium.

"We've got it!"

Estrella looked serious.

"This is inside the Reserve," she pointed out. "Very, very harsh ter-rain. Interesting."

"How so?"

"It is a region the Inca never conquered."

"Perhaps that's why they chose to go there," Emma observed.

"Perhaps." Estrella said thoughtfully.

I carefully measured the scale on the map's legend and then drew a dark exact circle, three centimeters wide, around the small peak.

"If Richardson's notes are correct, the Q'ero are somewhere within that. As he said, 'always within sight of the eye.' The nearest town looks to be Tres Cruces. That's where we'll start." Estrella was barely listening, mesmerized by the circle I'd drawn on the map. Perhaps she felt it was all too good to be true.

"You still with us?" I asked her.

"I'm sorry. It's Viedma. He'll probably pull his nose out of the mud long enough to smell what we're up to."

"Shoot," said Emma. "I forgot about him."

"Hey, what's happened to my intrepid explorers? Forget Viedma. Forget the journals. Listen, looking for an emerald would have been like trying to find a walnut somewhere in British Columbia. But a city. A whole city with buildings, temples, houses, storehouses, and maybe fortifications. That we can find! We've got a real shot to succeed here! The four of us are going to find the tribe, we're going to find the city, and we're going to find the OS-187! Joel, you don't doubt we can do it. Do you, bud?"

"Not at all."

"Em, are we going to find this?"

"Absolutely!" Their optimism was back.

"What about you, Ace? Afraid to find what you've been searching for these past six years?"

"No! For the first time I am convinced the Jewel can be found!"

"That's better. Tomorrow, we're off to find the last living direct descendants of the Inca."

CHAPTER 16

▼

EMMA
CLOUD FOREST

We were entering the eyebrow of the jungle.

Uncle Jake and Estrella explained to us why the Manu Cloud Forest, where we'd be searching, was one of the most astonishing places on the planet. Between cold mountain highlands and the humid jungle lay a belt of stunted forest evergreens that was draped in lichens and moss—the eyebrow. Here, frigid air collided with warm, creating swirling clouds and mist that almost perpetually shrouded these miniature forests. When the sun occasionally managed to break through, it was filtered through a dense canopy of leaves (as through stained glass). The forest became a glistening green cathedral.

Jake's plan was simple. During our first trail day, the four of us would hike along a ten-mile traverse through the highlands on the Andes' eastern side, staying above the outer boundary of the cloud forest. On the second day, we'd descend into the heart of the misty preserve, toward Suchana Peak, with our eyes peeled for the elusive Q'ero. It had been over fifty years since Richardson tripped across them. I wondered what, if anything, we might find.

Uncle Jake had organized so many expeditions that pulling together the essentials to survive our week in the Peruvian wilderness only took a half-day. Thank goodness. We were in a race with Viedma. Once all our gear was spread out on the hotel floor, I couldn't imagine it all fitting into our backpacks. But, by tying tents, rope, and sleeping bags onto the outside of our packs, we were able to cram everything else inside.

Between the four of us, we had two blue tents, some red climbing rope—300 feet worth I think—a first-aid kit, a small portable cook stove with a few liters of what Jake called "white gas" for fuel, a compass and a GPS, a satellite phone, compact binoculars, maps, an aluminum cooking pot, and a few lightweight eating utensils.

For "sustenance," as Jake called it, we had a weird Peruvian instant drink mix, tea, hot chocolate, instant oatmeal, energy bars, salt, pepper, sardines, and a huge pile of dehydrated food packages. Oh, we also had iodine tablets so we could purify water for drinking.

We'd carry our own sleeping bags, inflatable ground pads, gloves, hats, toiletry stuff, sunscreen, sunglasses, lighters (Joel's job is not to waste his), flashlight with extra batteries and bulb, two refillable Nalgene water bottles each, and a few small candles.

Plus our clothes. Mine included waterproof hiking boots, a wool shirt, sweater, windbreaker, one extra pair of socks, underwear, T-shirts, and polar fleece pants. I wasn't exactly excited about seven long days of perspiring under a heavy pack with such a limited change of clothes. By the end of the week, we'd all be pretty ripe.

We packed our gear in a small Cessna and spent the late afternoon flying from Lima to the outskirts of Cuzco. The next morning, we set out before dawn on a grueling six-hour, bone-jarring, butt-bruising ride in the back of a battered truck over an abandoned dirt road. It was a never-ending series of deep ruts, smelly mud holes, and washed-out, hairpin turns. It was long, slow, and painful. It was still morning when we reached Tres Cruces, a tiny village from where we'd launch our trek.

The first three hours on the trail, we slowly trudged up one steep switchback after another. Finally, we reached the crest of a narrow pass and got our first unobstructed view down onto the Manu Cloud Forest. It was amazing.

Roiling mists swirled at the base of the peaks and crags while fog drifted through endless ridges that receded into opaque obscurity. Atop the highest foothills, dwarf trees protruded through the floating mist. A constant chorus of bird calls from deep in the forest floated up to our ridge.

Even though the Manu forest is only half the size of Switzerland, it contains an astounding ten percent of all the plant species in the world—more than 5,000 different flowering types alone. Amazing. The cool, damp forests we were going to explore were also home to more than 1,000 different bird species. And a lot of Manu's plants and birds aren't found anywhere else on earth.

That view had an eerie, prehistoric timelessness; it was a window into the world a million years ago. I half expected a brontosaurus to lazily raise its neck out from the earthbound clouds or hear a pterodactyl screech overhead. It was definitely easy to imagine this forested terrain filled with ancient artifacts and treasure just waiting to be discovered…waiting for us.

Despite our seclusion in this isolated, untouched world, I trembled with a cold, anxious sensation that, hiding in the mists below, eyes carefully studied our every move as we traversed the high ridge.

By four o'clock, and with another three miles under our belts, we were ready to pitch our blue bubble tents along the mountain flanks and prepare dinner. That was one very long day.

Joel and I tossed potatoes into the campfire's coals and used sticks to cover them with glowing embers—the last of our *real* food. After tonight, everything was freeze-dried and dehydrated.

"I can't believe you two have never had these," Jake said, poking at the potatoes in the fire.

"We've got electricity at home, Jake. Even a stove. You oughta try *that* sometime." Joel hadn't lost his warped sense of humor. Uncle Jake laughed.

"Are you sure we don't need to cover them up with something?" I asked.

"Don't you want the skins to be crunchy?"

"Crunchy, yes. Black, no."

Estrella finished positioning the potatoes into the fire. "I haven't cooked like this since I was a girl."

"You're in for the treat of your life, kids. A little butter, pepper, and salt. It doesn't get any better than this. Did you two know the Inca grew more than 200 kinds of potatoes?"

"Uh, yeah. That's about the third time you've told us."

Joel and I exchanged a glance that questioned why we were entrusting our stomachs to Uncle Jake's dubious cooking skills. Then our minds moved in unison.

"Estrella…how come…if the Inca lived inland…in these mountains and stuff…well…how did the conquistadors find them?"

Joel had a knack for asking the same questions I was thinking.

Estrella didn't answer right away. She leaned toward the fire with a melancholy look. She either hadn't heard Joel or didn't want to answer. She finally spoke.

"For me, this part is the hardest, Joel. So many little clues, like loose threads in a fabric. A few chance encounters and the Inca were doomed. I've often wondered what might have been, if not for one or two random events. History often turns on such minor details." Absentmindedly, Estrella sucked on the end of her braid.

"It was 1511 when the Spanish first heard of a mysterious empire rich with gold. Balboa, who discovered the Pacific, was weighing gold stolen from Panama natives. A young chieftain, enraged by Balboa's enslavement of his people, violently kicked the measuring scales, and the golden objects scattered across the ground. He shouted that, if the Spanish really treasured gold above life itself, there was a legendary kingdom far to the south where gold was as plentiful as iron. Foolish words."

How many other seemingly insignificant events had changed history through the ages? It made you wonder.

"Several years later, Balboa heard again of this mythical empire to the south. He was shown native drawings of llamas, which the Spanish thought to be a strange species of camel. This added to the mystery."

"In the following years, the legend grew. Native traders frequenting South American shores provided brief accounts of an opulent empire in which gold and emeralds were commonplace. Still, no Europeans pursued the legend. This mythical land lay behind the Cordillera Blanca, which was considered an impassable stone barrier to the interior. Also, the few seamen that had sailed south of Panama spoke of a dismal land, barren shores, and endless swamps with poison air that was inhabited only by swarms of bloodthirsty insects. For a time, the Incan empire remained safe."

Uncle Jake plucked the blackened potatoes from the glowing coals. I hadn't eaten since lunch, so, when he split them open, the aroma overwhelmed me…and my salivary glands.

Estrella paid no notice.

"In 1524, Francisco Pizzaro, an illiterate soldier turned fortune hunter, made his first attempt to locate this empire." Bitterness bit through Estrella's voice as she spoke Pizzaro's name.

"Sailing far to the south, Pizzaro's ship encountered small native villages along the shore. From these simple, trusting Indians, Pizzaro was told of a rich country further south, a journey of ten days across the mountains. There dwelt a great monarch, a powerful emperor who was considered a 'Child of the Sun.' Low on supplies, Pizzaro was forced to return to Panama. But the stories had whet Pizzaro's thirst for gold."

"Food break."

Uncle Jake handed out our thin plastic plates with huge split potatoes, slathered in butter and generously salted and peppered. I gorged on a steaming forkful.

"Mmm. These are great," I mumbled with my mouth full.

"*Muy bien.*" Estrella wiped the butter running down her chin and then giggled.

"How many can we have?"

"Got plenty, Joel." Jake took a large bite. "After a long day on the trail, there's nothing better than food cooked over an open fire."

He was right about that. The hot, buttery potatoes were heaven. We devoured our dinners in silence, serenaded by the hissing fire and occasional crunch of crisp potato skin.

Eventually, Joel was spudded out and resumed his questioning amid finger licking.

"So what happened after Pizzaro went back to Panama?"

Estrella stretched back against a rock and, after an appreciative glance at Jake, continued.

"Two years later, sailing further south than any European before him, the Conquistador sighted a huge raft of balsa with enormous masts. He overtook it. Upon boarding the vessel, the Spanish discovered natives wearing exquisitely crafted jewelry of silver and gold. Their clothes were woven from a woolen cloth finer than anything found in Europe and delicately embroidered with flowers and birds. The threads were dyed in brilliant colors. Here was proof of a rich and civilized culture. Unfortunately, one of the Indians naively bragged that, in the palaces of their monarch, gold and silver were as common as wood."

"What happened then?" I finished the large potato and set the plate aside.

"That is enough for now."

Jake began gathering up the utensils from dinner. "She's right. We need to get going early tomorrow."

I was beginning to wonder if Uncle Jake had *ever* slept late his entire life.

"But we're not tired," Joel complained.

"Maybe you're not, but I am." Estrella wearily rubbed the back of her neck. "We have many nights ahead of us. There is plenty of time."

It seemed just talking about the downfall of the Inca drained Estrella. Maybe Joel didn't see that.

Estrella and I were cozy in our tent, brightened by a cute candle lantern. Even with our sleeping bags foot to head, we were practically on top of each other. So much for privacy! I needed to take off my arm to sleep, but I didn't want an audience.

"Can you blow out the light?"

"Do you need any help?"

No, I'm okay."

Estrella obligingly blew out the squat little candle. Silver moonlight and starlight filtered through the thin nylon walls, giving me just enough light to see what I was doing.

"Thanks." I began unfastening the prosthetic's straps.

"Emma, I owe you an apology. I didn't mean to stare when you first came to my apartment."

"That's all right." I placed the plastic arm next to me inside my sleeping bag. "A lot of people stare. Losing an arm is pretty noticeable, compared to a leg. I can't hide it under my jeans. I sort of stand out." Even though, for all the world, I wished I didn't.

"Your uncle says you were very brave."

"I don't know. I just try not to get discouraged. After my accident, I met this little boy at the clinic. He was probably four years old and really cute. He was being fitted for new legs. I think he'd been born without them. But you should have seen him. He was all excited to get fitted for new prosthetics. He acted like it was Christmas. You could tell it really didn't bother him at all. If he was so happy, I don't have much room to complain. Do I? That probably sounds corny."

"No, just the opposite."

We laid in the dark for a few moments.

"What is your Uncle Jake like, Emma?"

"Uncle Jake? What do you mean?"

"What is he like inside?"

"Well…" I had to think about that for a second. "When I came home from the hospital after the accident, everyone started telling me all the things I couldn't do or shouldn't try. They said I needed to lower my goals, not to set my sights too high. They said that I'd only be setting myself up for disappointment and failure. I know they meant well. But I started to feel like I was being smothered."

"I remember when Jake first visited. He'd been out of the country on some treasure hunt. He walked right into my room and sat on the edge of my bed. He didn't even say 'hello' or 'how you feeling' or anything. He just started telling me an incredible story about a warrior, Queen Vishpa, who lost her leg in a terrible battle. But she refused to quit. She ordered that she be fitted with an iron leg. She returned to battle, leading her armies to victory. Sorry. I don't tell it as good as Jake. But she didn't give up, even after losing a leg."

"He told me the legend of Queen Vishpa was part of a sacred poem from India written more than 4,000 years ago in Sanskrit. It's the first written record of someone using an artificial limb."

"I didn't know that," Estrella said quietly in the darkness.

"After that, whenever Jake visited, he'd tell me stories about an amputee climbing a mountain, winning a race, or doing something no one thought was possible. That's my uncle."

"Yes, I see that in him."

Our tent flap blew open in the wind. Estrella reached from her sleeping bag and zipped it shut. I decided to be frank.

"You like him, don't you?"

I wondered if she'd answer or change the subject. She seemed pretty evasive about stuff like that.

"Perhaps. He is certainly not what I expected. But now it is time to sleep. I think your uncle is right about you. Good night, Emma."

After a little while, I heard Estrella's slow, measured breathing. I rolled onto my back to sleep and snuggled into the sleeping bag's hood to keep warm. I wished it was all as easy as I pretended. To be as brave as Uncle Jake and Estrella thought I was. Maybe someday it would be. I just hoped *someday* would arrive sooner, rather than later.

CHAPTER 17

▼

EMMA
MIRAGE ON THE RIDGE

I could see my breath inside the tent as I rose and began getting dressed. The pale, pink-blue light of dawn had just softened the cold morning air. Estrella, still bundled in her sleeping bag, opened one lazy eye as I unzipped the flap.

"What time is it?" she asked.

"5:20. I'm just going to the bathroom."

"I'll be up in a bit." She burrowed back into the warmth of her down-filled cocoon.

Tired, I stumbled across the rocky terrain surrounding our campsite until I reached the far side of a certain large boulder. Our community bathroom. This was by far the worst part of the *Great Outdoors*. Baring it all in the cold morning wind was bad enough, but Jake had given us strict orders as to disposal. That meant, among other things, burning the used toilet paper. I flicked my disposable lighter and watched as the small, windblown flame consumed the refuse. Fun. Once we entered the cloud forest though, burning wouldn't be enough. Jake wanted us to pack it all out. Even more fun.

That done, I bundled up and wandered a little further from camp to watch an awesome sunrise. The crisp, sapphire sky created a dramatic backdrop for the stunning white peaks of the Andes. I don't know which was more breathtaking—the cold air or the view.

Nearly fifty yards in front of me, along the top of a small ridge and directly in line with the blinding morning sun, I saw something. The dark silhouette looked like a llama, although thinner than those I'd already seen on this trip. I tiptoed toward it. It remained so motionless. Perhaps it was only a rock formation that was being aided by my over-active imagination. As I approached, I could shield my eyes enough to see that it was indeed some scrawny sort of llama. It stared directly at me, lifeless as a statue.

"Emma!" Joel's shout echoed across the rocky landscape. He was running from the direction of camp. "Breakfast!"

I only looked away for an instant, but, when I turned for a final glimpse of the creature, it was gone. Joel's voice must have frightened it. Back at camp, over steaming hot chocolate and instant oatmeal, I asked Joel if he'd seen the mysterious creature. He hadn't seen any-thing.

Later in the day, after we'd packed up camp, Estrella and I set out together on the narrow trail. Jake and Joel walked behind, well out of earshot. I'd found myself beginning to like Estrella, like the big sister I never had. She wasn't anything like the angry, in-your-face professor who berated Uncle Jake when we first met in Lima. She was actually very approachable.

"Uncle Jake said the Incan armies outnumbered Pizzaro's forces 500-to-1. Why didn't they fight back?"

"It had been foretold, Emma. Many of the Inca believed it was fate, the will of the gods, and therefore useless to resist. It is said that, even before Columbus reached the New World, Incan oracles foresaw that, following the reign of the twelfth Inca monarch, a race of bearded, fair-skinned men would destroy the empire. The twelfth ruler, Huayna Capac, sat on the golden throne prior to the Spanish invasion of Peru.

When the first tidings of the white men reached Cuzco, many believed it was fulfillment of this ancient prophecy foretold 100 years earlier."

Her speech was warm, not haughty.

"At the same time, there occurred an abnormal number of unexplainable supernatural events. Comets flamed through the night skies. The land trembled with earthquakes. The moon was ringed by fiery clouds. Lightning struck a royal palace and left it in ashes. To the Inca, such things were signs from the heavens of the empire's pending doom."

I couldn't understand why the Inca—or anybody for that matter— didn't think they could control their own destiny. I'd learned the hard way that life is a matter of choices. People choose how they act or react to dark times. After my arm went, I could have chosen to give up and wallow in self-pity. That was one choice. Or I could move forward and make the best of a cruel situation. I would choose. I would determine my fate, not the stars.

"Huayna Capac received word of the white men while they still probed the shores of Ecuador, years before they ever entered the Inca empire. He heard of their great ships and powerful weapons and assumed these men represented a civilization far more advanced than his own. He believed they would eventually reach the Inca, and, when they did, the throne would be lost. Huayna Capac believed the visions of the oracles and the astronomers."

Uncle Jake joined us. His shirt was heavily stained with perspiration from the huge pack he carried.

"Can I join you?"

"*Sí.*" Estrella returned to her story. "A few years later, Huayna Capac lay dying. He called together his greatest officers and chieftains. He beseeched those huddled about him to accept the decrees of heaven and the future events, which had been foretold. He asked his court to give their complete obedience to these bearded messengers of the gods."

"Is that true?" I could usually rely on Uncle Jake to get to the bottom of legends and myths. I didn't believe in oracles that could foretell the future, but Estrella's story was kind of eerie.

"No one knows for sure, Em." Jake walked close to Estrella. Even though they didn't agree on a lot of this historical stuff, it was obvious they had a thing for each other.

"You mind, Ace?"

The adults exchanged smiles.

"No. Please go ahead. I'd be interested in your perspective."

"Frankly, some scholars believe Incan historians invented the vision of the oracle, the supernatural events, even Huayna Capac's dying wishes as a way of rationalizing the ease with which the Spanish conquered so vast an empire. Basically, it may have been a way for the defeated Inca to save face."

Estrella bristled.

"That is nonsense! There is no other explanation for the passivity with which the Inca allowed themselves to be butchered. Huayna Capac was considered a direct descendent of the Sun, a god in his own right. If he had directed his vassals to subvert themselves to the visitors, they would have done so. His word was law, and the Inca were an obedient people."

Jake continued.

"Then there was the factor of weaponry and military tactics. The Spanish had breast armor, guns, steel swords, and approached on horseback, which terrified the Inca. The Inca were armed with only crude stone hatchets. Supposedly, they were awed by the soldiers on horseback and simply fled in disbelief. And remember the most important point. By this time, Pizzaro had seized Atahualpa, the Incan ruler, and held him hostage under threat of death. Don't you think the Inca would have feared retaliation against their emperor?"

"Jake Morgan, that is so typically male. You have no sense for things that cannot be explained in facts and figures. You think nothing exists except that which you can see with your eyes or touch with your hands."

Uncle Jake let out his big rolling laughter. "That's me. Just a simple treasure hunter, Ace."

"When we find the Q'ero tribe, then you shall see the truth. The Inca were proud and courageous. They forged one of history's great empires. They carried themselves with the proud bearing of warriors and kings. You shall see, Jake Morgan." Estrella gestured forcefully with her hand.

"I sincerely hope so."

Jake excused himself and dropped back to walk back with Joel again.

"Your uncle can be very frustrating, Emma. Does he do this on purpose?"

"I don't think so." I could see where Uncle Jake might be difficult for someone like Estrella. "But I can tell he likes you."

Estrella let out a long sigh. "He is confusing as well."

"Estrella, can I ask you a question?"

"Since when have you asked permission?" She gave me a wide grin.

"When we were in your apartment, you had a bunch of pictures of little kids on your desk. Those can't be all yours, could they?"

"Ah, my little children."

"Your children!" There were at least ten of them. How could Estrella have so many kids?

"My foster children, Emma. I pay a little money each month to help support them."

"Oh. That's great. Have you met them all?"

"Almost all. And they are wonderful."

We walked in silence awhile while Estrella pensively pondered the ground beneath our footsteps.

"Peru is still a very poor country by your standards, Emma. The great wealth from the nation's resources has not been well-distributed. President Toledo has tried. He truly has, but half our people live in terrible poverty. It is heartbreaking to see the shacks of the desperately poor in the shadows of glistening new office buildings."

Estrella kicked an occasional stone as we walked.

"Our Indian peasants are the poorest. They face discrimination and exploitation. Peru's elite ridicule our traditional language and clothing as signs of backwardness and ignorance. You must remember that this was our country, Emma. Now we are considered inferior, outcasts in our homeland. It is not right. It is my hope that if we find this metal…"

"The OS-187," I volunteered.

"Yes, the OS-187. It is my hope that it will benefit all the people of my country, not just a few industrialists, but, in particular, the Indians that have been brushed aside for so many years by the modern world. That is my hope."

"It's a wonderful dream, Estrella." I wanted her to know I admired her unselfish goals. All this time, I'd thought she just wanted to be famous for discovering the lost city.

"And who knows?" I said encouragingly. "If anybody can find the OS-187, it's Uncle Jake. He's a world-class treasure hunter, even though he jokes around a lot."

By late afternoon, we had fallen into a monotonous routine. Walking single file, we plodded along, stoically bearing the weight of our packs and losing ourselves in our own private thoughts. Conversation had long since passed. Joel was all eyes taking in our new surroundings—the mountains, the mist-covered forests, strange plants, colorful birds, and the occasional gust of wind when we traversed a ridge. Estrella methodically walked the trail with her head down, sweetly humming to herself.

However, since late morning, Uncle Jake had been oddly tense, less relaxed and cavalier than his usual self. Every half hour or so, he would hang back from the group, scramble atop a boulder, and carefully scan the horizon with his binoculars. He never said what he was searching for, but it wasn't Suchana Peak. He spent most of his time studying the terrain behind us, where we'd already walked.

As the day wore on, I began to feel more and more anxious. It was a nervous, uneasy feeling like those crazy dreams I'd have where I was on my way to school and realized halfway through the semester I'd never attended one particular class and had no idea where to find it. My insides felt the same, like there was something I needed to do or something I had to do, but I'd forgotten what it was. Some unfinished task gnawed at me. My stomach churned until that gross bile taste was in my mouth.

After only a few bites of dinner, I excused myself to the tent, carefully folded my clothes, cleaned off my boots, and snuggled into my sleeping bag. There wasn't any point telling Jake or Estrella how I felt. It was probably all in my head. I'd feel better in the morning.

CHAPTER 18

▼

JAKE MISSING

Viedma strutted arrogantly into the clearing with a silver .38 caliber gun in hand. They'd surrounded us before we could react.

Emma and Joel stopped; they were in the middle of stuffing their sleeping bags into their packs. I was cinching a tent to my pack frame. His four armed accomplices quickly picked positions around our perimeter. All avenues of escape were gone.

Ever since we'd left the trailhead, my gut told me we were being watched and followed. So much for my caution the first two days. I'd scanned the trail behind us, trying to get by with only a few hours sleep. This morning, I'd dropped my guard. How could I have been so damn stupid? It was going to be tough to talk my way out of this one.

Our only sliver of hope was Viedma's hired guns, obviously no para-military professionals or fanatical remnants of Shining Path. Sloppy layers of shirts hung at varying lengths over their dirty blue jeans. Their nervous faces hid under dark, broad brimmed hats; they'd hiked here in badly worn work boots. There was nothing sure in the way they held their government-issue .45 caliber automatic revolvers. They were probably hungry peasants Viedma had hired for a palm full of *sols*. Good men pressed into bad labor.

"*Buenos dias*, Señor Morgan."

Viedma's smile was unconvincing. "Your resourcefulness impresses me. My compliments. But you have something my employer requires."

Estrella interrupted, not intimidated by Viedma in the least. Her voice was harsh. "Our government and the Canadians have authorized our use of the medallion."

"I doubt Mr. Viedma's employer is still the Ministry of Antiquities. Or am I mistaken?"

There's no way he'd be hijacking us with Lima's blessing.

"Very observant, Señor Morgan."

Viedma paced the campsite, his sick, self-pleased smile ever-present. "I resigned my post with the Ministry several days ago…to pursue more lucrative endeavors. Now, I must ask you for the medallion."

"Very well, Eduardo, but your business is with me. Let the kids and Professor Maroto go. Once they're a safe distance, you'll get the medallion. You have my word."

Viedma didn't answer. He relished us twisting in the wind while he wallowed in his new found *machismo*. In his mind, this showed his accomplices he was the big gun. Casually, he dug at his scalp, got whatever he was after, and intently scrutinized the scab of dead skin under his nails. Total cretin. But, instead of flicking the residue to the ground, he popped it in his mouth like candy. Damn. Joel gaped. Estrella simply shook her head, expecting no less.

"I am not a murderer." Viedma's voice was overly gracious. "My employer has been very specific in his instruction. In fact, we intend to pay you for the piece. One hundred thousand dollars."

"It's worth two million," I countered.

"Perhaps. But only to one who knows how to dispose of the metal. Regardless, the time to negotiate is past."

"My last offer was $250,000."

"Yes, so I understand. But I must extract a small handling fee. In fact, I insist upon it. You wouldn't begrudge me that, would you?"

"Do I have a choice?"

"No. I advise you, Señor Morgan, that I am being unusually lenient in this matter."

I couldn't trust Viedma. With the amulet in his hands, there was nothing to stop him from putting a bullet in each of us. The medallion was our only leverage.

"I'm the only one who knows where the amulet is, Eduardo. It's not here. Search us, our gear, and the area. You won't find it without my help. Let the kids and Maroto go and I'll give you the medallion. No questions asked. And you can keep the whole $250,000."

It was a test. If he truly planned to let us go, this was a no-brainer. But, if he hesitated, even for an instant, we had a real problem. And I'd have to try something desperate.

"He'll take it." Estrella hoisted her pack onto her back. "This *puta* will do anything for a few *sols*. Emma, Joel, get your packs."

Christ! Couldn't Estrella just cool her jets and keep her mouth shut? Didn't she realize how serious this was?

"*Alto!*" Viedma shouted as he strode to Estrella and thrust his glistening face within inches of hers. So much for my strategic diplomacy. "No one will leave until I have the medallion. Do you understand? *No eres nada a mí, así que no empujes la suerte.*"

Viedma's cohorts shuffled uncomfortably. I doubt they'd bartered for abusing an innocent woman and two children, and I hoped they weren't up to the task. Viedma remained cocky.

"Your terms are unacceptable. I have fulfilled my employer's request. Now we will do things my way. We will begin with a thorough search of the women." Viedma grinned. "And I assure you, I intend to be most thorough."

Estrella met his lecherous gaze with defiance. "Your pathetic fantasies do not frighten me."

But I couldn't stand by and let this sadistic son of a bitch grope Estrella or my niece. I had to stall and think of something.

"Hold it! Joel, remember that large flat rock behind where we pitched the tent? There's a metal box under it. Bring it here, will you?"

"Jake, don't!" Estrella pleaded.

"Go ahead, Joel."

"Sure thing, Uncle Jake."

Joel was scared, but he put on a brave front. Good for him. He returned, lugging the small, metal box. It had a five-digit combination on the front.

"It's heavy."

"Yeah. Half-inch plate steel. Thanks, Joel."

As I grabbed the cumbersome container from Joel, I leaned and whispered, "When I grab the amulet, you and Emma run for it."

The moment I placed the box in Viedma's greedy hands, his face lit. He was jubilant. He'd won.

"And the combination?"

Viedma was salivating.

"Five, four, three, two, one."

"How quaint."

I hoped this wasn't a fatal mistake. Viedma's word was no good, but we had to try something. I was outnumbered and outgunned. No good options—for me anyway.

Damn. What a crappy way for things to end. At least I'd go down fighting for the kids. It was a gamble, and I was wagering Viedma's hires wouldn't shoot two children—or Estrella for that matter—if there was a juicier target. Me. I was about to become one big, dumb decoy. Joel looked tensed. Good. But I couldn't catch Emma's eye. I counted on Estrella to follow the kid's lead. I sucked a deep breath. I was ready.

Viedma's bony fingers turned the tumblers in careful sequence. First to five...next to four. Joel was ready to run. Viedma kept turning. Three...two. I nodded, slightly, at Estrella. Did she understand? The last dial clicked into place, releasing the internal bolt. I shifted my weight onto the balls of my feet, prepared to strike. Viedma shoved back the lid.

"It's gone!" he cried.

"Gone?" I nearly keeled over. Where was it?

For a split second, Viedma and I, both dumbfounded, stared at the empty lockbox. That split second gave me time. I lashed out with a solid right hook and connected hard with Viedma's face, just above his left eye. Pain shot up my arm as he collapsed backwards and onto the ground. The heavy box tumbled from his hands.

"Go!"

Joel grabbed Emma, dragging her toward the forest.

"Shoot them!" Viedma screamed, his face screwed with pain.

I jumped the man closest to me and spun him around in order to use him as a shield. He was stronger than he looked. I had to reach his gun.

Estrella was caught. She thrashed violently within one thug's iron grasp. Then Joel and Emma blindly crashed into someone at the edge of the woods. They fell back into the clearing. Perfect targets. At the same instant, cold steel pressed against my neck—the business end of a gun.

"It's over for you, Morgan."

Viedma!

I released my captive, expecting the worst at any instant. A deafening roar, then nothingness. We'd lost.

But Viedma lowered his gun.

Where Joel and Emma lay sprawled in the clearing, a middle-aged man—black-haired, dark-skinned, and oddly dressed—emerged from the forest. A heavy wool tunic hung to his knees, a faded red cloak loosely draped his shoulders, and crude leather sandals wrapped his feet. At one side, he held a long, wood-handled stone club. In his other hand, he held a long staff. Then, two graying men who were dressed similarly stepped from the woods behind us. As the first man approached, we could see that a large gold breastplate adorned with the unmistakable image of Inti, Sun god of the Inca, hung at his chest.

CHAPTER 19

▼

JAKE
LOST TRIBE

The man with the breastplate seemed to be in charge. He spoke sternly in *Quechua*. I could recognize the language, but not a single word. And judging by Viedma's expression, he didn't speak it either.

Estrella quietly translated. "He is offended we are here. This is Q'ero tribal land. We are forbidden upon it. He is especially angered at the local peasants." She looked at the man who held her. "They should have known better."

The scene was astonishing. The Q'ero leader wielded only a ceremonial club, yet Viedma's armed men cowed in shame.

The Incan descendant pointed at me.

"*Quinquin qhechunkuy, quinquin maqanakuy.*"

I didn't like the sound of it, whatever he said.

"He wants to know why you were fighting. Why you hit Viedma."

"Well, tell him."

Estrella spoke haltingly. The man nodded, satisfied with her answer.

"I told him they intended to rob us. I told him we wished to speak to the tribe's *sutinchaj*, their prophet or wise man, on a matter of great importance."

Viedma shouted at his men, brandishing his gun.

"*Qué es esta tontería? Diles que corran, que se vayan si quieren quardar la vida. Diles que yo les envie a sus antepasados.*"

"Viedma is threatening the Inca. He's warning them they must go," Estrella softly translated.

The wiry man I'd tangled with angrily accosted Viedma. "*Callate! No esta hablando a niños.*"

Estrella looked surprised.

"What?" I hated this. It was bad enough I couldn't speak *Quechua*, but, without Spanish, I was completely in the dark.

"The peasant told Viedma to shut up. That he could not speak to the Inca in that manner."

"*Cholos estúpidos! Hagan lo que digo,*" Viedma shouted.

The Q'ero spoke again for several moments, pointing to Viedma and his men. One of Viedma's men turned…and then another…and obediently walked away from the clearing.

"He told them they must leave and never return. We are now under protection of the Inca."

"*Tontos! El medallón vale millones.*" Viedma shrieked with rage. His eye was already bruising where I'd hit him. He aimed his gun directly at the chest of the Inca. "I'll kill you myself!"

Like a snake striking its prey, the peasant nearest me flashed his gun to Viedma's temple, the hammer poised to fire. His tentative uncertainty was gone. The man held the gun steady; his finger was firm on the trigger. He was no longer Viedma's puppet. Fierce determination glinted in his eyes. "*Haga daño al Inca y morir á usted.*"

Another peasant raised his pistol, aiming it at Viedma. Finally, the third pointed his weapon right at Viedma's chest. Viedma had run out of friends.

"*Deja el fósil, Senor Viedma, por favor.*"

"He said…"

"I got it, Ace."

I didn't completely understand what was happening, but I was flooded with an enormous sense of relief. We just might get out of here alive.

After several more tense moments, Viedma slumped and lowered his gun. One man took it and tucked it into his belt.

"*Lluchina!*" The Inca commanded.

Two of Viedma's men retreated down the trail. The smallest one, who had faced down Viedma, signaled with his gun for Viedma to follow. "*Ya ha terminado usted. Siga a los otros.*"

Our attackers left. As they were disappearing into the underbrush, Viedma turned and shouted, "I'm not finished with you Morgan. Not yet. Not because of these superstitious *cholos*."

The wiry peasant pushed Viedma forward to move faster, just before they completely disappeared.

"*Cholos?*" I asked Estrella.

"It is what those of arrogant Spanish blood call Indians. It is very degrading."

To my absolute relief, they were really gone, and Emma, Joel, and Estrella were safe. We'd dodged that bullet, but it had been too close. The thought of Viedma's gun against my neck—his manicured finger tensing on the trigger—made my stomach lurch, even now. I hoped I'd have the chance to even the score.

The Inca spoke while Estrella quietly translated his words to English.

"He says we are to follow them. They will take us to the tribal elder. It sounds like it's a long way, Jake. We probably won't get there until dusk."

"Tell him we'll be greatly honored to go with them. Tell him I'd like to shake his hand…as a sign of my gratitude for his saving our lives."

Estrella quickly translated. The man looked a little puzzled, but he nodded. I shook his hand enthusiastically, smiling, even laughing. He smiled and laughed as well. Did he realize he'd saved our lives? The formalities over, we hoisted our packs and fell in line behind the Q'ero. Their pace was fast. One of the older Indians brought up the rear to ensure we didn't deviate from the narrow, well-worn trail.

"Dude! You really laid that guy out." Joel walked at my side. "That was excellent!"

"I just wish he'd stayed down after I hit him. But that only happens in the movies." I looked at my swollen knuckles and then showed them to Joel. A head wasn't the softest thing to smash with your fist.

Joel gave me a thumbs-up. "It was awesome."

"You and Em didn't even bat an eye. You did great. We almost pulled it off."

"Yeah…well…maybe I was a little shaky about that part." It was good to hear Joel wasn't completely full of bravado.

"I was proud of you, Joel."

I was too. I couldn't imagine how I would have fared at the age of eleven if someone had pulled a gun on me. The kid had guts.

After a while, we spread out along the trail, and Estrella and I walked alone.

I still floated with a euphoric, intoxicating sense of relief that we'd escaped. Swollen knuckles were a small price to pay. I smiled at Estrella.

"Now that it's just you and me, you want to explain what exactly happened back there?"

She sucked on her braid another moment before answering. "It is the Inca, Jake. It is at the heart of us. It runs in our veins. Its hold on us is stronger than money, possessions, or centuries of Spanish teachings."

"In some ways, it is like your hockey, where men fight with one side against the other. Yet, when your national anthem is played, all is forgotten. The men stand together as one, bound by something larger than the sport. It is something like that, but deeper than your nationalism. Much deeper."

Estrella's eyes burned with an intensity I'd never seen in her.

"The Inca are our essence, Jake. They stir something basic in our core. Something primal. Direct descendents of the Inca are revered. Back there, once the Inca spoke, those men were no longer under Viedma's control. Their ultimate allegiance is to the Inca. Can you understand?"

"Yes."

We walked in silence a while. Estrella put a tender hand on my arm.

"What you did back there to try and save us was very brave. The Inca would say, *wapu*, a brave warrior. Thank you, Jake." She gave my arm a long, affectionate squeeze and gazed at me with those beautiful, deep brown eyes.

It wasn't even 9:00 AM yet, and we'd already found the Q'ero tribe, our tenuous link to the OS-187 mine. I'd decked the weasely Viedma, which I enjoyed more than I'd let on. We'd escaped being shot. And, to top it off, Estrella was coming around. This was going to be one great day. With one "minor" problem: What happened to the pendant?

CHAPTER 20

▼

JAKE
FATHER

Emma was unusually subdued during our forced march through the forest. She normally bubbled with enthusiastic questions. This afternoon, she was quiet and withdrawn. I worried she was getting sick. We'd been lucky so far, not to come down with something. Tourists in South America seem to be magnets for intestinal bugs. It looked like Em had finally been bit. On our next break, I'd give her some Imodium and antibiotics. Then she should be fine by nightfall.

We entered a small clearing and stopped cold as we saw it. Our first glimpse of Suchana Peak, perhaps a mile away. The pinnacle's sheer sides and jagged ridges rose several hundred feet above the mist and fog. In the spire's uppermost was a dark indentation in the rock. And, even though the peak was partially obscured by afternoon shadows, each of us realized we were gazing at what Professor Richardson described in his journal—the sacred Eye of Suchana Peak.

Thirty minutes later, we descended into a narrow valley surrounded by steep hillsides, only a quarter-mile from the peak. Estrella showed signs of anxious anticipation as we neared the Q'ero village. We smelled life first. Then we saw it.

The small encampment was punctuated with a dozen or so small cooking fires. Bluish smoke lazily curled into the overhanging treetops and then dissolved in the Cloud Forest mist. A thick, stagnant brackish mud lined both sides of the footpath. The stench of fecal matter mingled with the smell of the wood fires. I worried again about Em's stomach.

Outside the first ramshackle stone hut we passed, a young mother squatted in a tattered alpaca shawl, lethargically grinding maize in a heavy stone mortar. She blankly looked up from her monotonous task without a pause in her tedious grinding. Two dirty-faced toddlers ran for cover behind her and then peered over the top of her weary shoulders. Nearby, a hunchbacked gray-haired woman, perhaps the grandmother, stripped kernels of maize into a broken wicker basket. All four of these Q'ero watched us with suspicious, nervous eyes. All the while, they attended to their tasks.

We passed another hut of stone that was set off the muddy footpath. Slouched against it were two, shabbily clad, wire-thin men—perhaps in their fifties—lazily gnawing enormous mouthfuls of coca. They stared back at us with hollow, apathetic eyes. I could hear Joel whisper to Emma, "They look like zombies."

Tied to a corner of the hut was a llama yanking against a frayed cord, its only barrier to freedom. Two spotted guinea pigs, no doubt a future meal, squealed softly in a wood cage next to a basket half-filled with yellow potatoes. The men's clothes resembled traditional Incan costume, but they were drab and frayed. A reflection of the entire sorry encampment.

After listening to Estrella along the trail the last few days, I had formed a mental image of a primitive but dignified people who were content and thriving on the bounty of the land, as had their forefathers. This squalor and despair was a world away from legendary Incan pride and honor. Seeing it must have been agony for Estrella and her inflated expectations. Only halfway into the tiny village, Estrella's proud demeanor evaporated. She cast her eyes down to the narrow trail, looking neither to the left nor the right.

We passed more run-down structures. More elderly men mechanically chewed coca and watched us aimlessly as we quietly filed past. Every single circular thatched roof stone hut was in some stage of decay and disrepair. Partially finished masonry, the task apparently long ago abandoned, was smothered with overgrown vines and various kinds of vegetation. The forest was reclaiming the land from the Q'ero, whose ancestors had carved this village from the wild.

A solid young man, probably eighteen years old, led us into one of the round huts at the end of the narrow path. A small fire smoldered inside, giving the smoke-filled interior an acrid, campfire odor.

Seated in the center of the hazy structure was a decrepit old man, his dark puckered face withered and withdrawn. The sickly yellow eyes that followed us were flat and lifeless, though wary. I thought of an old-fashioned pioneer doll with the cloves poked in an apple-head that converted the dehydrated fruit into a shriveled mass of wrinkles. What few teeth the old fellow had were discolored a sickening dull gray. His knotted fingers, twisted and bent with arthritis, attempted to rest in his lap. Wisps of white shoulder-length hair tickled his long threadbare cape, a faded remnant of the Inca's prior glory.

The young man spoke to the old man in *Quechua*. The elder momentarily pondered. Then, in a hoarse, raspy voice, he addressed us. Estrella translated when he was done. She extended a hand to the elder.

"This is Intuto, the tribal elder and chief. The boy is his grandson. He says we may stay one night and only one night. That is all. He remembers the old stories of contamination, disease, and death."

"Disease?" Joel asked.

"Smallpox, pneumonia..." Estrella began.

"We don't have any of that stuff," Joel insisted.

"...and influenza."

"Oh." That seemed to satisfy Joel.

I couldn't blame the old man. The Inca once numbered seven million. The population plummeted to less than half-million in the early years of Spanish conquest.

European diseases, for which these people had no immunities, had devastated them.

Estrella spoke.

"Where are your people? Where is the rest of the Q'ero tribe?"

"They are gone. They lost faith in the Inca. There was nothing here to sustain their hearts. When the outsider found us, we numbered several hundred. We are now only twenty-three."

Only twenty-three. We had to ask him. Now.

"Ask him if he has any knowledge of the Seventh Jewel...the seventh capital of Pachacuti."

While Estrella spoke, I glanced at Emma, concerned. She still didn't look her usual self. Here we sat with an Incan elder, and she was completely disengaged, absentmindedly daydreaming.

When Estrella finished her inquiry, the old man frowned and slowly shook his emaciated face.

"*Mana, mana,*" His voice was dry and brittle.

Joel tugged at me.

"Jake, ask him what used to be in the eye, or the cave."

"Shhh, Joel. That can wait."

I understood Joel's anxious curiosity, but that was way down on our list of priorities. The Peruvian Andes were honeycombed with ransacked archaeological sites. Most of those were long ago looted by smugglers and thieves. Unfortunately, according to Richardson's journal, the Eye of Suchana Peak was just one more plundered site...empty.

"Ace, tell him we're searching for a rare metal that can only be found in these mountains. Tell him it can save the mountains and forests from dying. But tell him we need their help to find it."

I didn't want to sound desperate, but this last link to the Inca was our only hope. We had bet the farm on Estrella's hunch, and it wasn't looking too promising.

Estrella translated, but, midway through, a high-pitched, cackling laughter burst from Intuto's gaping mouth. His misshapen fingers pointed at us, accusing. Then, as the old man spoke slowly and deliberately, the color drained from Estrella's face.

It was frustrating not understanding more than a few rudimentary *Quechua* words.

"What's the story?"

"He said we have been here before…many, many years ago…seeking that which the Inca possessed, breaking our promises, stealing their wealth, and destroying their way of life and their hope. Soon the Q'ero will be gone, yet we have returned, wanting more. He said they have nothing left for us to take."

Later that evening, Estrella and I stood outside our hut. The smell of boiled corn and potatoes floated in the air, mixed with the distant sound of Andean flute music.

Dejected, Estrella surveyed the encampment. Her eyes were red and swollen. I leaned against the railing next to her.

"You going to be all right?"

"*Sí.* I suppose."

She continued gazing out across the wooded landscape.

"When I was a young girl my family lived in a small village outside of Lima. My father would come to the public market each week to sell the meager crops we'd grown on the hillside. Many times, he let me accompany him to town. The city was a wonderful place for me. There were so many people, all busily hurrying about. And I could peer into the shop windows at all the beautiful things we didn't have at home."

"On the way to the market, we would pass the city's oldest hotel and, in it, the Mira Mar Restaurant. I would press my dirty face against the window to capture a brief glimpse inside. It was beautiful. Golden chandeliers, crisp linen tablecloths, sparkling crystal, and white china plates. Tiny, flickering gas lamps shone on ornately framed paintings and gilt-edged mirrors. Handsome, moustached waiters in starched uniforms carried trays of exotic foods and drinks. And the people inside! Sitting in those red velvet chairs were European monarchs, American movie stars, and rich and famous people from Buenos Aires, Santiago, Sao Paulo, and Caracas. It was magic. Magical."

"I never thought we were poor, but my mother and father told me we could not afford to eat at such a place. The hotel was only for the very rich. Yet still, I gazed inside whenever we came to the city and longed to dine there someday."

"When I was grown up and attending the university, I starved myself for months to save enough scholarship money to order a meal at the Mira Mar. Finally, I would satisfy so many years of desire to dine at this magnificent place."

"But the Mira Mar was not as I remembered from childhood. The velvet upholstery was tattered and ripped; the thick carpet was faded and worn. My crystal glass had lipstick stains. Bits of dried food were stuck between the tongs of my fork. The white tablecloth was stained with old wine and coffee circles. The waiters were ill-mannered, and their uniforms were ill-fitting. I looked around at the other patrons. They were not movie stars, but mostly shopkeepers with scuffed shoes and dirty trousers. It had all been an illusion…a little girl's dream."

I put an arm around Estrella and pulled her closer. "I'm sorry."

She took my hand and squeezed affectionately. She slumped against me, accepting support.

"There is no hope or spirit here. The Q'ero are a dying people."

Joel burst from the hut, looking frightened.

"Uncle Jake, you better get in here. Em's getting worse. A lot worse."

We rushed to Emma's bedside.

"I kept her bundled up, like you said, but she isn't any better."

Emma's face was bloodlessly pale. Her lips and fingernails were purple. Her eyes were dilated.

Estrella put a hand on Emma's forehead. "Did you two have all your immunizations before you left?"

"Yes. I think so. She got all the same shots that I had."

Estrella removed her hand, shook her head.

"This isn't a fever."

I'd seen this before in high-altitude first-aid class. "Looks like advanced hypothermia. She's freezing to death. Estrella, crawl in next to her. I don't know what else to do."

I tried to stay calm and think clearly and logically. I never expected this. My own niece.

"Today? Taytay? *Taita?*" Emma mumbled through clenched teeth. Her voice was pleading with desire.

Joel rolled his eyes.

"She's been saying that again, too."

"Again?!" Estrella was alarmed. "She has spoken this before, Joel?"

"Yeah, back at Uncle Jake's. She was yammering in her sleep the first night in his apartment."

I took Emma's hand.

"I heard it, too, but later. The next night."

"What was she doing when she spoke these words?"

"Well, she seemed to be sleepwalking, looking at this awful painting I have. There's a safe behind it. In my wall."

Joel's eyes widened.

"A safe?" That answered that. Joel and Emma hadn't accidentally discovered my hiding place.

"And in the safe?" Estrella prodded.

"A few odds and ends…and the necklace!"

Joel jumped into a higher gear.

"Dude! When Em talked in her sleep in the bedroom, she was staring at the closet. That was the same day we got Tom's climbing stuff."

"And the box had the medallion in it!"

It was that damn necklace! We were losing Emma now from my own stupidity.

Estrella frantically unbuttoned the top of Emma's heavy flannel shirt. There it was. The leather string around her neck disappeared down under her T-shirt. I removed the cord from around her head and withdrew the shimmering silver-green amulet.

Instantly, Emma's teeth stopped chattering, and the color seeped back into her cheeks. The Incan artifact had been sucking the life from her. But why? Was OS-187 radioactive? My research never mentioned it, but no one knew much about this stuff. Whatever the reason, I was determined to keep the OS-187 away from the kids and Estrella.

Estrella felt her forehead again. "She's already warming up."

I tucked the blankets around Emma. "She just needs some rest and something hot to drink when she's able."

Estrella slowly stood up. "Jake, has Emma been studying *Quechua*?"

"*Quechua*? No, of course not. How would she?"

Estrella was troubled as she looked down on Emma. "*Taita* means father, Jake. She was calling for her father in the language of the Inca."

CHAPTER 21

▼

EMMA
TREASURE TUNNEL

I sure didn't remember taking Uncle Jake's amulet, let alone wearing it like a necklace. Joel, with his warped sense of humor, could have slipped it on me while I slept, but I could tell he didn't do it. I guess maybe I did it sleepwalking. But that didn't answer how I would have found it. Joel and I had no idea where the amulet was hidden. Maybe I was cracking up. Emma Morgan, schizophrenic, meet Emma Morgan, your other personality…who is apparently a kleptomaniac. Great!

I stood outside in the crisp night air wrapped in a short alpaca blanket. It had only been a few hours since my fever had broken, but I was feeling better. I was still a little cold, but Jake and Estrella said a little fresh air wouldn't hurt.

Above me, a brilliant canopy of stars twinkled through an indigo-black sky. I wanted to get away by myself, just to think things through for a few minutes.

I didn't want Jake and Estrella—or even Joel for that matter—to think I was some sort of thief. We all knew how valuable the medallion was, and it didn't look very good that it disappeared and I wound up wearing it.

I jumped. A dark figure appeared from nowhere and walked toward me. It was old Intuto's cute grandson. I'd been so absorbed with questioning my sanity that I hadn't heard him approach.

"*Ima shutitac canqui?*"

"I'm sorry, I don't understand. *Se habla espanol?*"

"*Jay? Cani* Putaq." He spoke slowly and pointed to himself. "Putaq." He then pointed to me. "*Conqui...?*"

"Putaq?" I pointed back to him. He was telling me his name.

"*Arí,* Putaq!"

"Emma," I pointed to myself. "Emma."

"Emma," he repeated, pointing back at me. "Emma. *Alli shuti.*"

It felt like "Me Tarzan, you Jane." And, with that one brief exchange, we'd exhausted our possible topics of conversation. I shivered under the blanket, still trying to warm up from my earlier ordeal.

"*Conqui chiri?*"

"What?" I wish he spoke just a little Spanish.

"Emma *chiri. Acha chay!*" He imitated a freezing person with chattering teeth and shivering arms. I guess that's how I looked. "*Chiri.*"

"Cold? Yes." He was right about that. I couldn't seem to stay warm. "Yes. *Chiri. Arí.*"

Putaq smiled, pleased. I smiled too. It was nice to have company.

"*Arí, chiri,*" I answered again.

Putaq seemed much taller, now that he wasn't stooped over in his grandfather's hut. He reached out and tightened my blanket, which was more like a large, heavy shawl around my shoulders. "*Alli catana,* Emma. *Q'onichiy.*"

"Thanks, Putaq."

He looked at my hands, clutching the heavy shawl. And, as expected, he stared at my prosthetic. Oh well, it was nice while it lasted.

"*Ch'ulla rigra. Imashina? Wit'uy?*" He reached out to my prosthetic hand. I recoiled from his touch. Tonight I couldn't deal with the rejection—the gawking, morbid fascination for the poor crippled girl. I shivered again. Not tonight.

"I lost my arm, okay? And I'm sick and tired of explaining it and having everyone stare at it and everything." I was on the verge of tears, practically shouting.

"*Mana, mana, mana.*"

He waved his hands protesting, realizing he'd upset me. Gently, he grasped the blanket around my neck and looked down into my eyes. I had no idea what he was saying, but his voice was calming. "*Qum munaycha sipas.*"

Then, just as gently, he held strands of my hair in his fingers.

"*Sumaq puka accha jina antawara. Ch'aska nawi.* Emma, *munaycha mirka uya.*" As he smiled, he slowly ran his finger down around my eye and to my cheek. We were standing so close that we were touching. He took the blanket in both hands and pulled me even closer. I could feel my heart racing, and I thought I could feel his as well.

"*Qam sumaq sipas*, Emma. *Qam chunkitu yurak waita.*" I felt like he was looking right through me with those brown eyes. "*Manchana?*" he whispered.

"*Manchana?* I'm sorry. I don't understand," I whispered back.

"*Manchana.*" He leaned forward and gave me a long, gentle kiss on the lips. I felt warm inside and light-headed. "*Manchana. Allin?*"

"Mmmm...*allin.*" I answered a little dreamily. He leaned down and kissed me again, but more deeply. After a moment, I suddenly realized I didn't know what I'd answered or what I'd just agreed to. I pushed him away.

"No *allin!* What did I say?"

Putaq laughed, but it was not mean laughter. Most of the laughter was in his eyes. He pulled me back toward him.

"Emma *llullu. Yuruk waita manchakuy cuyana?*"

This he asked me with childlike innocence, but he looked as if it was more a statement than a question.

Estrella walked into the moonlight from a part of the trail hidden in shadow.

"Well, Emma, you certainly seem to have broken the Q'ero language barrier."

I was embarrassed and moved away from Putaq. But he didn't seem to be the slightest bit embarrassed by Estrella's appearance. The two exchanged a few words in *Quechua*, and Putaq backed away to leave.

"*Alli tuta*, Emma. *Paqarin, yurak waita.*" Then Putaq smiled again and returned toward his hut.

Putaq had no way of knowing how much his innocent kiss meant to me. It was the first time anyone had ever looked at me like that and the first time I'd been kissed since my accident. There were so many days and nights I thought I'd end up alone for the rest of my life. That no one would want anything to do with someone like me. That I'd never have a normal life. For the first time in more than a year, I felt whole. Putaq made me feel whole. I smiled. It was a wonderful feeling.

"You've made quite a conquest," Estrella teased.

"How long were you standing there?"

"Oh, a little while. I didn't mean to eavesdrop, Emma. I apologize. But you were both standing right in the trail. At first, I thought I'd just wait, but I then thought I'd better interrupt while I had the chance."

I wasn't sure how I felt about Estrella's presence. I certainly didn't like being spied on, but she would know what Putaq had been saying.

"So…what was he saying?" I tried to ask nonchalantly, but I was dying to know. Estrella smiled and took my arm, and we began walking back toward the shack.

"He was being very nice, very chivalrous. He is very taken with your hair color. And he has given you a nickname, *yurak waita*, the white flower." I could feel myself blushing and was glad Estrella couldn't see.

"And *manchana* means kiss."

"Yes, I sort of figured that one out." I smiled.

"He thinks you're very…cute…I think you say. He seems like a very nice young man. And cute."

We continued toward our thatched roof hut. It had been a long day, and we were both tired.

"Did he say anything else?" I felt awkward fishing for compliments, but they were rare lately.

"Well…"

Estrella paused, deciding whether to translate everything.

"What?"

I hated it when people started to say something and then tried to withdraw it. Back home we had a rule: If you started to say something, you had to finish it. "You can't start something like that and then not tell me. That's not fair."

Silently, we walked back to the doorway of our small hut. Estrella gave a big sigh and then relented. "He said you should not be afraid to love." She sighed again. "Perhaps that is my lesson as well. I'm going to walk a bit. Good night, Emma. I'm glad you're feeling better."

I lay in my sleeping bag, unable to sleep, clinging to Putaq's words. I thought about all the times this past year I'd been standoffish to the boys at school. I mean really, totally aloof and distant. I hadn't given anyone the chance to get close since the accident. I realized all the barriers I created. I'd been so absorbed feeling sorry for myself about the prospect of romance that I'd been making everything worse than it had to be. Putaq made me realize it didn't have to be that way. I didn't have to hide, aloof. Unlike my physical situation, this was something I could change. For the first time in a year, I went to sleep thinking about boys without wanting to cry.

The next morning, Estrella had agreed to cook breakfast—if Joel and I washed up everything afterwards. It was the first time I'd seen her wear her hair down and unbraided. We were just about finished washing when Putaq approached.

"*Alli tutamanta, yurak waita.*"

Joel looked surprised by Putaq's greeting. "Are you talking to us?"

But I wasn't.

"Good morning, Putaq."

"What's this? How come you guys are such big pals today?"

Joel looked back and forth between Putaq and me. Thankfully, Estrella hadn't told everyone what she'd overheard and overseen last night.

"Don't be a jerk, Joel." At times, those were not easy orders for my brother.

Putaq spoke quietly. "*Tairy urcu nawi?*" His eyes darted around the area. He acted nervous, not like last night. He stooped down and sketched a pyramid with a circle in the top of it in the dirt. He pointed at the peak and then back to his own eye. "*Lerq'o urcu jaqay.*"

"The Eye of Suchana Peak?" Joel blurted.

"Yes! *Arí. Arí.* Can you take us there?" I excitedly asked.

"Shhh. Putaq *sat'ikuy,*" he whispered.

"Joel, I don't think he's supposed to take us there. I don't think he's even supposed to go there." I didn't care if Joel and I got in trouble, but, if the tribe's punishments were as bad as Incan justice, Putaq could get into serious trouble.

"*Jacu!*" He motioned for us to follow.

Joel grabbed his knapsack filled with our flashlights and a bottle of water. I threw on my coat and followed. When we got to the base of the rock peak, Putaq pointed toward the spire. "*Wichariy urcu. Jacu!*"

From the base of the pinnacle, I couldn't even see the eye, the entrance to the cave. An overhanging ledge or something was obstructing it. That wasn't the only impediment. The first 100 feet or so didn't look too bad. "Steep scrambling," I thought. I could do it so long as I was careful. But the remaining sixty feet looked impossible, at least for me. Looking up at the rock face, there was no possible way I could climb. I didn't think Joel could either. How did Professor Richardson make it to the top?

"Joel, I can't do this. There's no way. I'll have to stay here."

I was dying to know what might be in the cavern, but not literally.

"I don't think I can either."

Joel squinted up at the formidable peak. Normally, Joel was willing to try anything. I didn't feel like such a chicken after all. I tried to make Putaq understand that the pinnacle was beyond our abilities, but he was insistent, saying, "*jacu, jacu, jacu.*" None of that white flower business now. This felt like another Q'ero forced march. Putaq had offered to take us to the cave, and he was going to get us there— whether we liked it or not.

"Let's just go up the first part, Em. Then we can turn around. We'll just see how it looks." Reluctantly, I agreed.

Putaq held my hand tightly, virtually pulling me up the rocky incline. Joel scrambled behind us. I hoped Putaq wasn't going to like me less when I couldn't make the final climb, but how could he possibly think I could do it? I wasn't even sure how he was going to climb it. The route got steeper. We slowed our pace.

"*Pajtataj! Llusk'a.*" Putaq pointed down to the slippery ground.

"Em, any idea what he's saying?"

"Sorry. Absolutely clueless." Putaq squeezed my hand harder.

"I thought you knew some words." Joel had seen me struggle with Spanish. I don't know why he thought I was suddenly fluent in *Quechua.*

"Well, just a few, like *manchana.*"

I smiled to myself, thinking of last night. The thought of Putaq's kiss made me glow inside. Putaq whirled around on the steep trail.

"*Manchana?*" An eager expression filled his eyes.

"No. *Mana, mana.*" I'm sure Joel would love to see that. I motioned Putaq to keep going uphill. Inca, maybe, but he was still a boy.

When we reached what I had figured would be my turnaround point, where the trail turned into a cliff, I was amazed to see crude steps and handholds carved in the stone face. They traversed the cliff at a forty-five-degree angle. I might actually be able to make it up the spire. They'd been cut into the rock at a downward angle, so, from below, they were invisible. I was more and more impressed with resourcefulness of the Q'ero. Here was yet another reason the cave had remained so secret.

"Cool," Joel said. "It's like they're invisible. Em, you can do this, easy!"

Putaq looked expectant.

"Well, maybe I can." I wouldn't say easy. I had to make sure I didn't look down, or I'd freak out for sure. This would be like a heart-stopping ride at Knott's Berry Farm. If I just stayed focused, I'd be all right.

Putaq protectively climbed behind me, ready to help if I should slip. I felt much safer knowing he was there. It was funny to think someone could lead from behind.

I gripped the handholds with each carefully placed step. As we climbed higher up the face, I fantasized about the cave's treasure…and wondered, as Estrella hoped, if it would point us to the Seventh Jewel.

Two-thirds of the way up, I made the mistake of looking down. As predicted, it totally freaked me out. It was a sheer drop, straight down. I panicked and hugged the rock face, frozen and unable to move either up or down. I felt like, if I tried to move the slightest bit, I was going to fall. Behind me, I could hear Putaq talking, gently encouraging me and trying to get me to go. After a few more paralyzed moments, I slowly reached for the next handhold and then stepped up to the next step. I took a deep breath and repeated it. Another deep breath…another step higher. I was climbing again.

Finally, I cautiously crawled up over the ledge, and I was there in the mouth of the cave. The floor was gray and felt chalky. I stood and wiped my hand on my jeans.

As my eyes adjusted to the dark interior, I could see Joel leaning against an interior wall. The cave was about twenty feet by twenty feet. Its ceiling was not quite twice my height. I heard a peculiar squeaking. Just as Putaq scrambled up behind me, I noticed Joel was staring at the ceiling with an odd expression on his face.

"Joel, what's the story?"

He gave me a look—as if to say "Don't you have any brains?"—and pointed up. The ceiling was moving! Clinging upside down to the rocky ceiling, almost close enough to reach up and touch, was a solid mass of squirming, screeching, jet-black vampire bats. Hundreds of them. They blanketed every square inch above us with their pointed ears; black, beady, rat-like eyes; and those creepy, flesh-covered wings folded around hairy bodies. Tiny needle-sharp teeth flashed everywhere in the dim light. The whole cave stunk. I loathed these revolting creatures, and I made a noise to express it.

"There's zillions of them," Joel whispered, sounding just as apprehensive as I felt.

"Shhh. *Chhichhinakuy.*" Putaq put a finger to his mouth.

I forced myself into calm. I was acting like a two-year-old. I knew they wouldn't hurt us—if only there weren't so many of the nauseating little vermin.

Vampire bats aren't the monsters portrayed in the movies. They did feed on blood, but not from people's necks. Supposedly, they only bit cows, horses, pigs, or other livestock. What made my skin crawl was knowing that there's something in their saliva that keeps blood from clotting. They bite sleeping animals and then lap up the blood that continues to ooze from the wound. What's even more creepy was that there's also something in their saliva that numbs the skin—like novocaine at the dentist—so the animals don't even feel anything as they bleed and don't wake up. Gross!

Putaq looked at me, and I settled down and remembered the reason we'd climbed here in the first place. I turned on my flashlight and crept in further, trying to ignore the beady-eyed bats overhead.

"Anything in here, Joel?" I asked in a whisper so as not to spook the bats.

"I don't think so." Joel switched on his light.

The rough rock walls didn't seem to conceal any treasure passageway or secret tunnel. Professor Richardson's notes had been correct. The Eye of Suchuna was empty, a hollow shell.

"*Cushac.*" Putaq made a wide sweep of his arm, referring to the interior of the cave. I surveyed the barren interior, wondering what the cave once might have held. What had the original members of the Q'ero spirited away from Cuzco and Pizzaro's insatiable grasp? Perhaps this room had overflowed with jewelry of silver and gold, encrusted with jungle-green Ecuadorian emeralds. But not now.

Everything was gone, stolen by Spanish invaders or treasure hunters from centuries earlier or, disappointingly, even by outlaw castoffs of the Q'ero itself. The Incan heritage, of which the grizzled old sage had proudly spoken, had already been gone when Professor Richardson scaled the peak fifty years ago.

Perhaps the cave had always stood vacant. And the stories of a vast treasure were just that. Empty tales of a desperate people clinging to the past. Just like stories about vampire bats, the treasure was little more than fabricated folklore. I felt sorry for old Intuto, who clung so faithfully to his ancient dream.

Putaq figured out we didn't like the bats and probably thought he'd do us a favor by getting rid of them. Standing at the mouth of the cave, he violently clapped his hands and shouted into the enclosure. "*Cayacu! Riccharina! Cayacu! Riccharina!*" Again and again.

The stone cavern exploded with the frightened creatures. Dim turned to the blackness of night in a churning frenzy of black wings as the frantic bats screeched hysterically in a panicked flight to escape. I crouched to avoid their tiny teeth and claws. Thankfully, very few flew into me. Their piercing screeches echoed within the chamber. I hoped the tribe didn't hear.

Within moments, the cave was silent again, and I uncovered my eyes. The odorous creatures were gone. Putaq still stood at the mouth of the cave, covered in bat droppings. So was Joel. Crap! Me too. Those stupid bats were like a flock of frightened pigeons, raining poop as they panicked and fled.

"Gross! I'm covered! Ugh! It's even in my hair!" I felt the small clumps of sticky goo. "It's all over me!"

Joel wasn't any more pleased than I was. "It stinks."

Putaq laughed at us both. I think he enjoyed my embarrassment. Today, he was the last person I wanted to be humiliated in front of.

Putaq held his nose and made a contorted face. "*Chhini ishpana. Asnay!*" Putaq thought the whole incident was one big joke. I guess he wasn't so different from the boys back home.

The floor of the cavern was slimy with bat dung. It was already beginning to dry and blend in. I kneeled and dabbed a dry patch. It had the same chalk-like texture as the stuff I'd first wiped off my hand. It covered the entire floor of the cave. Staring at the cave floor, I grasped the secret!

"Em, if you're looking for samples, you've got plenty on your shirt."

Didn't Joel understand? Hadn't anyone understood? There were hundreds of tiny blotches drying on the floor. Each day brought another thin layer of dried bat guano…dropping and drying…dropping and drying…day after day…year after year…decade upon decade…century upon century…until…well…who knew how far down the original stone floor might be? And what might lie buried below?

CHAPTER 22

▼

EMMA
VIRACOCHA

Digging with bare fingers through five hundred years of bat poop wasn't exactly how I'd planned to spend my vacation, but this was so exciting I didn't mind. The only "shovel" we had was Joel's dull hunting knife, a gift from Jake. Luckily, the dried guano came up in large chunks. We started excavating on the easternmost wall, nearest the mountain's core.

The digging was slow work. Putaq and Joel took turns muscling the blunt blade into the petrified dung and then working it back and forth to break off hunks of the hardened stuff. Within a short time, they were bathed in perspiration.

An hour later, we'd chiseled and scraped a narrow trench about a foot deep along the base of the wall where remnants of rotted thatched sticks lay flush against the cave's wall. Joel and Putaq dug furiously. We uncovered more and more of the brown matting, and eventually ripped the decaying sticks away from the wall. Behind was a deep, black hole cut into the cavern.

I could barely contain my excitement. "The treasure tunnel!" We'd found what had eluded Professor Richardson fifty years ago and who knows how many centuries of other treasure hunters.

Joel shined his flashlight down the long, black shaft and poked his head through the narrow opening. "It's a tunnel all right." For his sake, I hoped it wasn't filled with snakes. "Let's see. It goes down a long way. It's filled with cobwebs. Nope, I can't tell how far. I can't see the end of it from here."

"*Yana jutca.*" Putaq stared down the hole with wide eyes.

Joel extracted his head. He and Putaq dug furiously again, prying, chiseling, and slowly widening the mouth of the passageway. Another fifteen minutes of burrowing through the guano unearthed enough of the steep, black shaft for Joel and Putaq to slither through and stand upright in the tunnel. Then they helped me squeeze through the hand-dug entryway.

The passageway was like a giant wormhole bored through the rock, approximately six feet in diameter. It dropped off steeply, probably a fifty-degree angle—down to who knew what.

I'd read stories in travel magazines about spelunkers, or cave explorers, getting lost in underground labyrinths. "We ought to have a rope before we go any further." I was anxious about the treasure, but, frankly, I had no desire to get permanently lost underground.

"Em, you worry too much."

"*Allimanta, yurak waita.*"

It sounded like Putaq was trying to warn us. I was stepping sideways on the lip of the tunnel, when I turned my foot on a stone and stumbled into Joel. We fell against Putaq. Then the three of us toppled over like bowling pins. Everything after that was a blur. Our flashlights were knocked loose, and we were immediately immersed in blackness. We half-slid and half-tumbled, banging into each other down the shaft through the darkness. My screams and the boys' yells reverberated deafeningly off the stone walls. Blindly, we careened downward, faster and faster, banging and bumping on the rocks and each other. An instant later, we toppled onto a hard, flat place. My forehead smashed into someone's head with a dull clunk. In the darkness, Joel let out a loud yelp. We were a jumbled heap of tangled arms and legs. My prosthetic arm was especially twisted. Thankfully, Putaq couldn't see me as I fumbled in the dark to correct it.

"*Chuta!*"

I didn't have to speak *Quechua* to know swearing when I heard it.

"Joel, are you okay?" I rubbed the swollen knot on my forehead. "Where are you?"

"Right here. I guess I'm okay. Was that you who hit me?"

"Sorry. If it makes you feel any better, I've already got a huge lump on my head, and my elbow really hurts. We need to find the flashlights."

"*Uncupi chaupi urcu.*"

Putaq didn't sound very thrilled about our situation.

"Em, how far do you think we fell?"

"I don't know, maybe thirty feet or so? Not too far."

"That'd be an awesome ride if we were sitting on cardboard or something. You could set up little lights inside..."

"Joel!" We'd just about been killed and here was Joel, concocting a carnival ride. How could he forget we were on the verge of discovering lost treasure?

"I found my light, Em, but it's broken." I could hear Joel shaking his flashlight. I heard the shattered pieces rattling inside. That left mine.

After blindly groping in the dark, I felt the smooth, cool shaft of my flashlight. I carefully stood up, pressed the "on" button, and, at the first beam, recoiled in terror as a lurid skull stared at me. I stumbled back with a jolt, tripped, and fell backwards onto the floor. Joel's laughter echoed all around.

"You should have seen yourself jump!"

"Jeez, Joel! That thing scared the fricken' crap out of me. The least you could do is help me up."

Putaq pulled me off the hard floor and then gave Joel a dirty look. "*Qam cuchi oqoti.*" It didn't sound very complimentary.

Mentally prepared for whatever the cave might hold, I shined my flashlight back in the direction of the skull, determined to be calm this time. Where Uncle Jake's mummy looked like it was peacefully sleeping, the two mummies seated before us were downright ghoulish. Empty, lifeless eye sockets pierced us. Hideous, blackened teeth grinned through petrified lips. The nose was shriveled, like dried leather, but it was still there. Skin clung to the bones in random patches like dirty parchment, stretched beyond the breaking point. Gaps in the brittle flesh exposed gray-brown bones. Skeletal fingers clutched a faded bundle of unraveled colored cloth.

I held the flashlight as steady as possible, almost gagging at the thought of breathing the same stagnant air surrounding these decomposing corpses for hundreds of years. I knew Joel's spurts of laughter were just bravado. This stuff creeped him out as much as it did me.

Capping one of the dirt-colored skulls was a rough hewn, decomposing material with blue and green feathers attached. The figure sat draped in a large cloak or cape comprised of tiny feathers—black, red, and white—intricately woven together in patterns resembling fish. Discolored ribs were visible through gaps in the decayed clothing.

The two figures sat rigidly upright upon ornately carved, throne-like wooden chairs. At each corner of the "thrones" were holes through which poles could be inserted to carry the lifeless passengers.

I expected Putaq to ridicule my squeamishness, but his reaction was another surprise. He knelt on one knee, subdued by the mummified Inca.

"*Aya pambana. Putaq k'umuykur. Chullpa.*"

Putaq sounded humble and meek. His young warrior's defiance and confidence had evaporated. This was his heritage. His ancestry. His blood.

Following my flashlight beam, I surveyed the rest of the chamber. Whether it was the cool cavern temperature or the two mummies seated nearby, I don't know, but I was suddenly covered head to toe in goose bumps.

This hidden chamber was even larger than the cave above us, roughly thirty feet in diameter and ten feet high. We could see rows of dust-covered wood scaffolding, all blanketed with long, thick cobwebs. The far side of the cave was strewn with rotten matting, thatched material, and other dirty debris.

But, as we picked our way through the musty chamber, I realized those weren't cobwebs at all, but thousands and thousands of strings. Strings of various lengths in muted, faded colors with small knots at various places along the strands. Most of the strings were bunched together, like miniature mops. Hundreds of others littered the floor, having rotted away from the others.

"Joel, don't you know what these are?" I held a few strands in front of my flashlight.

"No. What is this place? Some sort of torture chamber?"

"They're called *quipas*," I explained.

"*Arí, quipas.*" Putaq walked to my side.

"It's like Incan writing, Joel. This is how they kept track of stuff. Don't you remember Estrella talking about the little mops made of strings? Archaeologists thought they were just an accounting system, for census taking and recordkeeping and stuff."

"Sort of like an abacus?"

"Right." I always talked faster when I was excited. "But she said some Incan experts, including her, suspect these *quipas* are a lost writing system, different from any other civilization."

I didn't really understand some of the stuff Estrella told me that night. She thought the language was based on a binary code system, like computer language. But no one had been able to decipher the complex Incan writing system, and only about 600 *quipas* were known to still exist. But there must have been at least a thousand right here.

"Joel, don't you get it?" I didn't give him time to answer. "If the Q'ero took these from Cuzco, this could be like the Incan library. I mean, maybe it's a whole record of their history and culture."

"And…" Joel was a quick study. He was with me now.

"And maybe it's got something about the Seventh Jewel."

It was time to get help.

Thirty minutes after Putaq left to retrieve Uncle Jake and Estrella, I heard their voices coming up the face. Joel and I had crawled back up the steep passageway with Putaq before his climb down the pinnacle. I'd intended to do the same, but, when I'd peeked over the ledge at the sheer drop-off, I acted like a cat in a tree. I was going to play it safe and wait for Uncle Jake. But I had no intention of hanging around those mummies alone. I made Joel stay with me.

Putaq was the first to return over the ledge. Estrella was next, breathing hard and looking flushed with beads of perspiration on her forehead. Her long hair was tucked beneath her Nikon strap, and a small knapsack with her tattered *Jewel Journal* was strapped tightly to her back. She never let that cryptic collection of clues out of her sight. Joel and I helped her over the ledge.

"*Qué subida!*" Estrella wiped sweat from her brow.

"You won't believe what we found!" I blurted.

"Hey, I'm the one who dug up the tunnel." Joel wanted his share of the credit.

"I believe, I believe." Although still winded by the climb, Estrella rushed to where we'd dug without waiting to catch her breath. "Is this it? The entrance to the tunnel?" I'd never heard that frantic tone before.

Uncle Jake brought up the rear. He quickly pulled himself over the ledge, stood, and surveyed the interior. He looked as fresh and rested as if he'd scaled the pinnacle in an escalator. His red nylon climbing rope wrapped his torso, two high-intensity lanterns were clipped to his belt, and a collapsible shovel dangled behind him. This was obviously his idea of fun.

Joel was practically bouncing.

"We found it, Jake! A secret passageway right inside the mountain. It's awesome! A couple of mummies and a bunch of those string things." Joel was as excited as me.

"*Quipas*," Jake corrected.

"Right, tons of 'em."

"You guys didn't have to get so dressed up for us," Jake smiled. I'd been so excited that I'd forgotten we were completely covered in bat crap.

"This stuff will wash out, won't it?"

I couldn't wait to get it out of my hair.

"I'm sure of it."

"*Apurate!*" Estrella was already waist deep in the hole leading to the passageway. "What are you all waiting for?"

"This might help?" Jake handed Estrella one of the lanterns.

"*Sí.*" Estrella made a long sigh. "Please understand. I've dreamed of a discovery like this all my life."

One by one, we squeezed through the narrow opening that led to the hidden chamber. Excitedly, Joel and I explained how we'd found the tunnel, fell into the second chamber, and discovered the mummies. We constantly interrupted ourselves in our rapid-fire description. Putaq stood by quietly. I smiled a "thanks" for his role.

When we stepped down into the second cave, we shined our lights around the interior. The *quipas* seemed to glow in the high-intensity light beams.

"*Qué maravilla.*" Estrella was dumbstruck. "You have no idea what this means, the importance of this. This might be the Rosetta Stone of the Incan language. For the first time, we might unlock the secrets of the *quipas*, read the language of our ancestors, the history of the Inca as recorded by them, rather than through clumsy interpreters. Amazing."

Estrella removed the lens cap from her Nikon and began shooting the cave, the *quipas*, and the mummified figures. Putaq was uncomfortable with the blinding flashes. Next, Estrella focused on the wooden throne of the nearest mummy, her long lens zooming in and out. Suddenly, her expression softened from excitement to wonder. The camera fell to her side.

Estrella leaned across the petrified figure to scrutinize the carving on the high-backed chair. I don't know how she could stand being so close to the leering skull. The carving depicted crude figures with spears or clubs, fleeing from other warriors flying in the air.

Estrella gasped.

"*Dios Mí! Emperador de mi gente.* These are the mummified remains of Viracocha, Inca Emperor! We have found Viracocha!" She wrapped Jake in an enthusiastic, celebratory hug, burying her face in his chest. Estrella was half-laughing and half-crying with joy. Then gently, she touched the cracked wooden panel with tender reverence. Her voice came out in a hoarse whisper.

"It is revealed in the carving. The dawn of our empire. The Inca nation was small, little more than a group of tribes. The powerful Chanca threatened to attack the Inca. Viracocha's aged father fled from Cuzco, leaving the capital in the hands of his young son."

Estrella paused to collect her thoughts.

"The Chanca attacked Cuzco. Incan chroniclers said the battle was hopeless for Viracocha. The Inca were outnumbered many times. But, with the Chanca on the verge of a great victory, the gods sent invisible spirit warriors in defense of Viracocha and crushed the invading army. It was a terrible battle. The field was named *Yahuarpampa*, meadow of blood." Estrella made sweeping gestures to illustrate the destruction of the Incan enemies.

"Later, when the Inca finally understood the intent of the conquistadors, they hid the sacred remains of all the emperors. It was believed they were all found and burned in 1571 by Viceroy Toldeo. But not all of them. Not all."

"Isn't this kind of creepy?" Joel read my mind again. "It's like keeping mummies of all our dead prime ministers or something. What's with that?"

Jake filled the chamber with big, rolling laughter.

"I agree with you, Joel. But, to the Inca, the emperors were considered gods, descendants of the Sun. Their mummified remains were considered holy. Estrella?"

"*Sí*. They were *huacas*, holy shrines. It was the Incan way, Joel. High priests waited on the mummies, attending to the emperors. Even in death. The deceased emperors were treated as if they were still alive."

"Dude, that's twisted."

"It is unusual, yes." Estrella began taking more photos and then abruptly stopped. "Damn."

"Out of film?" Jake asked.

"No. I am wondering what will happen to the Q'ero if these picture are published and if my notes are published. What will happen to these people? They'll be descended upon by the government, forced to modernize, and forced to assimilate into the twenty-first century. Perhaps displaced from their ancestral lands. I had never considered this before. I dreamed of a discovery like this for so many years, and I now don't know what to do."

"It's not something you have to decide today." Jake caressed her shoulder.

In the brief time I'd known Estrella Maroto, I never doubted her work came first, and, given the opportunity, she'd do everything and anything to locate the Seventh Jewel. She was obsessed. But her hesitation to exploit these innocent, simple people made me wonder if I'd misjudged her intensity.

"Estrella, the kids are right. These *quipas* may give us our answers. This is our last shot. But there's only one way we're going to know what they say."

"*Sí*, we need to get the old one up here to decipher. Perhaps this will give him peace."

Back at the village, Uncle Jake rigged an ingenious Z-shaped hoisting mechanism with two small pulleys. He said it was standard mountain rescue stuff, but the rest of us were impressed.

Estrella worried the hoist would be too demanding for the frail chief, but, to our surprise, he loved the ride, waving his arms and laughing loudly as Jake hauled him up the precipice. It looked like the most fun he'd had in a long time.

As we slowly raised the Q'ero elder up the face of the peak, I felt like I was peering back through time. This must have been how the tribe's ancestors had raised the Incan emperors into the cave. It made me feel closer to the tribe and the mountain somehow, being part of something that hadn't been repeated for a half-millenium.

Once we were all inside, Jake and Putaq carefully led Intuto down the steep passageway. Joel had widened the entryway while Uncle Jake was securing the rope hoist. As we expected, the frail leader knelt reverently before the mummies, uttering a long, barely audible prayer. The *quipas* must have represented an enormous collection of knowledge because the old man was speechless and then tearful when he saw them. But his initial expression faded as he slowly shuffled through the cave amidst the knotted strands.

The old man's eyes were moist with memories that filled the room. He quietly spoke; Estrella haltingly translated. His fingers stroked the strings.

"So much sadness. So much unnecessary sadness. The fate of our people should not have come to this. We were betrayed by our own and doomed by the wealth bestowed upon us. So much could have been different." Intuto ran unsteady fingers down the length of a hanging string. He spoke. Estrella interpreted. "I will share with you what I was told by my father and he by his father and by his father before that. This is the way of the Inca. Our legacy is written in the heart. I am the twenty-third son to pass on the word of the Q'ero. Putaq is the twenty-fifth."

Ruefully, the tribal chief examined a brittle portion of scaffolding. He absentmindedly picked at the delicate wood with the dirty nail of his thumb.

"In his youth, Huayna Capac, Emperor of the Inca, heroically served the people with strength, with courage, and with wisdom. Yet, as he saw the end of his own life with greater clarity, he grew sentimental and weak. As Huayna lay on his deathbed, he summoned his most loyal counselors and generals. With his final command, he destroyed everything his predecessors had built, dismantling the empire's very foundation—its unity."

Though I couldn't understand the *Quechua* language, I could feel his bitterness and sense of betrayal. I felt sorry for him—for all of the Q'ero tribe.

"Huayna declared the empire would be split. The northern provinces would be ruled by Atahualpa, his stepson, who was not of royal Incan blood. The southern provinces would be ruled from Cuzco by Huascar, true son of Huayna, and rightful heir to the throne."

"When was that?" Joel quietly interrupted.

"Shhh." Estrella put a finger to her lips. "1527."

The chief spoke again, and Estrella continued.

"By these words, Huayna brought war and bloodshed to the empire he loved. Atahualpa was ambitious and combative. After five years of political bickering, the two regions went to war, as many had foretold."

Intuto's knees buckled. His grandson caught his frail arm in support.

"The two armies met in a final desperate battle on the plains of Quipaypan, just beyond the gates of Cuzco. Atahualpa's troops were disciplined and battle-tested. Huascar took the field with inexperienced recruits and volunteers—the old, the young and the sick—in a last desperate stand to preserve the Inca. The battle raged from sunrise to sunset." The old man closed weary eyes, which flickered, as if seeing the battle raging before him. "The earth was shrouded by great heaps of the dying and dead. These mounds of dead covered the plain for a hundred years. But Atahualpa's seasoned army won the day."

All the while, Intuto fingered the *quipas*.

"Atahualpa claimed Cuzco and dominion over the empire. But he had not finished his slaughter." The old man wearily rubbed his scalp.

"Atahualpa then invited the royal Incan chiefs, advisors, and generals to meet in Cuzco for a great counsel to determine how to most wisely rule the empire. But, as these nobles arrived, they were butchered. Atahualpa feared heirs to the Incan throne would rebel, so he ordered all the women of royal blood—including his very own aunts, nieces, sisters, and wives—be put to death by torture."

"Jeez, the guy was a real Stalin or something."

Even after all this time, Atahualpa's butchery was sickening.

"The empire was in disarray, the wisest counsel and generals had been murdered, and the lifeblood of the empire, the Incan nobility, was gone. The empire had become an empty shell. It needed time to heal. That is when the Spanish landed upon our shores."

Estrella seemed nearly as weary as the elder.

"So much might have been different, perhaps not the empire's eventual fate, but the final journey of the Inca might have lasted for centuries, instead of days."

The old man put a trembling hand on Uncle Jake's arm. Estrella continued her translation of his slow words.

"Who can say what is right? For twenty-three generations, the Q'erohave waited for the doorway between the two worlds to open again. We have hidden from the world, unable to visit our holy shrines for fear of discovery and contamination. We have faithfully clung to the ancient ways. But the doorway to the stars has not appeared. Now we are dying. How is one to know? Would the Inca have changed, even if the white man had never entered the four corners? I do not know."

The chamber fell silent as the old man disappeared in thoughts of the distant past.

Once the frail chief was situated in his sling to descend the face of Suchana, Uncle Jake handed him a drawing. Jake must have sensed this was perhaps our best time to learn some of the carefully guarded information of the Inca. On the paper was an enlarged picture of the snake engraving from the necklace. Upon seeing it, the old man sprung to life.

Jake jumped at his chance.

"Estrella, does he know what it is? Ask him if this has any significance for the Inca."

Estrella translated. The leather-faced chief answered in the affirmative, nodding vigorously like a bobble head doll.

"*Arí, Arí, Arí.*" he laughed. "*Katari.*"

Jake's impatience with all the translating back and forth was beginning to show.

"Well?"

"It's called 'the serpent.'"

Joel and I exchanged a look of "Well, duh." On the ledge next to me, Putaq quietly said, "*katari*, serpent." We smiled.

"Does it mean anything?"

Estrella started to speak, but the tribal elder raised his hand to silence her. From his robe, he withdrew a small, sharp stick and, with effort to steady his trembling hands, meticulously poked five holes through the paper along the outline of the snake.

"*Katari, katari.*" The old man waved the paper under Jake's nose.

"What do you mean? Was the serpent shot? What happened to it?"

Intuto held the paper high, allowing the morning sun to shine through the five small holes in the paper. "*Coyllur, coyllur.*"

"Of course!" Estrella slapped her forehead with her palm. "How could I have been so stupid?"

"Estrella?"

"They're stars, Jake. It's a constellation called the serpent."

"Okay, now ask him about the fish, the jaguar, and the insect."

She frowned at him.

"Where did these come from?" Estrella wasn't happy Jake had been safeguarding information from her.

"Just ask him Estrella…please."

She did.

The old man spoke for more than a minute, gesturing toward the sky. Finally, he paused and looked to Estrella to translate.

"They're all constellations, Jake. The fish, or *challhua*, lies to the northeast. It's not an insect, but a spider, or *uru*, to the southwest. To the northwest is the cat, *misi*, not a jaguar. And your serpent is in the southeastern sky."

When she finished, the old man spoke again for a few moments. As he did, Estrella's eyes grew in amazement, and she let loose a yelp. Her long, black hair was swinging.

"Jake!" Joyous, she grasped both his arms, her dark eyes blazing into his. "This is it! They used the stars for mapping. These constellations are in four different directions, like compass points.

"I don't get it," I asked.

"Depending where you're located, some of the stars are above the horizon. Others are below, out of sight." Obviously, Jake now got it as well.

"From the earth being round?" Joel added.

"Right! It's why the stars down here are different from the ones back home."

"So…" I finally understood.

"So the four constellations are never all visible at the same time," Estrella finished my sentence. "Unless you happen to be standing in one specific point in Peru. And that point is where we'll find the city!"

CHAPTER 23

▼

EMMA
TWIST IN THE RIVER

Uncle Jake pounded away at the keyboard. His eyes were glued to the enormous, high-resolution monitor. Estrella watched from behind. Her hands sat comfortably on my uncle's shoulders; her body casually leaned into his back. Joel and I watched from across the room in wing-backed, polished leather chairs in front of a massive stone fireplace with a hearth so clean I wondered if a fire had ever warmed the chilly room. It was almost five o'clock in the afternoon, but the windows were shuttered, and the heavy curtains were tightly drawn. A bubbling percolator near our stack of dirty lunch dishes filled the room with the aroma of fresh-brewed coffee. We'd been working in this secure room at the plush Canadian Embassy in Lima all afternoon.

After the cave, Putaq and his aging grandfather had guided us back through the Cloud Forest's maze of twisting trails to the hidden entrance of the tribe's secret valley. The old chief amazed us with his slow, steady stamina. Just when it seemed we'd have to stop, he'd draw on some new reserve. I'm not sure Uncle Jake would admit it, but, without Putaq, we would have been hopelessly lost—even with his global positioning handset. We couldn't have guessed our way out of the Manu wilderness. And, by taking Putaq's route, we'd successfully evaded Viedma.

At our final good-bye in the wilderness, Putaq gave me one last *manchana*, right in front of everybody. I thought Joel's head would explode! It gave him endless ammunition for teasing during the two days it took us to return to our trailhead. By the time the six-seater plane shuttled us back to Lima, we'd been gone in the unmapped Peruvian interior six days. It was good to get back to the hotel, to talk to my mom and dad on the phone, and sleep in a real bed again. With Putaq, I had nice dreams.

Speaking of which, Jake's and Estrella's relationship was definitely now more than business. Personally, I thought it was great. I'd really grown to like her.

But our remarkable discoveries were a mixed blessing for Estrella. The mummies we found, even the tribe itself, were a huge archaeological discovery. Yet, to reveal our find to the outside world, the onrush of amateur archaeologists, fortune hunters, and opportunists would permanently doom the fragile remnants of the Q'ero. Estrella was torn.

Back in Lima, Uncle Jake insisted we find a high-speed, absolutely secure communication link. The stakes were too high to be intercepted or overheard. We were racing with Viedma to locate the OS-187. Jake was confident we had the means to find it, but we all sensed Viedma was close by, lurking like a coiled snake in tall grass.

Jake finished printing the data, stood, stretched, and walked stiffly to the fireplace near an oil portrait of the prime minister.

"Okay, troops, let me bring you up to speed. The chief was right. The four constellations are at opposite corners of the compass. Essentially, the Inca used this as a crude method of triangulation. By identifying planets or stars that were just visible on the horizon, you could pinpoint a specific location anywhere in the world—so long as you had four points of reference."

The light finally went on. "That's why they needed the last piece of the necklace so badly." No wonder someone had been willing to kill to get our medallion.

"Exactly, Em. The last amulet is extremely valuable all by itself, but, if it leads to a mine filled with the osmium isotope, it could be theoretically worth billions."

"Why'd the Inca go to so much trouble?"

"Joel, whoever made the necklace for the girl on Huascaran wanted her to be able to find some exact place."

"In this life or the next," Estrella added sadly.

"Unfortunately, that may be true, Ace."

Estrella elaborated. "But the stars will only reveal the location at one specific point in time."

Jake led us to the globe.

"Estella's correct. As the earth rotates, that one specific point will change. The key is to plot the various points along the arc from which the four constellations would have been visible."

"Yeah, but couldn't we have just done this at a planetarium?"

Wow. I had to hand it to my little brother. That sounded like a great idea.

"It's not quite as simple as it sounds, Joel."

With Uncle Jake, nothing was ever quite as simple as he said it was going to be. "Over time, the earth gradually shifts its position, sort of like wobbling on its axis. It's called precession. The points from which the four constellations are visible wouldn't be the same today as they were in the mid-1400s. A planetarium would have to go backwards, re-creating each day's evening sky, one day at a time. Even if it was sped up, that process could take months."

"So that's why we needed the high-speed data line?"

"Exactly," Jake said. "In fact, it's embarrassingly easy with the computer. The key is knowing which stars to track, and, at the moment, we're the only ones with that information."

My mind jumped back to Putaq, but I recovered.

"The young woman was left on Huascaran sometime between 1449 and 1462," Estrella explained.

"Right. So analyzing that entire period gives us a band, or an arc, about six miles wide." Using a thick red marker, Jake slowly drew an arc, bisecting the top third of Peru, on the map we'd taped to the wall. "The necklace pointed to some location along that red line. That's where we'll find the OS-187 mine."

"It will be in the narrow central corridor." Estrella marked on the map, reducing the search area even further.

"It's still a lot of ground to cover, guys. That's where the second portion comes in and the real reason for the high-speed connection. On foot, it would take months, even years, to narrow the search in such rough terrain. Normal aerial reconnaissance would take weeks and weeks, assuming the weather was always clear."

Over the years, I'd come to realize this was Uncle Jake's specialty—applying up-to-date technology to unsolved mysteries and ancient puzzles. And he always seemed to know someone who could give him access to whatever data or systems he needed.

"However," Jake continued, "by using infrared satellite photography, I'm hoping we can find what we're looking for in a matter of hours."

"What exactly are we looking for?"

Joel was right. It's the one thing Jake and Estrella still hadn't explained, if they knew themselves. Were we trying to find a city, a mine, or what?

"Any evidence of man-made structures. Any remnants of the city. That would be the most obvious," Jake said. "But it might be a landmark that looks unnatural or even an area honeycombed with tunnel entrances. The city may be completely overgrown with vegetation. It may not even be visible."

I'm sure Estrella hoped that wasn't the case.

The computer made its doorbell sound, announcing the receipt of an e-mail.

"Here's what we've been waiting for." Uncle Jake hustled back to the monitor. "Close-up satellite images of our target area."

"Cool!" Joel followed close behind. "Are they from a spy satellite?"

"Officially, they're from a U.S. weather satellite. Unofficially speaking, you're probably right. My contact was adamant that no one outside this room could see how much detail the satellites can photograph. I'm told it's pretty amazing, like reading a license plate from 600 miles up."

That wasn't very comforting. "Jeez! That's kind of frightening."

"Well, in this case, it may be a good thing, Em. We'll just have to see."

As we all leaned over his shoulders, Jake opened the large (compressed) image, and the screen filled immediately with wild patterns of vibrant color—red, orange, yellow, green, black, and white.

"I'm sure this looks weird to you guys because the colors depend on how each thing reflects infrared radiation. Water is gray or black, see here? Deciduous foliage is white. Cone-bearing trees appear dark, although clouds appear white."

We stared at the mind-numbing colors for a good twenty minutes while Jake scrolled through countless satellite images. But he abruptly stopped and zoomed in on a light gray river, twisting in a horseshoe-shaped loop. From there, the river widened, forming something like a small lake, before it returned to its narrow, crooked path.

"Interesting." Jake rubbed the stubble on his chin.

"What?" We squinted at it.

"Look at this flooded area of the river. It's probably a quarter-mile across." Jake pointed to the screen. "The river's gray color gets darker and darker toward the center. It's completely black in the middle."

"So?"

The rest of us had no idea what he was getting at. Jake's thinking out loud always drove me crazy. He liked to feed us clues a little bit at a time, rather than just telling us what was on his mind.

"Meaning the flooded area isn't flat. It gets deeper, much deeper toward the center. Based on its coloring, it could be 100 feet deep at the center."

"Zoom in again."

Now I wondered what we'd stumbled upon. We leaned in closer. Magnified three times, the dark concentric rings were even more obvious.

"A large pit in the middle of nowhere. That doesn't follow the natural contour of the land…" Jake began.

"A mine!" Joel blurted.

"Or a quarry." Estrella squeezed Jake's knee. Her eyes were on the screen.

"It's definitely in the right area," Jake added confidently.

"But they couldn't mine underwater."

Was I missing something?

"I doubt it's always been covered by water, Em. See where the river makes that big loopy turn? Something diverted the river. The Inca may have done it purposely, or it might have occurred from some sort of natural disaster."

"Then we've found it!" Joel exclaimed. "A slam dunk!"

"Piece of cake!" I was imitating one of Uncle Jake's expressions.

"Are there no structures anywhere in the area?" Estrella asked hopefully.

"Sorry, Ace. I don't see anything. It's probably overgrown, like you said."

"But it is close by, I know it. I just know it is. The lost city of Parachuti. I'm sure we'll find it! Excellent!" Estrella was beaming with confidence. Her eyes were dancing across the satellite image.

Estrella, Joel, and I were ecstatic! Considering everything we'd been through the last ten days, both here and in Vancouver, and how much of the mystery we'd single-handedly unraveled, I was swelling with pride. Uncle Jake was surprisingly subdued. He just kept staring at those darker and darker shades of gray in the lake, and he kept on rubbing his chin. Estrella practically pranced to our large wall map and, with a big smile, circled our target area.

"The river doesn't even appear on this. Without the aerial photos, you'd never know it was there. We can reach it in two days." She closely studied the map. "And somewhere nearby lies the seventh city."

"Yes," Uncle Jake absentmindedly replied. He glanced at his watch and then quickly picked up the desk phone.

"Who you calling?"

I assumed Ottawa. To report our fabulous success.

"My contingency plan, Em. It's just a hunch. I'll just be a second."

Jake gave the operator a Canadian number and waited for the connection.

We were interrupted by a knock muffled by the heavy door. Jake motioned Joel to check it out.

"Awesome! Chocolate chip cookies!"

The ambassador's personal chef efficiently wheeled a tray into the room, delivering a chilled carafe of ice-cold milk and a large platter of warm, fresh-baked cookies.

"For the children, with my compliments."

He bowed his head. I could definitely get used to this kind of treatment. The chef was about Jake's age and wore a spotless, pressed-white shirt and a small, dirty apron. A *la toque* chef's hat added dash to his balding head.

Joel helped himself to a handful of cookies. "Excellent! Thanks!"

I guessed one cookie wouldn't hurt. "*Muchas gracias.*"

The chef gracefully gestured toward the leftover lunch dishes as he unloaded the desert onto the end table. "May I take these?"

"*Sí,*" Estrella answered.

The chef bowed politely and quietly stacked the plates onto the cart.

"Steve?…Jake Morgan…No, I'm in Peru. It's a long story. Hey, I need a favor." Jake glanced in the direction of the chef and lowered his voice so even I could barely hear. "I need the *Moulton Equation.*"

A moment later, Jake was scribbling frantically, intent on the receiver wedged against his ear. He was up to something, but I didn't know what.

The chef's eyes fell on the map marked with the location of the underwater quarry, and he paused. Jake noticed.

"Thanks, Steve. I'll explain later." He placed the phone back on its cradle and quickly moved in front of the map.

Without blinking, the chef said, "May I bring Señor Morgan anything else?"

"The coffee over there will be fine," Jake said. "And the kids appreciate the cookies. Thank you."

"*Sí.* Very good, señor." He finished loading the plates, left, and silently closed the door behind him. Jake was quiet.

Having packed up all our notes, charts and maps, we walked with enthusiasm down the embassy's marble stairway. It had been a long day, and we should have been tired, but our discovery had given us a jolt of energy. In just a few days, we would locate the OS-187 mine and, hopefully, the lost city. I wondered if we might appear in any newspapers back home. Heck, maybe in papers all over the world! After all, we were going to be heroes—international heroes! The thought of it made me grin so wide that my cheeks ached.

As we filed out the main entrance, the gracious chef warmly smiled and made polite little bows to each one of us from behind the reception desk. I wondered what he was doing there as we passed through the doorway. I glanced back over my shoulder to see his smile disappear as he snatched the phone to call someone.

CHAPTER 24

▼

JAKE
QUARRY

Emma, Joel, and Estrella were only a few steps behind when I first crested the long ridge and saw it—the unmistakable river and lake from the satellite photos. A day-and-a-half after leaving Lima, we'd found it! Our search was over!

"We did it! It's the quarry!" Joel lost his teen cool. "We found the mine!"

Estrella sounded more surprised than excited and whispered reverently, "We really did."

But Emma's response didn't match her brother's. "It's different."

"Duh, Em. It's not going to look like the pictures with all those weird colors."

Emma softly spoke under her breath. "It's changed."

At the end of our search, we realized how tired we were and stopped to stretch out and relax atop the mile-long amphitheater, basking in the sun and our accomplishment. Six hundred feet beneath us, the green-brown waters made a long, lazy, horseshoe-shaped turn around the hillside. A cool breeze rippled the water. The sun sparkled on the surface. Downstream, the channel bulged, creating the small lake that had guarded the Incan secret for generations. The plateau beyond the river was thick with high jungle vegetation.

Joel perched himself on a high boulder. "Awesome view, Jake!"

"The Indians call this river *Upallagu churi*, the quiet son. I don't know why," Estrella said.

I stretched my legs out next to Estrella's long brown ones.

"I agree with Joel. After all we've been through, nothing has ever looked so good." I pointed downstream. "We'll make camp down there, at that clearing near the lake. I bet we can reach it in an hour."

Estrella took a long drink of water. "Can we rest up here a bit longer?"

"I guess there's no rush."

Emma sat apart from us, quietly sifting bits of crushed rock and dirt through her fingers.

"Em, you still with us? Looking for gold?"

"What? Oh, yes. No…I'm sorry. I'm just running out of energy."

Estrella leaned against me. Her shirt was warm from the sun. It was the most relaxed I'd ever seen her. "This will help the people of Peru more than you can imagine." She scanned the expanse below.

"One step at a time, Ace. We've still got a few unanswered questions." I was thinking of one in particular I'd never shared.

"I suppose you're right." Estrella sat up. "It's strange. I should be overjoyed, but the city still haunts me. The OS-187 is more important, I know. But I wanted the Jewel so badly." She tossed a pebble down the hillside. "Do you know how many years I've scraped and sacrificed? I gave up so much for it. I wanted to show all those arrogant professors. I wanted to prove I'd been right all these years."

"But you have." I grabbed her hand and swept our arms toward the hill's long embankment. "It's here, Ace, somewhere along this ridge."

"But there is nothing…"

Suddenly her eyes sparked with discovery. Elated, she grasped my arms. "*Dios Mí!* Jake, a mudslide! *Huayco!* Of course!"

"Bingo! That's why no one's been able to find it, not even you, Ace. Forget the overgrown bushes and vine theory. It's buried beneath a million tons of dirt and rock."

"*Mi precoso*, Jake. This would answer so many torturing questions." She stopped abruptly and pushed me away. "How long have you known?"

"It may be a while before we're absolutely positive...a long while. But this would explain why the city avoided detection for so long. And a mudslide could have changed the river's course to flood the pit."

"It is so sad," Estrella reflected. "Like Huaras and Caras."

"Can you guys let Em and me in on the secret?" Joel asked.

"Huaras and Caras were two towns destroyed by a great mudslide." Estrella said solemnly.

I picked up the storytelling. "Back in 1970, an area near Huascaran was the epicenter of a 7.5 earthquake. It created a massive mudslide. They estimate something like 100 million tons of mud, snow, and rock tore through a narrow valley. Huaras and Caras were in its path."

I hoped the kids realized this wasn't one of my tall tales. Prior to our fateful climb on Huascaran Norte, Jorge had taken us to the memorial commemorating the disaster. It had been a somber beginning to our climb.

"Twenty thousand people died," Estrella added. "I was only a baby then, but my parents spoke of it for years."

"The same thing happened here?" Emma asked in a weary monotone.

"It would have been before the Spanish ever arrived." Estrella looked out over the landscape. "It's such a huge area, Jake. It will take months and months to locate."

"Probably, but a lot less than six years."

"Yes." Estrella smiled.

"You smell anything yet, Jake?" Joel asked. "You know, the OS-187."

Estrella sniffed the air with a puzzled look.

"Whenever Uncle Jake is close to treasure, he says he can smell it," Joel explained.

"Fascinating." Estrella's eyes danced, challenging me. "And can you? Smell the treasure?"

"Almost guys. Almost."

I awoke to the sound of my tent door zipping open. Estrella poked her head inside. It was still dark out, but she was fully dressed.

"Jake! Wake up!" Her voice was urgent. "It's Emma. She's gone!"

Still groggy, I sat up in my sleeping bag. "What? When?"

"I heard her get up about an hour ago."

"An hour!" I checked the luminous dial of my watch. "It's only two-thirty."

"I thought she was going to the bathroom, but she never came back."

Joel muttered from his bag. "What's going on?"

"Emma's missing," Estrella explained.

"Okay, let's not panic." I pulled on my shirt and looked for my flashlight. "She's smart enough to stay put if she got lost. She's probably close by." I fumbled with my pants. "Joel, you'd better get dressed, too. Bring your light. We'll wait outside."

Joel emerged, squinting in the darkness. Clouds obscured much of the moon.

I called through cupped hands. *"Emma! E–m–m–a!"* My voice echoed off the rock ridge running the length of the valley. No answer. Damn.

"She probably got disoriented in the dark."

"Did she take her prosthetic?" Joel asked anxiously.

"I don't know."

I looked to Estrella.

"No, it's still there where she took it off."

"She never goes anywhere without it, Jake. I mean, never! She's totally paranoid about it."

"She may be sleepwalking."

"Sleepwalking?"

The idea surprised Estrella.

"She did it at my apartment. It's the only time I've seen her without the prosthetic arm."

Now I was worried. My biggest fear was the river. Missing persons—especially sleepwalking missing persons—and water were a bad combination. There were too many newspaper stories about missing persons, particularly kids, disappearing near a river or lake and being dragged ashore by divers days later.

Joel and Estrella looked desperate. I had to keep my head—think rationally and logically—if we were going to find her.

"Okay." I squatted on the ground, drawing our game plan in the dirt so there'd be no confusion where we each would search. "Joel, you follow the river upstream, but stay close to the water. I don't want you getting lost, too."

"Got it." Ever the good soldier, Joel sounded responsible and mature.

"Estrella, check the lake's perimeter. When you're done, work your way downstream for a half-mile or so. Do you remember what she was wearing?"

"A white T-shirt. I guess she'd have on her jeans."

"Good. That'll be easy to spot."

If she'd been in black, we could abandon any hope of finding her at night. "I'll head south on the trail and then make a big loop back here. Everybody understand?"

"Jake?" Estrella interrupted. "Is the amulet gone?"

"The amulet?" That was the least of my concerns.

"The necklace." Estrella was insistent. "Do you still have it?"

"Yes. I've been wearing it under my..." I felt my chest where the medallion should have been. "Christ! It's gone! How the heck..."

Estrella seized my arm. "She has it, Jake. That's why she's gone."

"Isn't that why she got so cold before?" Joel volunteered.

"Hypothermic," I corrected. "And she's already been gone an hour."

"You don't understand, either of you," Estrella snapped at us. "We're wasting our time searching the river and the trail. Something happened here connected to that pendant…connected to the mummy. That's what's been pulling Emma."

"The mudslide?"

"Yes, Joel. The mudslide. She steals the amulet. She calls for an Incan father. This must have been the mummy's village. This must be where she grew up. Emma won't be near the river, Jake. She'll return to the city or where the city was. She'll be up on the slope somewhere. That's where we'll find her."

I'd never believed in curses, black magic, voodoo, powers of the dead, or any of that junk driving Estrella's theory. But time was running out. Emma had somehow managed to find the amulet once before. And I had no explanation for her subsequent brush with hypothermia—at least no explanation I wanted to believe. I thought of her sleepwalking in my apartment, staring at the wall safe. Too many coincidences. Too many to ignore.

Estrella and Joel looked expectant. Emma's life hung in the balance. I had to roll the dice.

"Okay. We'll take the ridge."

Estrella breathed a sigh of relief. I'd worry about nursing my shattered ego later. We started out toward the long, sloping slide area.

"We need to fan out. Joel, you take the lowest level of the slope. Ace, you take the middle, say, about 200 yards above Joel. I'll go up top, just below the headwall. Stay in a line, keep your lights on, and yell if you see anything. Ace, if you start any rock fall, holler down to Joel. I'll do the same."

For forty minutes, we maintained our slow, steady sweep of the broad amphitheater. Far below in the darkness, I could only see the yellow spot of Estrella's light and, further down, Joel's light. I heard Emma before I saw her—a girl sobbing with grief. In the faint light, I couldn't tell where the noise was coming from.

Estrella called out, "I see her, Jake! It's her!"

Halfway between Estrella and me, a white T-shirt reflected in the thin moonlight that slipped through the clouds. Emma knelt on the slope, weeping and impotently clawing at the ground.

"*Mamay, taita, riccharina*! *Callpana*!"

I reached her first. Poor little Emma. She was doubled up. Tears were streaming down her dirt-smudged face. Her fingers were raw from pawing the rocky ground.

"*Imarayku chikiray Munray?*" She sobbed through clenched, chattering teeth.

I put my arms around her just as Estrella reached us. "Emma, it's Uncle Jake. You're okay, Emma. You're going to be okay." She was freezing; worse than before.

"Jake, the pendant!"

The amulet dangled from Emma's neck. I had it off in a flash. Joel bounded up the slope, out of breath. Emma's sobs turned to shallow, quiet whimpers. She spoke softly with great effort.

"*Kacharpari taita, kacharpari mamay. Munchay quam kukupacha. Musqoy winaypaq.*"

Joel looked grave. "Jeez, is she okay?"

"She offered blessings to her mother and father for their journey into the spirit world," Estrella quietly translated. "She had been trying to warn them."

"She's not physically hurt, Joel. But she's cold and exhausted. I think she'll be fine." I sounded as optimistic as possible.

Without being asked, Joel removed his heavy jacket and placed it over his older sister's shoulders. I helped Emma to her feet. She was in no condition to walk.

I gently shook her. "Emma, are you awake?"

"Yes," she answered without opening her eyes. "I'm so tired. I just need a little sleep. Just a little sleep."

I carefully lifted her in my arms, where she collapsed. She was utterly spent. Then the four of us picked our way down the dark hillside back to camp, a journey made easier by the fact that Estrella had casually slipped a finger through one of my belt loops. I smiled at her.

"You'll have to thank Emma in the morning, Ace."

"What do you mean?"

"She just pinpointed your city."

CHAPTER 25

▼

JAKE
KEEPERS OF THE TEMPLE

For an hour, I shoveled the brick-hard dirt until I struck the top of a large stone, three feet beneath the surface. Joel whooped. Excited, we all wiped away the remaining soil to reveal what I suspected was the uppermost ceiling stone of a temple or fortress.

After a good night's sleep, Emma awoke rested and relaxed. She didn't remember a thing. She compared it to the feeling right after finals, a great relief that a large burden was now off her shoulders. Whatever power the medallion held over her seemed to be broken. She was the same sarcastic, smart-ass Em that we all knew. It was good to have her back.

The stone was the size of a coffin. We removed a thick layer of rotten fibrous material—originally a layer of sticks and small logs—and immediately understood their purpose. This huge stone had been shifted sideways, creating a space large enough to squeeze through. That explained the scrapes and chip marks on its side. Someone had somehow levered the block from its original resting place.

I dropped a pebble into the blackness. It hit bottom in a few seconds. "About thirty feet deep," I estimated. Not bad. I leaned into the narrow opening and shined my headlamp toward the bottom. It was a large cavernous room, visibly murky with the dust we'd churned up. I'd have to go down inside.

I secured my climbing rope to a large boulder ten yards from the opening. I tossed down the line, cinched my headlamp in place, and tightened the leather straps on the small rucksack that held my prussic slings. Contrary to popular folklore, there was no way to climb hand-over-hand up a nine-millimeter nylon line. That was the stuff of Hollywood action films. However, with the prussic slings attached to the rope with a one-way slipknot, I'd be able to work my way back out.

"Be careful, Jake." Estrella gave me a quick kiss and hug. I should have told her there was no real danger, but I enjoyed her worried affection. "I wish I could go with you."

"You'll get your turn."

"Yell if you need help," Joel was serious.

"Relax, guys. I'll be right back. It's not much deeper than my basement."

"You don't have a basement," Emma corrected.

"Well, there you go! I'll be back before you know it. Half hour, max." I wanted to give them a time frame, just in case.

"And if you're not?"

"I will be, Ace. Count on it." I switched on my headlamp and slowly lowered myself through the crevice. The hole was lined with long-dead roots, dangling like stalactites. They were dry and brittle as breadsticks.

The smell was the first thing I noticed. The chamber's stagnant air had an odor reminiscent of my childhood. As a kid, when my family summered on Vancouver Island, I collected insects—grasshoppers, bees, butterflies, and beetles. Once they died, I mounted them with pins in paraffin-filled cigar boxes. After several years, those dried out bugs gave off a nasty, musty smell. This air reeked the same.

As I inched down the line, I thought of how ecstatic Estrella would be when she eventually excavated the buried city. This discovery justified the last six years of her life, paying off for the countless hours of solitary research. She'd uncovered what had been a whispered legend since the time of the Inca. Remarkable. No doubt she'd eventually pinpoint the date when the massive mudslide entombed the city, detoured the river, flooded the nearby pit, and wiped the Seventh Jewel from the face of the earth.

The odor intensified as I approached the bottom of the chamber. My imagination dabbled with the treasures or horrors I might encounter.

On a spring morning in 79 AD, the Roman village of Pompeii was just awakening when nearby Mount Vesuvius erupted. That volcano unleashed what geologists call a pyroclastic flow, a smothering avalanche of searing ash, pumice chunks, hot volcanic gas, and rock. The suffocating mixture hurtled down onto Pompeii at more than seventy miles an hour. Vesuvius instantly embalmed the city's inhabitants. But Estrella's Seventh Jewel would be different.

Rather than the lightweight ash that enveloped Pompeii, a mudslide releases tons of earth, rock, and debris with unimaginable force. All but the strongest structures in its path would have been swept away. The peasants' simple huts and communal cooking or storage areas would have been crushed and destroyed. Only a structure built with these immense stone blocks could withstand the onslaught. In truth, there might be very little for Estrella—or the rest of the world's archaeologists—to exhume.

My headlamp cast dark, shadowy images. I should have changed the batteries. The light was weak and feeble. I grazed monolithic stones as I lowered myself into near darkness. The Inca had never discovered the wheel, so these huge hand-carved blocks were dragged into place by sheer brute force. Wisps of ancient cobwebs still clung to the rough rock surface.

I reached the floor and stumbled on a dark clump of soft fibrous material.

"What did you find?" Estrella called down. Her voice echoed within the chamber. Her head was silhouetted against the tiny opening far above. "We can barely see your light."

I knelt to examine the dry lump at my feet. It was rope—very, very old, rough-hewn manila hemp. Gauging by its thickness, it originally came from a sailing ship.

"Rope."

"What?"

"It's a pile of old rope," I shouted toward the opening. Estrella would conclude the same thing I had. The rope could only mean the monk's diary was true. A small contingent of Pizzaro's force had somehow discovered this subterranean citadel. It also meant the conquistador's murdered comrades might be here.

In the faint illumination of my dying headlamp, I vaguely discerned larger shapes scattered sporadically across the length of the fifty-foot chamber. No need to look closer. They were the prostrate bodies of asphyxiated Inca.

The temple was disappointingly bare. No ornamental golden figures. No rich tapestries. No inlaid walls of silver. Based on my research of Incan opulence, I'd expected more.

Seated upon two wooden thrones, along the chamber's furthest wall, were the mummified remains of a man and woman dressed ornately in colorful macaw-feathered capes. They slumped together, as if comforting one other. Long gray hair covered both fragile, elderly figures. The fingers on their emaciated hands were still entwined, resting on the armrests between the thrones. Facing certain death, this couple had calmly, bravely remained united to the end—preparing for one last, final journey together. Here was the Incan courage of which Estrella spoke. In the face of a dark, suffocating terror, these two displayed dignity and grace.

I reflected on my own solo existence. These two Inca shared an enduring bond, apparent even now, countless years after they perished. Was this a treasure I'd never find?

In deference to these ancient soul mates, I retrieved the woman's white and blue headdress that lay on the temple's floor and gently replaced it on her peaceful brow.

As I stepped away, the room seemed to reel beneath my feet. I staggered. The simple task of reaching down now gave me severe vertigo. I steadied myself, and the room stopped spinning. But I still felt woozy and off balance. Lack of sleep? Altitude? Illness? I'd never experienced this kind of dizziness. That's when things deteriorated.

I remember hearing a muffled, roaring sound, like thunder through thick cotton. It grew louder and louder, but I couldn't identify the noise. It continued for a while and then abruptly stopped. Again the chamber was silent. Then, from my peripheral vision, I thought I saw one of the lifeless figures move. I jumped away, gaping at it. It remained motionless. Come on, Jake. Get a grip buddy. Was I losing it? It was harder and harder to focus, and the floor was still unsteady.

How long had I been down here? I looked at my watch. The hands and numbers blurred. I brought it closer, squinting at the luminescent face. Only fifteen minutes! That's all? It seemed like hours. Drips of sweat rolled from my brow onto the crystal. I looked at my shirt. I was covered with perspiration. What was happening?

Air exchange! Or lack of it, rather. My brain finally kicked in gear. These prostrate figures had sucked the oxygen from the sealed chamber ages ago. Why had I thought there would be oxygen in here now? I was breathing carbon dioxide. Dizzy, sweating, hallucinating, ears ringing. I was giving myself carbon dioxide poisoning. I had to get out!

Turning to leave, my dying light revealed a shallow alcove. I froze and then advanced clumsily. I had to be sure.

I stared at the compartment's contents a long moment, struggling to ignite my lethargic brain. There was no mistake. It was as I'd suspected. My second hunch was right! But I had only a few precious moments to escape before succumbing to the poisoned air.

From thirty feet below the ceiling's blurry opening, I saw no sign of Estrella, Emma, or Joel. My weakened calls went unanswered. Where were they? Why would they abandon me? Okay, Morgan, I'll just have to get out on my own.

Through a haze, I remember my thick, unresponsive fingers fumbling to attach the slings to the rope. I had to hold the ropes inches from my face to see well enough through the dizzying fog to tie and dress the knots. Clumsy as a drunk, I worked my boots into the slings, and began my shaky climb. Weight on my left foot first, I slid the right sling further up the rope and then stepped up with my right leg, shifting all my weight to that foot. Then I slid the left sling further up. Left then right...right then left. I gradually worked my way up the line. As I neared the opening, the air became cooler, and the musty smell grew weaker. With a final effort, I slivered through the thin gap, hoisting myself completely free of the corpse-filled temple. I'd made it! I was out!

But where was Estrella? And the kids? I had a bad feeling. I cautiously raised my head and peered down the hillside from beyond the ditch. There was my answer several hundred feet below. Two helicopters—so much for the roaring sound. Emma, Estrella, and Joel were held by three hard-looking military types. Even from my vantage point, it was clear their captors were no peasants—like last time—or farmers. They wore camouflaged jungle fatigues and high, lace-up boots. They looked disciplined, trained, and well-armed. Each carried a deadly looking semiautomatic rifle. Strutting amongst them, waving his arms wildly at the children, was Señor Eduardo Viedma. This time, he'd come well-prepared.

Okay, Morgan. Now what? My small caliber pistol was back at camp. How fast could I circle back to retrieve it? And what then? Lure a few of them into the poisoned atmosphere of the chamber? Or maybe sabotage the choppers? My frantic mind churned for a feasible rescue.

Then, directly behind me, I heard an unmistakable metallic click…click.

CHAPTER 26

▼

EMMA
PAYBACK

I figured, so long as Uncle Jake was free, we had a fighting chance. He'd think of a way out of this.

So, when I saw him between the two armed men staggering down the slope with his hands on his head like a prisoner of war, my heart sank. Joel slumped, too. Viedma was no longer just a crude joke. There was too much money at stake here to have us as witnesses to his thievery. Things looked pretty bad, but I was determined to act as brave as possible.

When we'd first seen the two helicopters, we left the buried temple's opening to greet them. The copters were emblazoned in white and red with *La Republic*, Lima's biggest newspaper. Reporters! But when we were close enough to realize the trick, it was too late.

Viedma greeted Uncle Jake with slimy false civility. "Señor Morgan, I am glad to see you again. I believe I owe you something from our last meeting."

His jaw clenched, and he angrily lashed out at my uncle, striking him hard across the mouth. I don't know what Viedma expected, but he was surprised when Uncle Jake hardly flinched. He instead stared back with a look that said, 'Is that the best you can do?'

"Okay, Eduardo, we're even." A thin trickle of blood ran down Jake's lower lip. "You now have the entire quarry of OS-187. Congratulations. You're going to be incredibly rich. Incredibly rich. Now keep me here as a hostage, and let the others go. Your secret is safe."

"I will stay, too," Estrella chimed in. "Let the children go."

"Very heroic, but I already know none of you will talk," Viedma said ominously. "And, this time, history will not intercede on your behalf. These men will not be swayed by local superstitions."

"Superstition? This area and the metal are shrines. They belong to the Indians, to the people, descendants of the Inca. Can't you see how much this would mean to them?" Estrella didn't plead for herself—or for us—but for the impoverished and the destitute.

Viedma's thin lip slid into a menacing sneer. "I have not descended from the same filth as you. My roots lie in Sevilla, Spain. My blood is pure. And, just like your beloved Inca, Professor Maroto, you shall die pathetically."

"If I have to die, it will be with honor. *Puta!*"

Viedma's face reddened. His jaw muscles tightened. The veins at his temples bulged; his fists were clenched white. He forced a thin smile and then spit—full force on Estrella! I couldn't believe it! If he wasn't such a creep, I would have laughed.

Estrella lunged at Viedma. Her hands were outstretched claws.

Jake's fist smashed the chin of his closest captor, snapping back his head. The guard crumpled to the ground.

Meanwhile, Estrella raked Viedma's face with deep crimson scratches before another mercenary restrained her, twisting her arms painfully behind her back.

Jake knocked another man to the ground and charged. Without any hesitation, Viedma held his gun up to my head!

"You'll watch her die!" he warned Jake.

The gun barrel was ice-cold against my skin. My legs trembled. I thought my insides were going to dump on the ground or I might throw up.

Jake stopped short. Two men were on him immediately, each tightly pinning one of Jake's arms. Viedma withdrew the gun, and my insides uncurled.

With those spidery fingers, Viedma fetched a linen handkerchief and meticulously wiped the blood from his face. That done, he conducted an efficient search of Uncle Jake, found the amulet, and promptly removed it.

"How predictable, Señor Morgan. You have lost."

"For now." Jake stared unflinching, into Viedma's rodent-like eyes.

"No, you are in error. For always."

Viedma raised the priceless medallion above his head, admiring the artifact as he would a huge gemstone. He was mesmerized. Probably calculating his newfound wealth, the creep.

The sun crested the ridge, flooding the valley with the brilliant warmth of morning. Then something really freaky happened. It happened when the sun struck the amulet.

The medallion reflected the sunlight in a blinding burst of silver-green luminescence. A hundred rays of light burst from the amulet like a Canadian Day skyrocket. It only lasted an instant, but I sensed something important had just occurred.

On the sheer ridge overhead, I could hear an irregular clattering sound, like something falling. And sure enough, a basketball-sized rock plummeted off the cliff, bounced dangerously close to us, and crashed with a loud bang into one of the helicopter's tail sections.

"Damn!" Viedma cursed at the collision.

Then, a second, smaller stone rocketed down the ridge, bounced unpredictably, and caught one of Viedma's men in the shoulder. He fell to the ground.

Jake stared at the ridge. His voice was quiet. "Déjá vu."

The sun's position made it impossible to see the ridge clearly. I thought I saw silhouettes of moving figures. Had someone, or something, intentionally thrown the rocks at us? I couldn't be sure. Viedma saw them, too. He fired his gun toward the ridge top, urging his men to do the same. In an ear-shattering volley of bullets, they sprayed the cliff to exact revenge on whoever—or whatever—might have dislodged the interfering rocks.

On Viedma's command, the men stopped firing. Silence. Even the faint breeze had abandoned us. It was too quiet. Dead quiet. It gave me the willies. Was this the calm before the storm?

Suddenly, a dozen rocks came crashing down around us. Luckily, we still had enough warning to avoid the projectiles as they flew past.

Joel grinned like he was playing dodgeball, clueless to the danger. The helicopters, stationary, didn't fare as well. The rocks smashed into them, though still inflicting only minor damage.

"Get the choppers out of here!" Viedma shouted.

Two pilots raced to the copters and jumped in. The great diesel engines coughed and sputtered to life while the long, sagging blades began to rotate in slow, giant circles.

Then I saw them again. Black, shadowy figures scurrying 400 feet above us on the ridge. I looked away. I'd go blind if I kept staring directly into the sun.

The constant banging sound of small rocks peppering the helicopters increased. Ten, twenty, thirty, forty. Rocks fell faster from the crest's entire expanse along the quarter-mile face. With irregular shapes, they bounced wildly and unpredictably. Estrella was struck in the thigh and knocked to the ground. Jake rushed to her and helped her back to her feet. All our eyes darted in defense. The rocks continued their banging sound as they ricocheted off the still-grounded helicopters.

Viedma stood, crazed. In one hand, he clutched his snub nose .38. In the other, he had the medallion.

By now, rocks were falling everywhere. The armed soldiers lost their imposing fierceness and looked more worried about saving their own skins than with Viedma's schemes. Nervously, they glanced back and forth between Viedma and the crumbling ridge.

A fist-sized rock struck Viedma in the neck, knocking him down on all fours. He inadvertently dropped the pendant, and it skittered to Estrella's feet. Everything after that seemed to happen in slow motion.

Estrella snatched the medallion, oblivious to the rocks falling all around her. Viedma waved his gun at her, screaming for her to throw him the amulet.

One of the three remaining guards abruptly bolted for the helicopters. Both choppers were close to being airborne to make an escape.

Estrella took a final look at the medallion and then flung it high overhead, past Viedma and directly into the path of the heaviest rock fall. His greedy eyes never left the amulet as it arced above his head and then disappeared into the scree-covered slope.

"Run!" Jake shouted. Man, had we been waiting to hear that! Joel was off like a frightened cat.

Viedma maniacally scrambled toward the necklace, madly clawing at the moraine in search of his prize. His two remaining mercenaries seized their chance to flee and sprinted at a dead run toward the helicopters.

Estrella sprinted toward the edge of the wide bowl.

Jake appeared from nowhere. "Em! Come on!" In one quick motion, he hoisted me over his shoulder and took off, shouting for Joel and Estrella to head for a concave stone wall on the boundary of the slide area.

Viedma hobbled toward the one remaining helicopter. The medallion's cord dangled from his bloody fist. In his panicked search he'd clawed off his nails. Gross! Viedma scrambled into the helicopter just as it lifted off. A large, cartwheeling boulder just missed them. Lucky rats!

Jake raced as well as he could toward the sheltered area. My stomach banged painfully against his shoulder with every jarring step. Miraculously, all four of us reached the outcropping safely and huddled in the small enclosure while a barrage of rocks crashed and rained nonstop around us.

"Can't we get further away?"

I didn't understand why Jake made us stay here, rather than making a run for it.

"If that ridge collapses, Em, these rocks are the least of our problem."

The two helicopters suddenly reappeared, hovering twenty feet above the ground like immense dragonflies hunting for prey. Us. Through the Plexiglas windshield, I could see Viedma, grinning from ear to ear. He was a jubilant jack-o-lantern. One of his accomplices leaned out the window and positioned a handheld machine gun. We were his targets. We were pinned from behind by the cascading rocks and trapped by Viedma from the front. Great. We could use a Hollywood escape just about now.

Then, as if on cue, the helicopters' occupants all snapped upright and gaped with terror at the ridge.

Next, we heard what they'd seen. A roaring, thunderous boom so deafening that the sound of the spinning rotors disappeared. I thought my eardrums might rupture. It was like being inside a cannon. The pilots maneuvered desperately to escape, but there wasn't time. Both helicopters hurled violently backwards, as if jerked on a cable. They crashed 100 yards downhill and erupted into giant balls of flame. With their volatile engine fuel, the downed machines were immediately engulfed in an inferno. No one escaped.

The solid rock we huddled behind shook and shuddered. For several minutes, it sounded as if the whole world was collapsing around us. Eventually, the roaring subsided, except for an occasional clattering of individual rocks. We emerged with caution from our rock cocoon.

Incredible! The entire ridge had separated from the mountain and collapsed in a gigantic avalanche. The sprawling hillside, the entire quarter-mile, was now twenty feet higher from the rock debris. The uppermost portion of the ridge was completely gone. Vanished.

A huge dust cloud enveloped the avalanche area. The four of us stared at the wreckage in wondrous disbelief. Gradually, the breeze began ushering the dust away. Further downhill, one of the helicopters still burned furiously. All that remained of the other was a crumpled, rotor section sticking pathetically from the rubble.

"Jeez," Joel whispered, interrupting our stunned silence. He had a cut over his left eye and would have appreciated the grimy gore of his face.

"The wrath of God," Estrella said quietly. "The wrath of God."

"Shouldn't we try to do something? I mean, see if there's any survivors."

It seemed uncivilized to leave them.

"Nobody could have survived that, Em. Even if we could move the rocks, there'd be no point. Sorry it has to end this way, kids. Really. I'm sorry."

"Uncle Jake?" Joel asked. "What happened to the helicopters?"

"Air, Joel. That's what did it. Big avalanches unleash air blasts that level everything in their path. Once that hit them, they were like leaves in a tornado."

One moment, the helicopters were hovering above us like killer bees; the next moment, they were barbecued wreckage. I thought it justifiably ironic. Viedma and his men took to the air to escape, and, in the end, it was absolutely the worst thing they could have done.

"What about the necklace?" I asked.

"It's over, Em. At least our part of it. There's nothing more for us here. Not now. Our work is done."

I was stunned. And exhausted. Talk about a grand finale.

"But we can't just leave it," Joel pleaded. "It's worth millions! It's inside one of the helicopters."

"The government of Peru wants it back. They can dig it out a lot easier than we can. We'll let them know where it is, Joel. I'm sorry, but we need to walk away from this one."

"But, Jake, the temple? What did you find inside the temple?" Estrella's eyes and voice were filled with hopeful optimism.

"Corpses. Suffocated Inca," Jake replied somberly and gave Estrella a sympathy hug. "Little of any material value, Ace. I've got a story for you, but it'll have to wait for later."

Of course, our group was divided about what triggered the mountain's collapse. And we debated the topic most of the way back to Lima.

Joel, freshly fueled with fifth-grade geology, was convinced an earthquake centered deep underground was the culprit.

"Earthquakes always cause rock slides and stuff in the mountains."

"But, Joel," I pointed out to him, "none of us felt anything. Not the slightest vibration. Nothing."

"Well, duh! How are we supposed to feel anything with a bunch of guns staring us in the face? We just weren't paying attention."

Jake was more analytical.

"This whole area's unstable. Look at the composition of the rock. It's rotten with cracks and fissures. That's why you never see rock climbers on this kind of stuff. It breaks up too easily. When they all started shooting toward the cliffs, the noise started a chain reaction. The internal pressure had probably been building for years. Cause and effect."

He was satisfied.

My brain told me one of those rational theories must be correct. But a little voice inside—to paraphrase Estrella—said, "typical male attitude."

"So, Jake," I questioned, "why did they shoot at the cliff?"

"Why?"

"Yes, why?"

"Well, they thought they saw…umm…well…I don't know…maybe they were just pissed."

Jake did a pitiful job of dodging my question, while Estrella clearly enjoyed my successful cross-examination.

"The defense rests," she smiled.

I still believed that someone—or something—was moving on the ridge when the first rocks began to fall. In a way, even if Jake was technically correct, it was those mysterious figures that indirectly started the avalanche by causing Viedma's men to shoot.

I suppose Viedma got what he deserved, though I'm not the revenge sort. We all knew that, if the avalanche hadn't happened when it did, none of us would still be alive.

I like to think that, if there was some mysterious presence atop the ridge that morning guiding the rocks, they weren't just aiming at Eduardo Viedma, but, in a sense, at all the men like Viedma who'd exploited Peru and its people over the centuries. Perhaps there is some justice in the world—or at least in this one small corner of it.

Obviously, the lost city's secrets would lie buried a little while longer. Estrella said it would take several years for an archaeological team to meticulously unearth whatever remained. But we couldn't call it lost any longer. Estrella had found her long-sought *K'anchis Llajpa*—her Seventh Jewel.

But Jake reminded Joel and me why we'd come. To solve the mystery of the OS-187. Not to participate in archaeological digs. Not to help drain the flooded quarry. Not to view initial excavations. Our job had been to find where the necklace had originated. Mission accomplished. And so, it was time to return home.

But there was still one unanswered question Uncle Jake hadn't shared with us.

CHAPTER 27

▼

EMMA
LAST MYSTERY

I couldn't believe it had only been two weeks since we'd first touched down at Lima International Airport. Now we were going home to British Columbia, way past the date Jake promised my mom and dad. Ugh! I didn't even want to think how far behind I was going to be in school. But Joel and I were both getting homesick for family and friends. We were ready to go, though I doubt anyone would believe everything we'd experienced. I was going to sound like some sort of mini-Jake. Telling stories too big to believe. Hmm. Maybe that wasn't such a bad thing.

Jake had been withdrawn during our final day. He refused to contact Ottawa about the mine or even the Peruvian government. And he didn't say a word about Viedma. He also insisted Estrella wait until we were well out of the country before speaking with the press. Because Uncle Jake had never been publicity shy, it made me wonder.

We sat in a small café at the Lima Airport, just outside security clearance. It was a calm oasis within the hectic, bustling terminal. Our baggage was checked all the way through to Vancouver, although in six hours we'd change planes first in Miami.

Estrella was more relaxed than I'd ever seen her. She wore a white short-sleeved blouse, faded blue jeans, and sandals. Her dark hair hung to her waist in a loose ponytail. Jake wore jeans, red T-shirt, and worn-out running shoes and had reminded Joel and me to wear something comfortable for the long flight, too.

He drained the last of his beer and then leaned back slowly with great solemnity. "Now that we're about to leave, this is as good a time as any to break the bad news. There's no mineral deposit of OS-187."

"What do you mean?" Estrella blurted.

"We found the mine!" Joel exclaimed.

Jake's bombshell had our undivided attention.

"Ever since the government briefing, I've been bumping up against a basic problem. The osmium derivative simply couldn't be manufactured by the Inca. Yet it also seemed far-fetched there would be a huge mineral supply of it because its creation requires such radical conditions."

"Which means what?" I asked. "Those are the only two possibilities, aren't they?"

"Exactly. But, if your two options are impossible, then it's time to look for a third."

"A third? Okay, Uncle Jake, just tell us!"

It drove me crazy when he purposely prolonged his explanations. Jake loved playing the part of a master detective, watching us squirm while he gradually revealed his discoveries.

"When I saw the infrared satellite photos, it got me thinking. The shape of the flooded area reminded me of something I'd seen in Arizona—steep sides, a flat bottom, and a raised lip around the perimeter."

"Aren't there old mines in Arizona?"

"It's not a mine, Joel."

"Or a quarry?" I didn't say it with much conviction. I had no idea where Jake was going with this.

"Nope, not a quarry, Em."

Estrella reached out and grabbed Jake's ear, giving it a hard twist. "*Jake!*"

He winced before she let go.

"Okay," he said rubbing his ear. "It's a crater."

"A crater?"

"A crater. Probably from a meteor that smashed into the area eons ago. Let me explain." Jake cleared the glasses from the center of the table. "Quite a few meteors are loaded with iridium and other platinum-based elements, which are the foundation of OS-187. The intense heat and extreme pressure caused by entering earth's atmosphere are the same forces needed to create OS-187."

"Cool! You mean somewhere there's a huge OS-187 meteor in the river!" Why hadn't Jake figured this out? He'd been on lots of underwater salvage projects.

"I wish that was the case, guys. But, when large meteors collide with earth, they're going about 40,000 miles per hour. Ninety-nine point nine percent of big, high-speed meteors are vaporized on impact."

"But the necklace…" Joel protested.

"I said 99.9 percent, not 100 percent. We're left with the key question: How big was the original meteor, and how much OS-187 survived impact?"

Jake's question hung in the air. He was getting into stuff that was way over my head. Estrella and Joel had blank expressions, too. Jake answered his rhetorical question.

"There's a formula called the *Moulton Equation*…"

"That's what you were copying down!" I remembered it from the embassy. Now it was beginning to make sense.

"Right. It's a mathematical formula. Based on a crater's depth and diameter, you can calculate the size of the meteor."

"So how big was it?" Joel was as hooked as me.

"Probably about ten tons, or 20,000 pounds. And, because of the density of iridium and osmium, probably something the size of a big refrigerator."

"Which would leave…" I began.

"Anywhere between twenty and thirty pounds of OS-187 in small bits scattered across the crater."

We sat in silence as Jake's heartbreaking message sunk in. I had a mental image of everything we'd hoped for—the catalytic converters, help for the impoverished Indians, and even my picture in the newspapers back home—swirling around in a great toilet bowl and then disappearing down the drain.

"That's the bad news," Jake said solemnly. "Here's the good." From his carry-on bag, Jake withdrew a crudely formed silver-green block, the size of a small paperback book, and set it on the table in front of Estrella. "Eighteen-and-a-half pounds of pure OS-187!"

The three of us stared at the ingot, mouths open and eyes bugged.

"Over the years, the Inca must have melted all the tiny fragments they found into this," Jake said, referring to the crude brick. "It must have been sacred. It was hidden in their temple, and no other city or province would have had anything like it."

"*Sí,*" Estrella said. "It would have been very special."

"I figure you could accomplish quite a bit with this."

"Me?" Estrella sounded shocked at the trust Jake was placing in her.

"Yes, for your people."

"Jake, I don't know what to say. I'm speechless. I mean, it must be worth…"

"An enormous amount. I don't even want to say it." Jake gave the restaurant a quick survey.

"But the exhaust emissions? The global warming?"

"There isn't enough of the metal. This is all there is. But, if it was sold and the proceeds were used down here by someone who cared, it could save the Q'ero and the other Incan descendents from extinction. If you choose to, Ace."

How fitting. This small remnant of Incan wealth would now aid the descendants of those who honored it. It seemed to complete a very long circle.

Estrella gingerly lifted the rough-formed lump.

"Do you think I'm too late?" she asked wistfully.

Jake leaned forward. "When I first visited Cuzco, the modern part of the city, my guide told me that, over the centuries, the city has had dozens of terrible earthquakes."

"*Sí*. Many," Estrella agreed.

"He said the earthquakes used to destroy the colonial buildings and now they ravage modern structures. Yet the Incan base structures, which these buildings stand on, always remain unharmed."

Estrella smiled. "You're right. The foundation is strong."

The public address system announced our flight. Fourteen days in Peru and my Spanish was nearly passable.

"Well, the kids and I better get going. There's a pretty long line to get through security."

We got up to leave, the four of us slowly walking to the checkpoint where only ticketed passengers were allowed to proceed. Jake and Estrella looked longingly at each other—those kinds of looks that make everyone else disappear. Finally, she took his hand.

"You won't change your mind?" she asked. "There's so much you could do here."

"How about you? Will you?" Jake asked. "Teach in Canada?"

They both looked down. Was this it? Were they splitting up just like that? Jake and Estrella had come to seem perfect for each other. They didn't agree on everything, of course, but they were both so stubborn that they were just going to say good-bye and that was it? They looked up, smiled, and tightly embraced.

"Hello!" Joel interrupted. "We're in public."

"Shut up, Joel."

My little brother still had a lot to learn.

"Good-bye, Jake Morgan, treasure hunter." Estrella gazed tenderly into Jake's eyes. "You were a pleasant surprise."

"You were too, Ace. You were too."

As our plane banked sharply to the east, I looked down one last time on the red tile rooftops outside Lima. As buildings became smaller and smaller, the sapphire ocean and Cordillera Blanca came into view. I wondered how many more Incan treasures still lay hidden in the mountains and cloud forests below. Would they ever be discovered? My eyes felt heavy as I gazed. I tilted my seat back. It would be another long flight.

*   *   *   *

I'd missed my parents, my friends, and even our crowded little house in Brackendale. But it was really hard to get back into my daily routines. School seemed pretty anticlimactic after the last two-and-a-half weeks with Uncle Jake. Joel and I had helped solve the OS-187 mystery. We'd found hidden caves, ancient mummies, and located a lost city. Well, then there was Putaq. After all that, it was tough to get jazzed about algebra.

A month later, Joel and I received a letter from Uncle Jake. A small newspaper clipping was enclosed, a short article from the international section of the *Toronto Star*, highlighted in yellow:

> "Reuters News Agency: Peruvian-born Estrella Maroto, PhD. Oxford, has established a private foundation, named Dignity of Man, to aid the indigenous peoples of Peru and to assist in the preservation of their cultural heritage. The organization, funded with over $140 million from an unknown source, is temporarily headquartered in London."

But it was the letter's last paragraph, written in Jake's jumbled scrawl, that really made me smile:

"Hope you two are doing well. Say 'hi' to John and Alice. I'm completing plans for my next salvage project, but I first have to attend to some unfinished personal business in London. As always, your Uncle Jake."

Glossary of *Quechua*

A

accha: hair
achachay: brrr! (cold)
achca: much
allimanta: slowly
allin: nice
alpaca: relative to the llama
ama: no (as a command)
anancu: ant
ant'awara: reddish clouds seen in evening or morning
arí: yes
ashana or *asnay*: stink
ayapambana: dead ground (cemetery)

B

C

callpana: run
cani: I am
canqui: you are
catana: blanket
cayacu: hey!
challhua: fish

ch'aska nawi: big, beautiful eyes
chasqui: messengers, runners
chaupi: middle, center
chay: that
chhichhinakuy: whisper
chhini: bat
chikiray: to separate baby animals from their mothers
chiri: cold
chiriyana: get cold
ch'ulla: having only one
chullpa: mummy
churi: son
chusi: blanket
coyllur: star
cuca: coca
cuchi: pig
cushac: empty
cuyana: to love

D

E

F

G

H

huaca: holy place, holy thing

huayco: mudslide
huichiyana: go up

I

ima shutitac canqui: What's your name?
imarayku: why?
imashina: how
inti: sun
ishpana: feces

J

jacu: let's go
jay?: what?
jina: like, as
jutca: hole

K

kacharpari: farewell
k'anchis: seven
katari: snake
kukupacha: spirit world
k'umuykuy: kneel, or bow
kuntu: condor
kusikuy: to be happy

L

laqha: darkness
llajta: city, town
llama: camel-like animal
lluchina: leave
llullu: not yet ripe, green
llusk'a: slippery ground

M

mamay: mother
mana: no
manchakuy: to be afraid
maqanakuy: to fight, to hit someone
maqui: hand
matararaju: mother's milk
mirka uya: freckle face
misi: cat
manchana: kiss
munaycha: pretty
munch'ay: bless
munray: (literal) beautiful
musqay: dream

N

nawi: eyes

O

oqoti: anus

P

pajtataj: warning to be careful
paqarin: dawn, morning hours
piacha: stone hatchet
puca: red

Q

qhechunakuy: to fight for possession of something
q'onichiy: to warm up
q'ori: gold
quam: you

quinquin: you
quipa: Inca records of knots made in string

R

riccharina: wake up.
rigra: wing

S

sat'ikuy: to enter without permission
shuti: name
sipas: girl, young woman
sisay: (literal) blossom
sumaq: beautiful
sut'inchaj: prophet, holy man

T

taita: father
tariy: to find
Tahuantinsuyu: "land of the four corners"
tutamanta: morning
tutu: night

U

ucupi: inside
upallagu: quiet
urca: hill, mountain
utca: quick

V

W

waita: flower

wanusqa: dead
wapu: strong, brave
wichariy: to climb
winaypaq: forever
wit'uy: to amputate

Y

yachayniyoj: wise
yano: black
yurak: white
yuyarina: remember

X

Z

Chronology of Incan Emperors

Manco Capac: Mythical founder of the Inca.

Sinchi Roca:

Lloque Yupanqui:

Mayta Capac:

Capac Yupanqui:

Inca Roca:

Yahuar Huacac:

Viracocha Inca: (?–1438)

Pachacuti: (1438–1471) Inca Empire historically begins. Built Machu Picchu and rebuilt Cuzco.

Tupa Inca: (1471–1493) Conquered vast lands, greatly expanding the empire.

Huayna Capac: (1493–1527) Willed the empire be divided upon his death.

Huascar: (1527–1532) Executed on orders of his brother Atahualpa.

Atahuallpa: (1532–1533) Captured and held for ransom. Executed by Francisco Pizarro, Spanish conquistador.

Topa Hualpa: (1533)

Manco Capac II: (1533–1545) Rebelled against Spanish. Set up a remote mountain capital at Vilacabamba.

Sayri Tupa Inca: (1545–1558)

Titu Cusi Yupanqui: (1558–1571) Only royal family member to dictate history of the Inca.

Tupac Amaru: (1571–1573) Last Incan ruler. Captured and executed by Spaniards.

Readings

Biggar, John. *The High Andes: A Guide for Climbers*. Kirkcudbright-shire, Scotland: Andes Press, 1996.

Cobo, Father Bernabe. *History of the Inca Empire*. Translated and edited by Roland Hamilton. Austin, TX: University of Texas Press, 1979.

Cock, Guillermo A. "The Race to Save the Inca Mummies." *National Geographic* (May 2002): 78–91.

Henty, G. A. *The Treasure of the Incas*. London: W. Foulsham & Co. Ltd., 1936.

Honigsbaum, Mark. *Valverde's Gold*. New York: Farrar, Straus and Giroux, 2004.

Jenkins, Dilwyn. *The Rough Guide to Peru*. London: Rough Guides, Ltd., 1997.

Lerche, Peter. "Quest for the Lost Tombs of Peru of the Peruvian Cloud People." *National Geographic* (September 2000): 64–81.

Lourie, Peter. *Sweat of the Sun, Tears of the Moon*. Lincoln, NE: University of Nebraska Press, 1991.

Prescott, W. H. *History of the Conquest of Peru*. London: Phoenix Press, 2002.

Sharman, David M. *Climbs of the Cordillera Blanca of Peru*. Aberdeen, Scotland: Whizzo Climbs, 1995.

Sullivan, William. *The Secret of the Incas*. New York: Three Rivers Press, 1996.

Vega, Pablo Corral. "In the Shadows of the Andes: A Personal Journey."

National Geographic (February 2000): 2–29.

About the Author

Jeffrey J. Pritchard lives on an island in Puget Sound. Author of six books, Pritchard is an avid outdoorsman and mountaineer. His previous books for young readers include, *Quest for the Pillars of Wealth*, and *The Secret Treasures of Oak Island*.

J. J. Pritchard

© 2005

PO Box 10771

Bainbridge Island, WA 98110

(206) 842-2201

JJPSR2@aol.com

0-595-33674-4

Printed in the United States
26956LVS00002B/37-57